A ZHONG FONG
MYSTERY

THE GOLDEN MOUNTAIN MURDERS

A ZHONG FONG
MYSTERY

THE GOLDEN
MOUNTAIN
MURDERS

DAVID ROTENBERG

McArthur & Company
Toronto

First published in Canada in 2005 by
McArthur & Company
322 King St., West, Suite 402
Toronto, Ontario
M5V 1J2
www.mcarthur-co.com

Library and Archives Canada Cataloguing in Publication

Rotenberg, David (David Charles)
The golden mountain murders / David Rotenberg.

ISBN 1-55278-522-X

I. Title.

PS8585.O84344G64 2005   C813'.54   C2005-903662-1

Design / Image / Composition: *Mad Dog Design*
Printed in Canada by *Webcom*

The publisher would like to acknowledge the financial support of
the Government of Canada through the Book Publishing Industry
Development Program, The Canada Council for the Arts, and the
Ontario Arts Council for our publishing activities. We also acknowl-
edge the Government of Ontario through the Ontario Media
Development Corporation Ontario Book Initiative.

10 9 8 7 6 5 4 3 2 1

For Susan, Joey and Beth without whom none
of these novels could have come into being.
And to my friend and business partner Bruce.
And finally to Michael and Kim whose faith
in the work has been unwavering.

PROLOGUE

BLOOD HEADS

Beneath the corrugated iron roof and inside the razor wire–topped fencing is a place of suffering. Wives nurse husbands, brothers sisters, and in the far corner of the large room a sun-scorched peasant father cradles the head of his twenty-six-year-old dying son.

Armed guards wearing surgical masks keep those outside the fence outside and those inside the fence inside.

If you suddenly begin to lose weight or feel inexplicably weak or break out in skin lesions in Anhui Province you will be rounded up and brought here or to one of the other two hundred–odd government-run compounds like this one.

And once you are here – you will never leave.

Blood trickles from the dying man's nose. His father begs for a bandage and some water. His pleas go unheeded. He rips a panel from his shirt and presses it hard against his son's nose. The man whimpers in pain. His cries simply enter the cacophony of anguish that forms the soundscape of this place.

The man's blood quickly saturates the cheap cotton of his father's shirt and sluices onto the older man's hands – hands that have been cut and nicked by so many years of hard labour in the fields that they never really heal. And the blood seeps into one of the open crevices it finds there – and deposits its contagion that will first make the man's father lose weight then extrude blood that can carry the virus to yet another victim.

The flies buzz in lazy circles awaiting their daily feast. The sun beats down on the metal roof and bakes the flesh beneath in preparation for the festivities – and Death lifts its spindle legs high, throws back its withered head in glee and dances its celebration to the symphony of sorrow that comes from within.

Fong was in a small mud-floored room in a small mud-walled hut in the far-off province of Anhui, whose major export may well be mud – or mud products. Fong didn't know.

If they didn't sell mud maybe they sold their second most abundant natural resource, bugs. There were bugs everywhere. Fong really didn't care for bugs. Especially country bugs. At least bugs in Shanghai were civilized. Here out on the very edge of nowhere who knew what bugs could do – had done – were about to do. Not Fong. He recalled reading an English-language picture book to his daughter Xiao Ming, when she was just two or three. Something about a boy who could fly who had a fairy friend called Tinker-something-or-other who also flew. Everybody flew. His daughter had taken one look at the print of the flying, winged sprite and pronounced: Bug!

Fong was tempted to smile at the memory – but didn't. Instead he readjusted his butt on the three-legged bamboo stool and wondered if country bugs were attracted to or repelled by human fecal matter. This thought entered his head because the peasant sitting on the stool on the other side of the rickety table had lost his bravura about half an hour ago, the logic of his lies about ten minutes back, and just moments ago control of his bowels. As the son of night-soil collectors, Fong was not bothered by human feces – but he was worried about the country bugs the material might attract.

Fong shook his head as he glanced at his colleague Captain Chen, whose face even in the dim light of the hut managed to astound with its ugliness. Fong left the hovel, watching where he placed his feet – the crunch of bugs underfoot always took his appetite from him.

The middle-aged Caucasian woman for whom he had sent awaited him.

He instinctively reached for his pack of Kents only to remember that he hadn't smoked for over nine years – since he'd killed the assassin Loa Wei Fen in the construction pit in the Pudong across the Huangpo River from the Bund. He made as if to brush lint from his shirt pocket and turned to the white woman. "You are from . . .?"

"Yale, an important American university."

Fong took that in, then said, "Anhui Province is a long way from America and its universities, whether they are important or not."

"Fine," she said as she widened her stance and put her plump fists on her waist. Then she changed tack. "Your English is very good."

"Yes it is," Fong said, refusing her compliment. "You are here in Anhui Province for what reason exactly?"

The woman reached into the pocket of her khaki pants and produced a folded sheaf of papers and held them out to Fong. The documents were festooned with official stamps and seals. Fong read the first page of what he thought of as Beijing wingo-wango and got the gist. "You're here to train nurses in dealing with a disease."

3

"AIDS. You Chinese have to start calling it by its name."

Fong didn't care for the "you Chinese" part of the nurse's statement but agreed with the rest of it. He accepted that to acknowledge a problem is the first step in solving it. So he said, "AIDS," then added, "happy?"

"Not much. What are you going to do with the man in there?"

"Are you concerned for his health?"

"Hardly. I want vermin like him stopped from coming to villages like this and collecting blood from these poor people."

"I understand your concern, but that's how he makes money. He's a blood head."

"Blood head? Is that what you call them? What he is, is a walking disease. An infected rat ready to bite these people."

Fong didn't agree. What this man was, was a poor man who had seen a way of making a few extra yuan. Extra yuan that could allow him to change his life. Although, now that he sat in his own shit, that opportunity was gone. Now he was no more than a link. Hopefully the first link in a chain that would lead Fong back to the money behind all this.

The American nurse lit a cigarette. Fong allowed himself to breathe in the smoke-scented air. "Do you want one?" she offered, holding out her pack of Marlboros.

"No thanks," his mouth said while his mind screamed, "Why not?"

"You're a better man than I," she said with a smile.

Fong almost corrected her, "than me, not than I" but was stopped when the nurse reached into her pocket and came out with a palmful of hard candies, each wrapped in cellophane. "Then how about a sweet?"

"Thanks, no."

"Come on, I'm trying to make peace. We're on the same side, you know."

Fong wasn't sure about that. "I have no taste for sweets anymore."

"Funny, isn't it? You crave sweets as a kid then you lose your taste for them."

"Until you get old."

"True. Until you get old. So, what are you going to do with that man in the hut?"

"Get him to tell us where he takes the blood he collects."

It didn't take long. The blood head was terrified. He kept appealing to Captain Chen as a fellow "countryman." To have a little sympathy, to just let him go.

"Tell us where you take the blood you collect from these villagers and we'll see what can be done."

The man began to cry. "They'll kill me and burn my house to the ground."

Fong knew that both were distinct possibilities. He turned to Chen, "Call the office. Get them to authorize the money to move this man and his family west." Chen pulled out his cell phone, turned away and placed a call.

The man turned to Fong. "You can do that for us?'

Fong nodded but did not speak. After all these years as a cop he still found bald-faced lying difficult, even though in this case he understood that a lie now could lead to a lot of good later.

Chen snapped the cell phone shut and nodded, "It's been authorized."

Fong turned to the blood head, "You heard him. No more excuses. Where do you take the blood you collect?"

Three hours of hard travelling later, Fong and Captain Chen stood across a dirt road from an inn that had been a point of commerce since the early days of Manchu rule back in the 1600s. Its sweeping roof, wide hardwood porch and open-slat exterior gave it a pleasing aspect. If you had to be in the country at least you could stay in one of the old Imperial Inns. Behind the inn a river widened as it made its way slowly towards the sea.

"Are we waiting for something?" Chen asked.

Fong ignored the question and watched a large brown bug with several million hairy legs wend its way up Captain Chen's pant leg. "You have a bug on your leg."

Chen shrugged, "It's the country – there are bugs in the country."

The thing curled into a tight ball about the size of a small plum. "Why does it do that?"

"It's scared, I guess."

"I've been scared lots of times, Captain Chen, and I've never done that."

"You're not a bug, sir."

Fong looked hard at Chen. There wasn't even a hint of sarcasm in this profoundly ugly countryman who now was married to his ex-wife, Lily.

"Say that again, Chen."

Without a moment of hesitation, Chen repeated, "You're not a bug, sir."

Still no hint of the sardonic. Fong suspected that Chen didn't even know what sardonic was or that such a thing as sardonic existed. Chen was the most honest man Fong had ever met and a fine influence over his daughter Xiao Ming, who lived with the Captain and Lily. "You're right," Fong found himself saying, then added, "Who did you call when the blood head thought you were calling Special Investigations?"

"Lily."

"Ah. How is she?"

"Good."

"And Xiao Ming?"

"Growing like a weed in spring."

After a moment Fong responded, "Yes." Then he seemed to drift off as if some completely extraneous thought had taken hold of him. Chen was about to speak when Fong returned from his reverie. "Have you got a gun with you?"

"Yes sir, we're supposed to carry them at all times."

"Really? I must have missed that memo."

"I don't think so, sir. I put it on your desk and you asked me to shred it."

"Did I?"

Before Captain Chen could reply Fong held up his hand and pointed towards the road. A man on a bicycle was approaching. A tall wicker basket was strapped to the rusted back fender. He stopped the bike across the road from the inn and rocked it back on its ancient triangular kickstand. Then he hoisted the basket on his back and headed towards the inn.

Fong nodded. Captain Chen moved towards the man, his gun raised. "Police, hold it right there."

The man stopped like a deer in a forest having heard a snake slither in the underbrush. He snuck a quick look to his left then dropped the wicker basket, which tilted over on the mud road and spilled its contents. Chen approached carefully, his gun pointing directly at the man's head. Suddenly, the man feinted to the left then ran right at Chen, knocking him to the ground then raced behind the inn and sprinted along the river.

Chen scrambled to his feet and turned to pursue, but Fong stopped him. "Let him go Chen, he's just a courier." Fong was looking at the basket's contents on the hard-packed mud road. Sealed blood packs, stored in dry ice.

Hundreds of hypodermic needles – used hypodermic needles, several with small pools of blood still in their chambers. "Don't touch them," Fong ordered. "Come around the back with me."

They circled the inn and emerged from a vine-covered alleyway on the river side. Two kitchen workers were cleaning utensils, woks and chopsticks in the slowly moving brown water. Beyond them, on a small dock sat four large wooden crates with markings on them in numbers and English letters. Three with V5S 9W2 and one with V6P 2Y7.

"Is it code, sir?"

"I guess." Somevhing itched on the edges of Fong's mind. He'd seen these codes before – or codes like them – but where? Before he could answer his own question, a voice boomed from the deep shadows of the inn's wraparound porch. "Are you the smart asses terrorizing my people?"

Fong looked to the shadows but could only discern a vague shape there. A vague fat shape.

The two dishwashers quickly gathered up their things and with much bowing and scraping made a quick exit down a set of steps that Fong assumed led to the inn's basement.

A man stepped into the light. He was a heavy-set Han Chinese male with a ruddy complexion. He either used rouge on his face or drink had had the better of him quite recently. Maybe both. The man was several years younger than Fong and already had a pronounced paunch and seemingly no muscles whatsoever. Like a pear rotting in a bowl. Fong couldn't help remembering the old days when no one was fat in the Middle Kingdom. Now obesity was a rising problem in the PRC – especially amongst the young. The man's silk suit cost more than Fong made in a month but there was a stain on one of the white lapels. Maybe from the soup he balanced in his left hand. He pointed his soup-spoon at Fong and said, "You. I asked you a question."

Fong wondered if this was the kind of man the Western press liked to call a warlord. He looked more care-fully at the man, but he could see absolutely no "war" in him and very little "lord." He thought of calling the man by an old slander – "monkey king" – then thought better of it and said, "Do you own the inn, sir?"

"Who wants to know?" the man asked, coming down the steps, careful not to spill his hot soup.

"Show him," Fong said to Chen.

As Captain Chen approached the warlord he reached into his pocket and withdrew his ID. He held it out at waist level for the man to see. As the warlord, evidently a short-sighted warlord, leaned forward to get a better look, Chen grabbed his arm and with surprising agility side-stepped behind the man's back, bending the arm as he went, and applying pressure. The warlord let out a cry, then fell to his knees. When he finally managed to look up, Fong was standing over him. But Fong wasn't looking at the warlord, he was looking behind him.

The soup bowl had landed right side up – seemingly without losing a drop of its steaming liquid. What were the odds against that? Fong wondered. Fong took one last look at the soup bowl, then knelt so he could look the warlord right in the eyes. "So. Are the boxes on the dock yours?"

"Communist!" the man shouted then spat straight into Fong's face. Fong sensed its wetness before it actually splatted against his cheek just below his left eye. Chen tightened his grip on the man's arm. "I'll take that as a yes," Fong said to the man. "Have you got a handkerchief, Captain Chen?"

"Yes, sir," Chen said, holding it out.

Fong cleaned his face then handed the handkerchief back to Chen. "Go back to the front of the inn. Bring me one of the syringes on the ground. Get me one that has blood in its chamber. Lots of blood. Use your handkerchief, don't touch the thing with your hand, and be careful not to prick yourself with the needle. That pleasure we'll save for this proud man." Chen began to move off. "Captain Chen?"

"Sir?"

"Leave me your gun."

Within five minutes of Chen's return with a bloody hypodermic, the warlord told Fong once that the crates on the dock contained blood products, and twenty-eight times that those blood products were totally legal and that "I'm just a businessman, a businessman conducting business – totally legal business." He also insisted that he had no idea where the crates went. It was his job to collect and send onward.

"What about the numbers and letters on the sides of the crates?"

"I've got no idea. I was told to mark three of every four with one set of numbers and letters and the rest with the other set of numbers and letters. But it's all legal. Totally legal." The man produced a series of stamped export licences with the contents clearly listed as: Blood Products.

Fong examined the documents. It was only then that he realized that the man on the ground had no body-guards. What kind of self-respecting warlord had no bodyguards – the businessman kind, he thought.

Fong considered making the fat man eat the documents, then thought better of it and simply ripped them into little pieces and dropped them into the soup.

The man looked truly hurt by this. Maybe he really liked soup.

As they walked back to their vehicle, Chen asked, "Was that smart, sir?"

"No, Chen it wasn't, but I'm tired of being smart – smart's not getting us anywhere with this."

And so their investigation went – over and over again, for month after month. From sick peasants to blood heads to blood merchants to blood packagers to local political officials who, for a cut, licensed the practice.

Back in his bug-free Shanghai office overlooking the Bund, Fong threw his files to the floor.

"Sir?"

"What kind of world are we living in, Chen?"

"The new . . ."

"There must be thousands, maybe tens of thousands of people involved in this, Chen."

"And many more than that quite sick, sir."

"Yes. Many more. But every middleman we put out of business is replaced by another in a week. The lure of the money is too great to stop the trade. There are always poor Chinese who are looking for a chance to better themselves."

"It is encouraged by the government," said Chen.

"What?" snapped Fong.

Then Chen added as clarification, "Bettering oneself, not collecting blood."

Fong thought about that. He wondered how much difference there really was between those two things: bettering oneself and collecting blood.

"Sir?"

"There's almost no use working from this side. As long as the money is available from the West we won't be able to stop this."

"But this is happening here, sir."

"Yes," said Fong as he turned his back on the setting sun. Then he pointed east towards the coming darkness. "But the money comes from there. The Golden Mountain."

Then his eyes panned down to the crowded streets and his heart skipped a beat. He blinked and it was gone. But for an instant Fong was sure he had seen a peasant man standing on a bench on the raised Bund Promenade looking right at him – no, through him.

CHAPTER ONE

ON THE WAY

ong's eyes soaked it in. The puffs of clouds over the shallow upland valleys, the sharp snow-covered ridges that, Great Wall–like, connected the coastal peaks. Then the high meadows followed by flatness – cut into rectangular demarcations of farms, then another set of wooded foothills.

So un-Chinese these Canadian mountains.

Where were the rice paddies climbing every hill, the fields growing right to the edge of the villages? But then again, through his airplane window he hadn't seen many urban areas since he'd boarded the plane in Vancouver.

Then yet more mountains and a river cutting deeply through it – and a single road – a paved highway in the midst of nowhere – very, very un-Chinese.

Wide dirt paths joined the upper level pastures, but in the valley a pristine, empty, paved blacktop cut through. Fong shook his head, unable to comprehend the logic behind spending vast numbers of yuan to build an unused road.

Here in the early-twenty-first century, a mere nine months after two airplanes brought down the World Trade Towers, Inspector Zhong Fong, head of Shanghai's Special

Investigations Unit was seeing North America – the Golden Mountain – for the first time.

He listened to the English spoken around him and marvelled at the variations in both the use of the language and the origins of the speakers. But what drew his attention most was the wealth – everywhere such wealth.

Another valley town, a river to the north, train tracks to the south, a four-lane highway seemingly through the centre, slid silently beneath the belly of the plane.

He was heading to an international conference on terrorism outside a place called Calgary in a canton called Alberta. He had to do a lot of prompting and cajoling to get the assignment, but finally the new powers in Beijing had relented – then in their inimitable style insisted – that he go. "Well, if you think this is important," he had said with a shrug. They had dismissed him quickly and he had been happy to leave their presence.

The next evening, well after office hours, his team gathered: Lily, his ex-wife and forensics expert; her new husband, the remarkably ugly but remarkably honest Captain Chen; Kenneth Lo, his info-tech guy; and two young officers whom he had, of late, taken under his wing. Joan Shui was back in Hong Kong settling the final details of the sale of her condominium before moving to Shanghai to join both Fong and Shanghai's Special Investigations Unit as their arson specialist. Even if Joan were in Shanghai, Fong was unsure if he could handle a meeting with Lily on one end of the table and Joan on the other. At this point he thought it unlikely that even he could ride those cross-currents without drowning.

The room's thick dusty draperies were shut and the lights on the table were all dimmed and hooded. The room was already thick with cigarette smoke by the time Fong arrived. Lily held a cup of steaming *cha* in her elegant hand.

Kenneth Lo had several small-screen gizmos in front of him and was busily tapping a tiny computer screen with a metal stick. Captain Chen hovered over Kenneth's shoulder, watching. The two young officers were supplying most of the dense cheap tobacco smoke that accompanied almost all meetings in the People's Republic of China. Fong recalled once telling a group of officers that there was no smoking. They took him to mean that there was no smoking, now – they butted out and within ten minutes lit up again.

Fong allowed his fingers to trace the edge of the familiar old oval table. He'd convened many meetings here before. But this was different. This wasn't a sanctioned departmental meeting. Fong shrugged off a shiver of tension and laid out the basics of the blood trade, just to be sure that everyone understood where they were with all this.

"It took me longer to get our Beijing compatriots to agree to my trip to the West than I'd anticipated so our time line is pretty tight." He reached into his pocket and put on his glasses, jotted a note on his pad and pocketed it. Turning to the two officers he said, "You're up."

The younger of the two cleared his throat and handed out copies of a newspaper article. "Everyone should give this a quick read."

The article was from the *Wall Street Journal*, Asia edition, under the headline "Blood for Sale":

Last December the residents of Appleton, Wisconsin, were told that their small town had a blood crisis and that everyone should chip in by rolling up their sleeves and donating blood.

The citizens did as they were asked and donated generously to help save the lives of their friends and neighbors.

What the Appletonians didn't know, though – don't know to this day – was that the same December their blood bank was appealing for blood, it sold 650 pints at a profit to other blood banks around the country. They also didn't and don't know that last year their blood center contracted to sell 200 pints a month to a blood bank 528 miles away in Lexington, Kentucky, and that Lexington sold half the blood it bought from Appleton to yet a third blood bank near Fort Lauderdale, Florida. Which in turn sold thousands of pints it bought from Lexington and other blood banks to four hospitals in New York City.

What began as a generous "gift of life" from people in Appleton to their neighbors ended up as part of a chain of blood brokered to hospitals in Manhattan, where patients were charged $120 a pint. Along that 2,777-mile route, human blood became just another commodity.

Fong took a pencil and circled the words "just another commodity" then said, "Okay. So that's the demand side. What's next?"

The other young investigator handed out a somewhat lengthy document. "This is the formal complaint registered by some members of the Canadian Chinese community with our government. Because all Chinese people technically remain citizens of the People's Republic of China and their complaint is against what are technically foreigners, we were able to make the case that their complaint falls under Special Investigations rubric since it's a crime by foreigners."

Lily whistled. Everyone looked at her. "And they bought that bullshit? Not to mention the crap about all Chinese technically being citizens of this country."

"They were anxious to get it off their desks, Lily," Fong said, "but I agree with you that it stinks. At the present moment I don't have time to go into it further. It's a gift that came our way, so I'm taking it as such."

"Don't kick a horse's gift in the mouth, huh?" Lily said in her unique varietal form of English.

Fong momentarily tried to decipher Lily's meaning

but he quickly gave up and said, "Right." Then he turned to one of the young investigator. "Do these Canadian Chinese have a case?"

The other officer responded, "A great case. Not only were Chinese people brought to Canada to build their railroad under totally false pretenses but once they were there they were treated more like slaves than workers. They were never supplied with the proper clothing for the harsh winters. They made less than 30 percent of what Long Noses made doing the same work. They were forced to do most of the dangerous tasks. Hundreds, maybe thousands, died on the job. Then when it was finally done, they all but kicked them out of the country and then charged them a head tax to return. And they wouldn't allow Chinese women in. Just men to do hard work." The man sneered as he added, "They didn't want us breeding in their pristine country."

"Is there more?" Fong asked.

"Lots. Laws denying Chinese the right to work and live in various cities were enacted. Laws everywhere to make sure that they came as slaves and stayed slaves."

"These laws are still in place?"

"No. But they were for years and years. In fact, from 1924 to 1947, Chinese were not allowed to enter Canada at all." He took a moment, then added, "No Canadian government has made even a mention of reparations."

Fong nodded. He knew the basics of the story. Every Chinese person did. "Seems legit to me," said Fong. "And what do the Chinese Canadians want from the Canadian government after all this time?"

"An apology," the younger investigator said.

"A formal apology," the other investigator added.

"And what has our government done about this?" asked Lily.

"Very little," said the younger investigator.

Fong stood, crossed to the nearest curtain and smoothed out the seam, "They'll hold this sort of thing and only bring it forward when they have something to gain by doing so."

"That may be soon," said Kenneth in his stumbling Mandarin. He was much more comfortable speaking English or Cantonese. The highly idiomatic Shanghanese dialect was quickly becoming the bane of his move to Shanghai, which hadn't exactly been a move of choice. When Hong Kong was handed back to China by the British, many businessmen – whose businesses were just on the wrong side of the law – were approached by the mainland authorities. The approach was none too subtle. It was an ultimatum. Jail or come work for the state. Fong was desperate for an advanced IT man and Kenneth admirably fit the bill. After thinking for twenty seconds about jail, Kenneth accepted the offer to work for Special Investigations, Shanghai District. Much to Kenneth's surprise he liked his new work and very much liked his new colleagues. It was a unique experience for him to be on the good guy's side of the law.

"Why is that, Kenneth?" asked Lily.

"China's economy is booming but we have very few raw materials left in our country. To feed our factories we must either trade for or, preferably, control sources of those raw materials. The Canadians have raw materials – iron ore, nickel, cobalt – you name it. But they have traditionally balked at allowing foreign governments to buy into their primary industries."

"So you think that Beijing will try to use the historical treatment of Chinese in Canada to shame them into allowing us to buy into their raw material industries?"

"That's quite a stretch, isn't it?" asked Lily.

"Is it? The British were shamed into honouring the contract to return Hong Kong – you may recall that event."

"It was what brought your wonderful self into our presence," Lily said, without a hint of a smile.

Fong thought about Kenneth's late arrival in Shanghai. He still wondered why it had taken Kenneth six months to settle some sort of business west of the Wall before he reported for work in Shanghai.

"Who exactly are the Chinese Canadians who are organizing this drive for an apology from the Canadian government?" asked Captain Chen.

The older of the two officers handed out several dossiers. Everyone quickly scanned them. Pretty standard stuff. Names, birthplaces, ethnicities, family connections both in Canada and in the Middle Kingdom, incomes, etc.

"Do you think they're organized enough to help?" Chen asked.

The officer nodded. "They've got money and lots of hands, eyes and ears."

Fong thought, naturally they have lots of hands, eyes and ears – they're Chinese. He took a quick breath and hoped everyone would leave it at that. His other contacts in the West and Lily's research on the Chinese-Canadian men weren't things he was prepared to discuss in this forum. He said, "How much do they need to know about what I'm doing?"

"I don't know, sir. You'll have to figure that out when you meet them. At this point all they claim to want is your assistance in getting them their apology from the Canadian government."

Fong returned to his seat. "Get them my Calgary information, Kenneth."

"Sure," Kenneth replied, "but it will be tracked. Every email is tracked, especially anything out of here."

That's why I ordered that raid on the Internet café last week and in the confusion sent that email to Robert Cowens, he thought. Then he looked at Kenneth again. He hoped the danger had passed for the man. Kenneth smiled for no particular reason – Fong realized that sometimes he did that to people. Then he said, "Repeat what you just said to me, Kenneth."

"Sure, Fong – basically that email out of the People's Republic of China is tracked."

A small shiver slithered up Fong's spine. Tracked – we're all being tracked, he thought, but again he said nothing.

"What, Fong?" Lily's voice was insistent. She knew him better than anyone else in the room and he was afraid she could see through any sort of lie he put forward, so he changed the topic. "What have you found for me, Lily?"

"Lucky you, Short Stuff," she said in her personal take on the English language. Kenneth smiled. She shot him a look that took the grin off his face. "Dead mom, no blood I claim, shoe fits, must convict."

Fong took a second to decipher that. Kenneth couldn't begin to guess what it meant. "Give me the details, Lily."

To do so Lily reverted to her beautiful lilting Shanghanese, "Poor Mrs. Jiajou was admitted to the Hua Shan Hospital six days ago with pains in her chest. Shortly after she arrived she had a stroke and they were not able to resuscitate her. When I checked her chart I saw that her son worked at the Port of Shanghai. That's why I called you. I talked to him and told him, as you told me to, that his mother had died because the hospital had run out of blood."

"Good, Lily. What's the son's name?"

"Jiajou Shi and, by the by, he's no ordinary dock-worker, he's third in command of the harbour facility.

What more could you ask for?"

"Not much, thanks Lily."

She reverted to English, "No problem, Short Stuff, care though be. No like I this one bite."

The next afternoon Fong used his Special Investigations ID to get him and Captain Chen into the restricted area of the Shanghai port facility.

The huge harbour was alive with activity. Cranes lifted massive metal containers high in the air then swung them over the open holds of the great ocean-going vessels. Men guided each container to its sea berth. The echoes of their shouts just made it to where Fong and Captain Chen stood and watched. In some ports heavy work was done solely by computer-controlled robotics, but this was the Port of Shanghai – in the People's Republic of China. There are few, if any, jobs that are too menial – too beneath the dignity of a Chinese labouring man in need of a wage to feed his family. The Shanghai port, the very centre of the world's foremost economic miracle, is still powered by the cheap and readily available sweat of men, Fong thought, as he struck a match and held it out towards the cigarette that dangled from the thick lips of harbour master, Jiajou Shi.

When Fong first produced his ID, the man's face had revealed no more than a rock reveals when you kick it.

Captain Chen stood to one side as Fong had instructed. Sure enough, the poor man's features acted as a conversation starter. Glancing at Chen, Jiajou Shi said, "If he was a fish and I was starving, I'd throw him back." The harbour master steadied Fong's hand and drew the flame towards the cigarette in his mouth. Fong sensed the smoke before he smelled it. The man smoked Snake Charmers. Fong had smoked them for years before he'd switched to Kents.

"So what's this all about, Inspector?" The man took a

bottle of Fanta from the railing and snapped the top off with his teeth.

"That's not the recommended way of opening those," Fong said.

"Yeah, well . . ." the harbour master said then emptied almost half of the sweet orange concoction in a gulp. The man waited for Fong to say something. Fong didn't oblige him. "Well, this has been fun but your cute friend over there is making my stomach turn so I'm going to get back to . . ."

"Your work," Fong said then put his hands in his pockets and stared at his shoes.

The harbour master looked at Fong's shoes too. Then he stopped looking and turned to go. "There's blood in three of the refrigerated containers. Chinese blood."

Jiajou Shi stopped and turned back to Fong. "Is that illegal, Inspector? If it is then arrest the offenders and get it off my ships. If it's not, then fuck yourself very much and leave me to do my work."

"It's Chinese blood taken from Chinese for almost nothing that will be sold to rich Long Noses so they can live an extra day or two."

The harbour master stopped at that.

"It's going to the West?"

"Yes, Chinese blood going to the West, in three of the refrigerated containers on board one of your ships."

"Which one?"

Fong looked to Captain Chen who took a computer printout from his pocket and handed it to the man.

The man read it quickly and then turned his head towards the ship at the far crane platform.

"I believe that blood is heading to Vancouver, Canada. Have you had many refrigerator containers heading to that port of call?"

Jiajou Shi didn't say anything, but nodded.

"I understand that blood and blood products need to stay refrigerated to maintain their efficacy."

"I don't know that word."

"Potency. The blood becomes useless if the refrigeration . . ."

"You wouldn't, as the head of Special Investigations, Shanghai District, be instructing me to interfere with international trade, would you, Inspector Zhong?"

"Absolutely not." Fong smiled. "Did you suggest that, Captain Chen?"

"No, sir, I did not suggest that this man reset the refrigerator temperature gauge."

"Although, Captain Chen, I'm given to understand that such things have been known to happen."

"Rumour has it, sir, that the mechanism of a thermostat is very delicate."

"Unreliable, sometimes."

Captain Chen made a face that Fong assumed meant "such is life" but with the intensity of the ugliness of his features it was hard to be sure.

The harbour master finished his Fanta, stubbed out his cigarette then spat on the ground. For a moment Fong thought he was going to tell them to go to hell. But he was wrong. What the man did was step on his own spit then grind it into the ground, an ancient curse. "Fuckin' Round Eyes have everything, even our blood." Then he stomped away.

When he was out of sight, Captain Chen asked, "Do you think he'll do it?"

"I think he loved his mother."

The two men headed back towards the Bund. "What exactly will hurting that shipment of blood do, sir?"

Fong wanted to tell Captain Chen about the rest of his

plan but decided it was safer for Chen if he didn't. He'd already put one of his men in jeopardy. Finally he said, "It will set the rats scurrying."

"And that will . . .?"

Fong ignored Chen's question. They walked a little farther, then Fong asked, "How long will that ship take to get to Vancouver?"

"It's scheduled to leave tomorrow. Should be there in five to seven days."

Fong thought about that. He hoped that would time out right, but he wasn't sure. He wished he knew Canadian geography better. On Chinese maps Canada doesn't look all that big. But then again Chinese maps are Afro-centric so that Europe looks tiny too. He'd just have to figure out things when he got there. This chat with the grieving harbour master and the raid on the Internet café to allow him a clean email line to Robert Cowens were the last pieces of his plan that he could put into play while he was still in the Middle Kingdom. The rest he'd have to do there – in the Golden Mountain.

Very late that night he and Lily met in his office. He filled her in on the details of his plan to trap the Vancouver money behind the Anhui blood trade.

"Once you set things going, Fong, it's hard to know when or where they'll stop."

"True, Lily, very true."

"What have you not told me, Fong?" Lily said in Shanghanese.

"What do you mean?"

She let out a long sigh. "I'm tired, Fong. But listen to me. I know you, Fong. I lived with you. I shared your bed. I gave birth to our daughter and I know you've held something back from me. Something that you're ashamed of.

Am I right?"

"It couldn't be helped."

Lily turned away from him. "It can never be helped Fong, can it?" Her voice was tight, angry. Fong couldn't meet her eyes.

It startled him when he felt her hand on his cheek. "Do you need my help?"

"Help me rearrange the pieces that I know."

Lily looked at Fong's desktop. She'd seen him work this way often enough in the past. There were three columns of three-by-five cards laid out on the scratched wooden surface. Long chalk marks led from the bottom of each of the three columns to a single card at the bottom of the desk marked with the dark thick title: THE MONEY.

She lifted her head. Over his shoulder, and across the Huangpo River, the new Pudong sparkled its enticement – its seventy cock-proud office towers, an open invitation to join in the glories of the New China. She crossed to the floor-to-ceiling window and placed her hand on the pane. Its coolness pleased her. She hadn't spent much time with Fong since they had separated. She was surprised how much she enjoyed his company – despite the fact that she fully understood that this was business, not pleasure.

She turned from the window. Fong was at his desk rearranging the cards, then making the three columns into three towers. "Don't change things, Short Stuff," Lily said in her unique brand of English. "No way better other than way."

Fong finally put the three-by-five cards aside. He'd thought and rethought his options but couldn't seem to increase his odds of success – and so many lives were in the balance. It frightened him. The weight of the responsibility bent him as surely as a heavy burden bends a coolie's back.

"Alone, feel, Fong?"

Yes, he certainly felt alone. There was so much money in all this that he didn't know who to trust. Only Lily and Chen at this point. And even they didn't know the full extent of what he was thinking about setting into motion – about what he'd asked of Kenneth Lo and the plans he'd set up with the two young investigators. Even the new woman in his life, Joan Shui – when he forced himself to be honest – was not totally in his circle of trust. The decades of propaganda he, like everyone else in the PRC, had ingested couldn't totally allow him to trust anyone from Hong Kong when it came to money. Even Joan Shui, his lover.

"Conference terror, when, Fong?"

He told her.

She blew a high-pitched whistle through her teeth. "Too soon, no?"

"What other choice do I have? You've completed your research on our people over there?"

Lily nodded and returned to Shanghanese, "But be careful. The boy is reliable but not his father and who knows about the grandfather."

"And he understands what we need?"

She smiled and in oddly accented English said, "He homosexual so he know." She smiled and said brightly, "I like homosexuals. Maybe I fag shag."

Fong thought that was highly unlikely but he responded, "Right." Then he glanced down at the three-by-five cards again. Each had writing in English in block letters: Robert Cowens, Apology from the Canadian Government, Dalong Fada, V5S 9W2, V6P 2Y7, three bills of lading for refrigerated containers, Newspaper Articles, Riots, Arrests – and others. Too many others. But too many cards had no writing on them, just wide, raw question marks.

The first of the three columns was headed by the name: CHIANG. Several cards were beneath it and then a long thick chalk line to THE MONEY. The second column was headed by a card entitled: THE LAYWER, which was then followed by many cards and again the chalk line leading to: THE MONEY. The third column was headed by a card with a large "?" on it. There were cards beneath and a chalk line to: THE MONEY – once again.

"Three lines," she said.

"Three possible ways to the money behind all this, Lily," he responded.

Lily let him sit with his thoughts for a moment, then said in Shanghanese "And you set this all in motion by inviting Kenneth Lo to your office with that computer for everyone to see."

"I didn't . . ."

"You did, Fong. Everyone knew he was working on the computer from the company that sold blood. Everyone knew that Kenneth is brilliant and would eventually break into that hard drive and get the hidden information there. Everyone knew that the moment you called him to your office that he had broken in and found the secret data. Everyone knew . . . and you knew that one of them might tell someone."

Fong sighed. "I didn't know how else to get this to begin. We were in Anhui for months but no one there is big enough to be important. The information in that hard drive might be big enough to rattle their cage so I can watch them scurry. Maybe I can detect their pattern from the scurrying. Scurrying rats leave tracks, Lily. Rats that are calm don't disturb the dust." He was tempted to move a card from the second column to the third but decided against it. "We need to stay in contact." It sounded funny in Fong's ears, as if he were inviting her out on a date.

She held out the electronic square that Kenneth Lo had been showing Chen in the meeting. "It's called a BlackBerry."

"Why?"

"Why is it called a BlackBerry?"

"Yeah."

Lily lifted her shoulders in a manner she always did before she let loose with a flurry of English obscenities, "Why fuck I know what, shit Blueberry, called. Who fuck care what fuck?"

Fong wanted to laugh but he didn't. He saw the worry in her eyes. "Chen will teach you how to use it," she said in Shanghanese. "Between it and your cell phone I should be able to feed you the information that you need. You have our Vancouver secure fax contact?"

Fong nodded. He didn't know what to do next. Then Lily put her finger beneath his chin and lifted his face so he looked right into her eyes – always so deep, so very very sad. "Be careful, Short Stuff. Be very careful."

Then she was gone and he was alone with his three columns and his doubts. Suddenly he was consumed by the feeling that he didn't even know what he didn't know. He worried that he had missed something terribly important – like who it was that was tracking him.

So here he was still not knowing what he didn't know, flying over more Canadian mountains, green valleys and regularly plotted farms that spread like a quilt over the few level areas by the rivers that sometimes took the breadth of lakes in their ceaseless meander to the ocean. To which ocean Fong wasn't quite sure.

Fong reached into the pouch attached to the seat in front of him. Maybe the airline magazine would have a map and at least he could answer that question. He found the magazine behind four identical copies of a cheap-looking magazine that claimed to be Canada's national magazine. If it was, why was it named after a Scottish man? Or was it named after a hamburger store? Fong didn't know or care.

He leafed through the airplane magazine to find a map. As he did, a flyer fell on his lap. It was an advertisement for a benefit performance of *Twelve Angry Men* at the Vancouver Theatre Centre. He stared at the picture – another theatre image in his life – another point of access back to his deceased wife, the famous actress, Fu Tsong. He shrugged off that thought and shoved the flyer into his pocket. At the back of the magazine he finally found a map that showed Air Canada's airline routes throughout the world, but it didn't help him determine to which ocean the river beneath him ran.

He stood and stretched. The plane he had taken from China was filled with people of one hue – one ancestry, the black-haired people. But this plane which he had boarded in Vancouver was a different story; all around him were people literally from the four corners of the earth. All of whom were evidently Canadian now. A maroon-turbaned Sikh sat across the aisle; directly behind him a black teenager nodded to the rhythm being delivered directly to his brain by a huge set of earphones. There were several Japanese couples and an elderly Korean woman – and children – always the great divide between people from the Middle Kingdom and the rest of the world – children, sometimes three or four from a single family.

He thought of his own daughter, Xiao Ming, now with her mother, Lily, and her stepfather, Captain Chen.

The plane tilted slightly and began a wide arcing change of course. A child cried that particularly high-pitched wail – so filled with betrayal – that some think only children feel.

The vast land, almost empty of people, continued to pass by his window, beneath the plane. The river was wider now, as if its effort was the achievement of girth. It elegantly seeks its end, its demise, Fong thought, in what had of late become his almost continuous inner monologue. He failed to add the two words, "Like me," afraid even in that private sanctum to give word to such thoughts.

A six- or seven-year-old girl awaiting access to the forward washroom first hopped up and down, then knocked at the closed washroom door, then decided that crying had more chance of getting the locked door to open. The girl was wearing shorts and a bright blue T-shirt with a red "S" within a yellow triangle.

Fong assumed it was a sports team of some sort and wondered where he could find such a thing for Xiao Ming.

Every time he saw his daughter it seemed that she'd grown. But not just bigger – somehow deeper. She'd always, at least as far as he was concerned, been wide awake to her surroundings. From the beginning she'd been fully aware. Her language was advanced for a five year old, and when she was with him they only spoke English. It was hard for him not to correct the mistakes she'd picked up from her mother, whose English was a wild mix mostly learned from CNN and American TV talk shows. Fong's English was textbook stilted but accurate – very accurate.

Lily and her new husband, Captain Chen, always made him feel welcome in their small rooms when he came to pick up Xiao Ming. They were strict about bringing her back at the appointed hour but that was understandable. They also insisted that she be kept away from anything that could bring back the days of near catatonia she'd experienced after her rescue from the arsonist who called himself Angel Michael. The poor thing still cringed when she heard loud noises or even saw a match struck. Just before he left for the Golden Mountain he had taken Xiao Ming back to the home in which he'd grown up.

As they had turned the corner and stepped onto Feng Beng Lu, Fong felt his daughter's hand curl in his. Quickly the new Shanghai faded away and was replaced by the old – the permanent, the ageless Shanghai – what was laughingly referred to by the locals as the Chinese concession. The ancient buildings gave the lie to the high bright towers across the river, the California-style condominiums in the embassy district and the English-language slogans on T-shirts and sweatshirts and pant butts. There was none of that here in the old city.

Fong and Xiao Ming hunched into the dankness of the place. Whispers followed them from behind pulled curtains; naked children being washed in bright red plastic tubs on the sidewalk openly stared at them; the five-spice egg seller gave Fong the evil eye as she had to a Japanese soldier who had raped her mother sixty years ago on this very street in Shanghai's Old City.

But as Fong and Xiao moved deeper into the Chinese concession they became more of the Old City and the denizens allowed them to pass. Fong had returned to from where he had come and where he had come from accepted him.

They passed by the Temple to the City God and the Old Shanghai Restaurant, then entered an unmarked alley. Immediately the smell of cooking engulfed them and Xiao Ming identified each smell. With each identification, she held her father's hand tighter and finally asked, "Where are we going, Father?"

"To my father's house. Your grandfather's house."

"Do I get to meet Grandfather?" she said, her voice alive with awe.

Fong stopped and picked her up. Then he said softly, "My father has been dead a long time. The last time I saw him I was your age. But he was a very good man. A kind man. I loved my father and still miss him." He paused. "I hope you don't miss me, Xiao Ming."

She shrugged in his arms then touched his face. "You are my father."

"I know, but I'm not always there for you."

"You are. Whenever I want you I call you and you always come."

"When I can."

"When you can." He put her down. They took a few more steps and the alley widened. Set back a few paces from the alley was the old archway that demarked the entrance to a family compound.

"Is this where Grandfather used to live?"

Fong stared at the archway. As a boy it had separated them from us. There was safety outside the archway and the wrath of his grandmother inside. He remembered when the family owned the whole compound. Now the place probably housed twenty families.

He pushed open the door and memory flooded him. His father had carried him on his shoulders in this open courtyard. He had told him the old stories. He had defended him from his grandmother. He had done the best he could to keep him safe from the diseases inherent in the family business, night-soil collecting. He had sat by Fong's side when he had contracted the cholera and had been thrown from the house with a blanket and a sleeping palette and been told by his grandmother to, "Get better or die quickly. There is work to be done."

Then his father had left to fight for the liberation. And had never returned.

Seven years later when the Red Army re-entered

Shanghai as victors, Fong had raced to the rooftops and waited and waited for his father to come marching by. But he had not come. Even hours after the last troops had passed, Fong stayed on the rooftop waiting. Waiting for the return of the man who held him on his shoulders in this courtyard.

"What can I do for you?" the middle-aged man said as he filled a metal pail with water from the courtyard's central spigot.

Fong explained that he had lived there and that this was his daughter and he wanted to show her . . .

"Show her what? What you and your bourgeois family had once owned but now belongs to the people. What you stole from us all and now we have regained?"

"Shut up, Father," said a young, well-dressed man carrying an expensive briefcase. The man stared at his son for a moment then pulled on his Mao jacket proudly, despite the heat, spat on the ground and left.

"You must forgive my father. The old ways die hard." The young man said, then introduced himself and listened to Fong's request. "No problem. Look all you like, those were the good old days and they're going to come back. Young people like me are going to make sure that they come back."

Alone in the room that used to be Fong's, Xiao Ming grabbed her father's hand. "This, this place and places like it are of us, Xiao Ming. Not of them. Not McDonald's or computers or Lexus automobiles. We made these places. We left our souls in these places. These places now must become part of you."

The little girl stared at the dingy walls and the exposed wood beams. Then she smiled, "I like it here, Father."

Fong took a breath – a deep breath – then lifted his daughter high into the air.

"It's like flying here, isn't it, papa? Flying into the past."

Fong smiled and looked out the window. He wondered if Xiao Ming would have to wait until her fiftieth year to fly in an airplane. Somehow he doubted it.

The plane droned on and on. Fong couldn't remember when he had last slept. His mind drifted to the beginnings of all this – all this blood.

It had been a cold night and Fong was working late. The knock on his office door had been soft – like a woman's knock. He quickly got to his feet, hoping it was Joan Shui. But when he opened the door he saw his IT man, Kenneth Lo. "What is it? It's late, Kenneth."

"Success has no correct time of day," Kenneth said in his stilted Shanghanese.

"You've lost me," Fong had said, covering the work on his desktop with a sheet of newspaper.

"That computer you gave me?" Kenneth prompted.

"The one from the man who was murdered by the woman who loved him?"

"The very one."

Fong had sighed and returned to his desk. "The case is over, Kenneth. The woman is in prison or executed. I don't know which."

To Fong's surprise Kenneth was undeterred. "I'm sorry to hear that. But I think you'll be interested in what the hard drive revealed about the nature of the dead man's business. The International Exchange Institute traded . . ."

"The case is over. Closed – not of . . ."

"Blood."

Fong was on his feet before he realized it. He went to

the office window and snapped open a latch. He pushed and the thing pivoted, letting in the sound of the traffic beneath. The Bund traffic, even at this hour, was very loud.

Finally Fong asked, "Blood?" although it wasn't really a question.

"Yes, Fong. The dead man's company traded in blood."

"Our blood?" Fong stepped from the window and smacked his hand against the wall. "I asked if it was Chinese blood this company was trading?"

"Yes, of course it was."

There was a long pause, the sound of car horns honking below and faraway. A siren sounded loudly then just as quickly stopped.

"They buy the blood in the provinces then sell it in the West, Fong."

"How do you know they sell it in the West?"

"All the figures on the hard drive, except one, are quoted in US dollars. And the figures are impressive, so where else . . ."

"What about quantities?"

"Huge and at the time of the man's death on a sharp ascent."

"Did they at least pay for the blood?"

"Yes, Fong, they paid. He kept immaculate spreadsheets – tiny yuan notes for pints of whole blood or platelets or plasma. Always from the distant provinces. Anhui seems a favourite place for them. They pay almost nothing for the blood products and then they sell them for top dollar. The profit margins are impressive."

"What else did you get off the hard drive? Nothing useful like names and places I assume. You said that some figures weren't US dollars."

"Estimates of the numbers of AIDS victims in Anhui.

They were evidently pulled down from an American university website that has nurses there."

Fong felt the rage move through his blood, like an animal released.

"Fong?"

"Yeah."

"Those figures seem to have been recorded by someone other than this Bob Clayton who ran the International Exchange Institute. They were stored in a different place on the hard drive from the business figures and were protected by a different password. So I figured . . ."

". . . that another person did the inputting . . . the secretary?"

"Could be – is that the woman who killed the man she loved?"

Fong turned away. "AIDS in Anhui Province? AIDS in the backwoods of Anhui? How the fuck did AIDS get to that part of nowhere?"

"Think, Fong. They collect blood. Blood transmits AIDS and most peasants don't understand that blood will replenish itself so they insist that when they give blood that they get re-injected with blood later. So the guys who collect the blood take it away and remove the commercial bits of it then mix all the blood that is left together and re-inject these poor fools the next day."

Fong hit the solid surface of his desk three, four, five times. Then he almost shouted, "I want names and places in the West that make profit off . . ."

"They're not on the hard drive. Only those two codes I told you about and collection schedules from Anhui Province and other . . ."

"Vulnerable places."

"Yeah. The only name we found in association with this company outside of the dead guy is not Western."

"A Chinese name?"

"Chiang Wo."

Fong nodded slowly.

Chiang Wo. An infamous name. So the Chiangs had returned to the Middle Kingdom.

And so Fong had gone to Anhui – which led him to this plane that was slowly making its descent into Calgary International Airport.

Calgary was a confusion to Fong. Were these people speaking English? Perhaps it was that he had been up for more than twenty-four hours. Then he realized that it was just past noon here. Morning was done. The morning of which day of the week he could only guess. Fortunately a large sign with his name in bold characters caught his eye when he left the customs area. The young Asian man with the sign smiled enthusiastically and grabbed Fong's bag as he led him to a waiting SUV.

"We're off to Kananaskis," the young man said.

Fong didn't completely get that but he smiled and closed his eyes.

When he awoke he was in some sort of mountain resort. The room they assigned him was so large that he expected several others to join him – although he knew they wouldn't. He quickly showered – amazed by both the volume and pressure of the hot water and the towels – so many white towels.

A knock at his door. Fong opened it. The young man who drove the SUV was there. He spoke a few words, in what language Fong couldn't guess.

"Let's speak English," Fong suggested.

"Fine, sir. The delegates are gathering in the lobby."

Fong took the stairs down to the lobby. He was never

very fond of elevators and besides he needed a little exercise after all the sitting – and on stairs you have a chance of spotting someone who is tracking you.

The lobby was filled with men, most of whom were his age or older. They all signed in and received packets, then the convention organizers herded them outside into the cold where a photographer waited. Each delegate was given a very large, white hat. Fong had seen cowboy movies before but he assumed that things like cowboy hats were just costumes like the headdresses worn in the Peking Opera. He never thought real people wore such impractical things. But before he could contemplate this he faced a more pressing dilemma. They couldn't find a hat that was small enough for him. Finally they stuck a hat on the back of his head and muttered, "That'll have to do, fella." The cowboy-hatted police officers from all over the world were posed on the steps of the lodge and the photographer finished his fiddling.

But just before the photographer took his shot, Fong picked out a young Chinese man several metres behind the photographer. He'd seen him on the airplane. So you're my minder are you, he thought. Well, welcome to the Golden Mountain, pardner. He allowed his eyes to sweep the crowd one more time and then returned to his Beijing "minder." The man was younger than Fong thought he would be. He had sat far forward in the plane. To stop me from running up and jumping out the front door or something, I guess, but the thought didn't humour Fong. This one's youth bothered him. Fong had thought that Party members would always remain older than him. Now here was this agile, well-tailored, nicely hair-cut young man.

The man took out a cigarette and lit it.

Fong smiled. Beijing hadn't briefed this one well enough. These Canadians don't like smokers much. As if on cue, the woman beside his young minder waved her hand in the cold air shushing away the smoke and said something that Fong couldn't hear but could guess at. The minder looked at the woman, clearly lost as to what offence of etiquette he had committed. Fong thought about walking up to the minder and snatching the cigarette from his youthful mouth, but decided to forego the fun stuff – he had bigger things that needed his time and effort during his short stay in Canada. Things that his minder would not appreciate.

Then without warning the Canadian woman reached over, plucked the cigarette from the young man's mouth and shouted, "Filthy, filthy, filthy habit." She threw the thing to the ground, then stomped on it as if she were driving it deep into the earth with a curse reminiscent of Jiajou Shi on the docks of Shanghai not five days ago.

Fong wanted to cheer. Instead he shook his head. That made the large cowboy hat slip from the back of his head and slide over his forehead.

Fong saw the photo flash from beneath the brim of the hat. The photo that appeared in newspapers around the world showed Fong sitting in the front row, his face almost totally obscured by the white cowboy hat.

The conference itself began with footage from the collapse of the World Trade Towers – but not the footage that had been broadcast to the world. This footage had never been shown on television or even mentioned in newspapers. This footage showed people jumping from the upper levels of the towers.

Hundreds of them.

Some holding hands.

Many alone.

Was there more alone than this? Fong wondered.

Person after person after person jumped.

The numbness of familiarity quickly set in – even horror can be rendered banal by repetition. Then the banality sundered and fresh bright waves of horror pulsed through Fong's heart. On the screen a young man with long hair stood on an upper ledge, some hundred stories in the air. He removed his suit jacket, folded it and placed it on the ledge. Then he looked up – something luminous crossed his face. He bent his knees and pushed – up and out. His body rose gracefully away from his perch, then his arms shot up and his body turned slowly so his feet were heavenward. Once the rotation was complete he opened his arms wide, puffed out his chest and pulled back his chin as if he were proudly accepting his death – as a groom does the arrival of his bride as she walks down the aisle to take his hand.

Fong stared at the solitary figure – the beauty – until it left the bottom of the frame. His heart was racing. He was seeing out of the man's eyes. Seeing the pavement approach – no – race towards his face. He thrust his arms forward as if somehow to mitigate the damage of the concussion.

Then Fong sensed the man seated beside him looking at him. Had he spoken aloud? Had he cried out? He had said something. His heart pounded in his chest so hard that he was sure the man could at least hear that.

The man removed his tortoiseshell glasses and polished the lenses. "Sad, huh?"

Fong nodded, careful to keep his mouth shut and his eyes away from the man. Then he looked up once again at the screen. The second plane entered the body of the second tower – and the world changed.

When the images stopped, Fong and the rest of the police officers were left to sit in the dark with their thoughts. Shanghai was already a huge and powerful city, its seventy-odd new towers seemed to have leapt from the ground itself. It was not hard to move from the images on the screen to the streets of his own city – to the Pudong, across the Huangpo River, where his first wife's body lay in cold obstruction in the cement foundation of an office tower.

The rest of the day consisted of speakers who moved from horror to horror. Dirty bombs, missing radioactive material, bioterrorism, the vulnerability of computer networks, the impossibility of protecting water, food, subways and on and on and on.

As the litany continued, Fong slowly retreated. At least in China there was a whole civil defence structure – granted it was not really there to protect the citizenry – but it was in place and could quickly be activated. As well, Fong felt it unlikely that China would be a target just yet. True, there were Muslim rumblings in the west but sheer numbers were against them as was the willingness of Beijing to use overwhelming force if necessary to subdue any uprising. Shanghai's new subway system was, no doubt, vulnerable and Fong listened carefully to the speaker from Japan when he talked about the Serine gas attack on the Tokyo subway that killed so many. The Russian speaker's detailed account of Chechen sabotage on Moscow's subway system also sent a chill through Fong's gut. Warnings of the need for evacuation routes and safe rooms for all skyscrapers followed. A tiny ray of hope came when a South African speaker addressed that issue, with a computer warning system called WATCHDOG that was linked to every computer in a building. On activation, it first flashed a warning on the screen with directions to the safe room then shut the computer down. So, as the man said, "You can't ignore the warning as businesspeople tend to do when fire alarms go off in their buildings. Because until WATCHDOG allows it, your computers will not work. See." With that, he switched a toggle and exclamations came from around the room. Fong looked at the blank computer screen on the lap of the man beside him. "That's what that little button we gave you as you came into the hall allows us to do. This system is already installed in many buildings in my country and in a few on the West Coast of Canada." Then he flicked the toggle the other way and said, "WATCHDOG sleeps," and sure enough the computer screen on the man's lap returned to its previous screen.

The American speaker snuffed out what little good feeling WATCHDOG had given the room with his talk on the danger of crop dusters, which was fortunately unimportant to Fong. There simply weren't many, if any, crop dusters in mainland China. The airline security analyst also left no impression on Fong. Air China had a very simple, very effective security system: when in doubt – any doubt – strip the passenger. Fong couldn't understand the resistance to this approach in the West. The idea of "sanctity of the body" must have come from Christian texts because it made no sense to Fong. How could a person's potential embarrassment about their body parts be more important than the potential safety of hundreds of people? Nonsense. Fong found it incomprehensible, but then again Fong was the grandson of night-soil collectors. That tended to make one sanguine about the niceties of human bodies.

Near the end of the conference, however, a speaker broached a calamity that could bring his city to its knees – the idea of a man infected with smallpox let loose amidst Shanghai's 18 million uninoculated souls.

That night Fong dreamt the terror. He was running in

Shanghai's vacant echoing night streets, quiet, oil slick iridescence on the pavement. A desiccated countrywoman steps out of an alley – one earth-darkened arm around a filthy child, the other hand out for a bit of money. Fong shouts at the woman, "Stand back!" She opens her mouth – lips already ulcerated with open smallpox sores, her pleas surrounded by mists of saliva – death floats towards him on the cool night air. Then she throws her baby, wrapped in rags, at him. In horror, Fong watches the baby rise and shake free of its blanket, then everything slows and the infant lays out and turns slowly, head over heels, a full circle, as it opens its arms and, chin back chest out, heads towards the pavement. Fong throws himself forward to catch the soiled child. But the filthy rag blanket lands on Fong's face. Fong calls out and thrashes, trying to get the infected thing off him until he awakens entwined in the crisp white sheets of his Kananaskis hotel room – the pale light of a cold dawn coming through the oversized window.

Fong was pleased when precisely at 9:00 a.m. that morning Robert Cowens, the Toronto lawyer who had helped him end the life of the arsonist who called himself Angel Michael, approached his table. It was gratifying to see that the effort that had gone into contacting Mr. Cowens had paid off, although he felt bad about the necessary damage he had to do to the Internet café on Han'an Lu. How else was he to send an email to Mr. Cowens without it being traced back to him by the Beijing authorities? True, the owners of the Internet café were out of business, but such is life in the rapidly growing economy of the People's Republic of China.

Their greeting in the hotel's snack bar – a turn of phrase that confused Fong – was warm but distant. The thing that had brought them together, the danger posed by the arsonist who called himself Angel Michael, was no more. Fong's first wife, Fu Tsong, had talked about the instant intimacy that actors felt when they worked on projects. He never told her that it was not only actors who experienced that kind of closeness. Danger either closes the heart down or opens it wide. The situation that Robert Cowens and Fong had found themselves in only seventeen months ago in Shanghai was nothing if not full of danger.

"You called, Inspector Zhong?"

"Well, I emailed . . ." he picked up the idiom and smiled.

Robert smiled back. "So you've been listening to the horror show?"

"You mean the conference?"

"I do."

Fong took a newspaper from his lap and put it on the table between them. "Well, yes, I have – been listening to the horror show."

"So what do you think?"

"I think all religions should be outlawed."

"Very liberal of you."

"Is that a reference to what you call civil rights?"

"Well, freedom of religion is thought by many to be a civil right."

"By you?"

Robert shrugged.

"I am a police officer, Mr. Cowens. I'm interested in the safety of the people I am paid to protect. I have no interest in what you call civil rights. What rights are there, civil or otherwise in a city of eighteen million people if panic sets in?"

"And you think religions cause panic?"

"They justify it. They propel it."

"How?"

"They claim there are rewards after death."

"Well . . ."

"They claim that if you follow them you get to sing forever in some sort of heavenly chorus or you get fifty widows in the afterlife."

"Virgins."

"What?"

"Virgins. You get fifty virgins or eighty or something."

"Who would want fifty or eighty totally inexperienced sexual partners?"

Robert sighed. "Let's leave this."

"Fine, but as a lawyer you should know that after death there is only dirt and decay and a return to the earth. Nothing more."

"No heaven?"

"More importantly, no hell. Just a good life lived to honour the creator."

"So you believe in a creator?"

"Of course. Where else could beauty come from? What I don't believe is that there are rules to please the creator. That the creator is so petty that he cares whether you bend one knee or two, that you recite his name over and over again, that he watches over one person's individual welfare and allows millions of others to starve to death. No. Only one thing pleases him – you live your life as fully and with as much respect as you can for others. Period. No other rules."

Robert nodded.

For the first time Fong caught the edges of sadness in the Canadian's eyes.

"How is your health, Mr. Cowens?"

Robert turned away as he said, "It could be better, Detective Zhong, it could be better."

Odd, Fong thought. In his experience most North Americans liked to talk about their problems. Another, very un-Chinese thing to do. But here was Robert Cowens closing down conversation about himself.

"But I'm sure you asked to see me for more than old time's sake."

And now he was changing the subject, Fong thought. For the umpteenth time in his life Fong had to remind himself that the omnipresent propaganda that claimed that Caucasians were stupid was just that – propaganda.

"I need your help," said Fong.

"I'm a lawyer, not a cop, Detective Zhong."

"You can drop the formality. Just Fong is enough."

"I feel privileged."

"Don't."

"Why not?"

"Several dozen con men, thieves and hookers in the Pudong also refer to me that way."

"Ah."

"Fine. I need your help."

"And again the Canadian says, I'm a lawyer not a cop."

"Cops have to obey rules over here – lawyers don't."

"That's not exactly true. Fong, what is it you want from me?"

Without so much as an ahem as a segue, Fong said, "We have an incipient AIDS epidemic in rural China."

"Are there that many gay men in rural China?"

"No. Very few, if any."

"Intravenous drug users then?"

"Rural China is extremely poor. If there is drug use, opium would be the drug of choice. Opium is smoked, not injected."

"Then how the hell is there an AIDS epidemic there?"

"They sell their blood."

"Who does, the peasants?"

"Yes."

"Okay, so they make a few bucks and blood is a renewable resource after all, so good for them."

"Good if you like them dead. Thin and dead."

"But how . . ."

"The men who buy the blood don't clean the needles they use to draw the blood. They don't take precautions. They just want to collect as much blood as cheaply as they can – tough luck if you give us your blood and we give you an American dollar and some diseased blood in return that will not only kill you but could infect others."

Robert sighed deeply. "So where does the blood they collect go to? Which comfy little American town?"

"Vancouver, British Columbia. That comfy little American town."

Robert looked sharply at Fong.

"I know who the Chinese partner is. But he's not the money. He's the conduit. But it's the money that drives all this. If I can't stop the money behind it I can't stop the blood trade. I can arrest the blood collectors – we call them blood heads. I can arrest fifty of them on Monday and by Tuesday morning there will be fifty different people out in the paddies replacing them. The money is just too great to pass up. The only way to stop the disease is to cut off the source of the capital that is pushing the whole thing. And that's in Vancouver, and that's what I need you to help me with."

"There's that much money to be made collecting blood?"

"No. The money is in selling it."

"How much?"

"Tons. They pay almost nothing to the collectors and

peasants in China to get the blood, then sell it at market rates throughout North America and Europe."

Robert's face darkened.

"What, Mr. Cowens?"

"You can call me Robert."

"What, Robert?"

"If the source was in Toronto or Montreal it would be easier for me to find out things, but Vancouver can be a hidden world to someone like me."

"Like you . . . a lawyer?"

"No. Like me, a Jew. But I do have an old friend who could be a good contact to the business community in Vancouver and another guy who . . ."

"Please contact them." Fong looked up sharply. Robert followed his eye line. Beijing's young watcher, this time without a cigarette stuck in his face, was approaching from across the snack bar.

"He your keeper, Fong?" Robert asked *sotto voce*.

"He is." Fong stood and shook Robert's hand, saying loudly, "Thank you for your advice on this matter. Thank you very much." Then as he turned he said in a practised undertone. "It's in the newspaper. Follow it carefully. This could get dangerous." Without looking back to Robert he said to his Beijing keeper in furious Shanghanese, "These Long Noses really don't know when enough is enough. And their smell – wooo."

"Ouch!" shouted the French tourist as she grabbed her stomach. All around her in the packed street market off Julu Lu, south of Shanghai's embassy district, Chinese faces looked away – just another damn foreigner making a fuss over who knows what.

The tourist, Francine Allaire, couldn't care less what these Asians thought. She pulled her blouse out of her slacks and looked closely at the pinprick hole just below her navel. It didn't make any sense to her but she could only think of one explanation for that kind of puncture. She turned to the mass of Asian faces and screamed in her high-end Parisian French, "Which of you fucking Chink assholes stuck a goddamned needle in me?"

CHAPTER TWO

THE ASSASSIN

He almost laughed at what the sparkling new Pudong International Airport considered a security check. Of course he was carrying no weapon. A folded piece of paper was a perfectly adequate weapon when in his hands – not to mention a credit card, whether the edge was filed or not. He held his hands out to either side so they could wand his body. Nothing bleeped or blopped or whatever noise this devise would make. He didn't know the appropriate sound – he'd never been on an airplane before. It was rare for the Guild of Assassins to take an assignment outside of the Middle Kingdom.

And this time the authorities had asked for him, the teacher – not one of his students. As he waited in line to board the plane he thought of his favourite student – perhaps the only one he'd ever really loved, Loa Wei Fen. The boy had slept in his bed for many years – although near the end the boy had pushed him away in the night screaming, "You stink of wet paper!"

An odd phrase that – stink of wet paper. He had thought of that exact phrase when first he heard that Loa Wei Fen had met his unlikely end in a construction site in the Pudong Industrial District. Back then the Pudong, across the Huangpo River from the Bund, was a place in transition. The old shanty towns had been pulled down and replaced with massive construction pits – teeming with labourers. Now, ten years later, those huge holes in the ground housed the foundations of seventy of the most modern skyscrapers in the world. Loa Wei Fen had helped that come to be – had been a midwife to the birth of the New China.

There is no notion of the nobility of martyrdom in China – but sacrifice, although not honoured, is understood. Dying for one's country is considered the act of a fool. The Guild of Assassins had mourned Loa Wei Fen's passing with a three-day fast and then a week of contests. But no one had mourned more deeply than Loa Wei Fen's teacher and bed partner who now, in his mind's eye, reviewed each of the one-on-one combats. Then he considered the surprise winner – a girl. He wondered what her future held as he handed over his boarding pass at the second security check in the boarding lounge.

He found this security check as ludicrous as the first one. He was not some moron with plastique in his shoes and matches in his pocket. He was a trained and practised assassin, and had been for many, many years.

On the plane the attractive cabin attendant offered him a hand, as if he needed help walking down the aisle. That was good. Age is a fine disguise for an assassin. Fong passed by him and he noted the man's gait, his slight stoop, his dark liquid eyes that were in constant motion – and the hands that had killed the boy he loved, Loa Wei Fen.

The old assassin closed his eyes. But he did not sleep. He roamed his memory leaping from one floating pod of images to the next. His mother crying as he was pulled from her grasp by his father and handed over to his uncle who recruited for the Guild. His uncle's strong hand and stern voice telling him that he had been greatly honoured. His early schooling in the province west of the Wall. The sudden move to Taipei. The first time the power had roared through his arms and his opponent had been flung clear across the room. The Tibetan woman who had taught him the use of the swalto blade, then the night she had come to his bed and first made him a man then rolled him over and cut the outline of a cobra onto his back. Even now he could will the ancient red welts to life, fangs dripping, hood full of blood. But no reason to – not here. Not now. Zhong Fong was at the back of the plane. His contract was to follow and execute when so instructed.

Fine.

He'd done it many times before when the government had seen fit. Although he preferred the old ways – swalto and strong hands – he had also adapted to the new. The disappearing plane with political opponents on board. The collapsing building when an executive board meeting is taking place. The unaccountable fire – like the one that would take place in just over seventy-two hours in the apartment of computer expert Mr. Kenneth Lo. But he preferred the old. Poison was a special interest of his – and snakes. Poisonous snakes. Without willing it, the welted lines on his back filled with blood and the cobra awoke.

The plane hit air turbulence and the "Fasten Seat Belts" sign came on. He made as if he didn't understand the announcement. The cabin attendant leaned over him and did up his belt. He allowed himself to take in her odour.

Sweet, like fruit left just a little too long in the sun.

She would suffice if he needed to use her – fleshy enough to be a shield. But he doubted he would need her "assistance."

The plane travelled on through the night but he did not sleep. The sense of movement that so few others on the plane felt was minutely evident to him. He felt every directional shift. At one point before dawn the plane ceased its northward march and turned east – towards the West. Turning east to get to the West – to the Golden Mountain.

He remembered the "party" at Tiananmen Square and the boy with the flower standing in front of the tank. His young assassins had infiltrated the protestors and awaited his order. A single dead boy with a flower might have been enough to do the trick. A murder from inside their own ranks would have scared the protestors in a way that an army assault would not. A murder from within is so Chinese – so recognizably Chinese – that terror would have sped through their ranks and unleashed the thing that Chinese people fear most: chaos. The protestors would have slunk away with wary sidelong looks at each of their comrades and a deep sense of betrayal in their hearts. How much wiser that way than the frontal assault that eventually was used by the authorities. Wiser and more generous to life.

The old assassin saw no contradiction between his job and the desire to save life. He was an arm of diplomacy. His people had marched with Q'in She Huang when the mad tyrant first united China. They had been there when the Chinese invented gunpowder. When a Chinese junk circumnavigated the world almost two hundred years before the silly Italian bumped into the Americas. A whole section of *The Art of War* was written by a direct ancestor and four chapters based on the exploits of another early member of the Guild of Assassins.

He stroked his whiskers. Yes, we are very old in a very old world, he thought, then added, we are surely the oldest weapon of state, the only one that existed then and exists now. An attendant asked him if he would like a pillow. He shook his head. In all his years he had never slept with the aid of a pillow, never accepted the need for softness.

Love – yes. He'd needed that but it had been taken from him. Now he would revenge the death of his love, of Loa Wei Fen – even if his political masters didn't want it so.

Zhong Fong passed by him, heading towards the bathroom in the front cabin. The old assassin studied him again. He had been tracking the inspector for the better part of a month. Nothing about him seemed unusual. But he knew this man was a worthy quarry. He must be. He had managed to kill Loa Wei Fen, the best student he had ever trained in the academy. Such a man must have some resources that he keeps to himself. A secret wellspring of knowledge – and perhaps power.

Women see it, he thought. And the man's little girl. I do not yet, and I will not attack until I do.

The attendant's hand came in front of him and lowered a table. Onto it she put a plate of what the old assassin thought must be food. He picked the icing off a slice of carrot cake and ate it. As he was losing his teeth, his love of sweets was increasing. He examined the rest of the "food" in front of him. He cracked a small hard paper tube hoping it would reveal a candy but was disappointed to find it to be salt. No more sweets. He sat back. He would not be eating anything else, although he looked at each dish closely and enumerated the number of ways that both the implements and the food itself could be used to kill an opponent. He was seventy-four years old. His teeth were bad but his body was as well toned as a well-conditioned man half his age. The enamel of teeth rots, but sinew and tendon, the real source of physical power, age well if they are looked after. And his sinews and tendons had been extended and strengthened by exercise every day for the past seven decades. He smiled, closed his eyes and waited. *"We began in patience,"* he heard his first teacher whisper in his ear. *"Be still. Listen to the room, feel the earth spin and sense the power of your* chi *deep within – like a cobra raising itself – then flaring its hood."*

CHAPTER THREE

A DEAR ROBERT LETTER

Robert slipped the newspaper Fong had left on the table beneath his arm and headed back to his hotel room. In the elevator he began to feel silly – like he was playing spy or something. But when he took out his card to unlock his hotel room door he wondered how to tell if someone had been in his room while he was gone. Something about putting hairs across the door jamb or something – he wasn't very fond of spy movies.

He locked his door, put on the safety catch and then spread the newspaper on the bed. There, in the innermost fold was a set of notes, instructions printed in remarkably tiny and precise block letters. Almost prissy, he thought. It occurred to Robert that Fong drew his letters rather than wrote them.

Mr. Cowens:

I have not yet involved you in anything dangerous. However if you choose to meet me at the place indicated at the end of this note then you are involved and perhaps in danger. I am not trying to frighten you. I am trying to give you what I believe lawyers call full disclosure. Read this and if you do not wish to proceed please destroy these notes. Cut them into small pieces then burn them in the sink of your hotel room. Not all at once as a lot of smoke may set off a fire alarm or worse a sprinkler system. Once the notes are completely ash, crush them then wash them down the drain. Allow the water to continue to run for a few minutes. I am not trying to be dramatic, Mr. Cowens, just careful.

All of this started during a previous investigation. At the time I impounded a computer from a Shanghai company named the International Exchange Institute. The owner of this company had been murdered by his secretary. I gave the computer over to our expert in these matters, a man named Kenneth Lo who had recently joined our office from Hong Kong like Joan Shui, who you met. Kenneth is someone who I think you would probably quite like.

Robert wondered what Fong meant by that.

Well, at the time of the investigation, Kenneth came to me and told me that if he worked too quickly on the hard drive from the International Exchange Institute that he raised the likelihood that the machine would self-destruct – something about tripping electronic erase commands, booby traps – I admit I didn't follow his technical talk. At any rate I informed him that he should take his time – that I wanted the information on that hard drive. I wanted to know what the dead man's company was trading.

Months later, well after the case had come to a successful but unhappy conclusion, Kenneth, knocked on my office door. It was very late and the cold of the winter was upon us.

Fong related the events of that meeting with Kenneth Lo that sent him to the back country of Anhui Province and then eventually to Calgary.

Robert you probably don't recognize the name Chiang Wo. It is an infamous name in my country. The Chiangs collaborated with the Japanese in the war. They bankrolled Chiang Kai Shek as he stole the wealth of the mainland and brought it to his island fortress in Taiwan. They were driven away after the liberation, but since the Beijing government set us on our capitalist path there have been persistent rumours that they have returned to the Mainland. They are a powerful, connected family that ruthlessly protects what is theirs. Profit has always governed their dealings in and out of the Middle Kingdom.

But there is more that you must understand before you agree to assist me. When I went to Anhui Province to investigate these charges I couldn't get over the feeling that I was being followed. No. Tracked. I felt the same when I boarded the plane for Canada.

At Kananaskis it was easy to spot the government watcher who was sent to make sure I behaved myself. The part of Beijing that monitors its nationals abroad could never be accused of excess cleverness. But it was not this man that I sensed tracking me.

Mr. Cowens, Beijing is set up in boxes and often what happens in one box is not always known by those who work in the other boxes. It is the way that those in power stop palace coups before they begin. You might recall that palace coups are a time-honoured tradition in my homeland.

Some government people are making real money off the blood trade and I'm sure that they are willing to defend those profits – ah, the New China. But the people of China are better informed now than in the old days. If it were to get out that government officials were getting rich by infecting their own people – well, revolution is a time-honoured tradition in the Middle Kingdom too.

All this is to say that it is very likely important to powerful people that I don't find the answer to who is behind all this. If you help me you will become a person of interest, as Americans like to say, to those powerful people.

Don't come to Banff unless you fully understand and accept the danger. I know it is unfair of me to involve you in this, but – I have no but. Either I will see you in Banff at Agnes's coffee shop – or I won't.

Then there were detailed instructions on how to make a safe approach to Fong in Banff and a copy of the article from the *Wall Street Journal*'s Asia edition entitled "The Blood Trade." Robert scanned it quickly then returned to Fong's final words.

Even if you don't come could you do me a favour. The photo at the bottom of this page is of the Beijing man who is assigned to make sure that I am behaving myself. My keeper if you wish. Could you possibly use your lawyer connections and have him waylaid for a few days?

Fong.

Robert looked at the picture of the trim young man who had approached their table in the hotel's snack bar. Robert looked out the window and took in the vista. He knew he should be thrilled by the natural beauty there – but he felt nothing.

He thought about that for a moment. Then about how alive he'd felt in Shanghai with Fong as they tracked down the arsonist who called himself Angel Michael. "Rage, rage at end of day," he said to the quiet of his room, then he reached for the phone and took out his address book. He picked out the private number of the immensely powerful oilman whose divorce he had successfully handled. He dialed the number and, after apologizing profusely for the late hour of his call, answered the man's question (What can I do for you, Robert?) by asking, "Do you know any police officers in the Kananaskis area?" The man's answer made him smile – the first time he had felt like smiling since his doctor had told him the bad news.

CHAPTER FOUR

LATER IN BANFF

T wo days later Fong stared out the window of Agnes's Fine Coffees on the main street of this peculiar little tourist town. Fong had purchased a Styrofoam cup of Agnes's special blend and sat at the raised counter by the window. He watched the parade outside. Down coats, baggy pants, toques, snowboards, blond hair, fleece vests, bright colours – and packages. Everyone carried packages emblazoned with the names of incredibly overpriced stores. Behind the two-storey buildings on the other side of street three steep jagged mountain peaks gave the lie to the surface civility of the place. The most southerly of the peaks shone white in snow. The other two were in shadow and bespoke the cold out of which the tourists were feverishly trying to buy their way.

To his right the Mount Royal Hotel modestly occupied a corner. Across the way the Ultimate Ski Ride battled for the public's attention with the Rose and Crown Pub, the One-Hour Film Lab and the Shirt Company. But it was a small store beside the pub that held Fong's eye: It's In The Cards.

Although Fong understood that the place sold greeting cards – though he couldn't for the life of him comprehend why anyone would need such a thing when all one needed was a pencil and paper – it wasn't the items sold that drew Fong's attention. It was the thought – It's in the cards – that bothered Fong. The deeply fatalistic idea that one's future is predestined, already in the cards – that the cards have already been dealt. The giving up involved in such a thought appalled Fong. The idea that trying diligently to make things better was futile, that hard work and honesty were useless in the face of predestination made Fong want to spit. The whole idea struck Fong as obscene. When he heard people accepting stupidity with a casual shrug of the shoulder or as in the case in Western China with the expression "Inshallah," he wanted to take the person by the ears, shake him hard then scream into his face, "Wake up. Do something. Don't accept. Fight back. Human beings are not dumb animals." There are some things above our power to change but not everything. A stupid government decision is not some god's will. A lazy, drunk, water controller who poisons his whole town is not enacting the will of some deity. Villages ravaged by AIDS are not part of the manifestation of some godly master plan. They are the direct result of human greed and have nothing to do with some heavenly will. They are not in the cards. They are the acts of men – acts that must not be accepted or excused. Acts that must be stopped, and pawning them off as some sort of predestination is nonsense and more importantly – dangerous.

The door to Agnes's Fine Coffees opened and Robert, dressed in a suit wearing a topcoat, the only one that Fong had seen in Banff, entered. He headed to the back and exited out the rear door as Fong's instructions had told him to. Fong waited and watched the street traffic. It all moved as before. No one stopped to stare into a store window across the way; no one stopped to tie a shoe. No car pulled over as if to adjust a rear-view mirror. And more importantly, no one followed Robert Cowens into the coffee shop then out the back door. A few minutes later Robert came around the block a second time. Fong nodded. Robert entered the shop a second time and took a seat at the back. Fong examined the street traffic again then moved back and took a seat opposite Robert.

"You're the only one in this town wearing a suit and tie."

"I'm the only one west of Winnipeg that even owns one."

"Is that good?"

"I never thought about it. It's one of those things that just is." Then Robert thought for a moment and said, "You know who Waylon Jennings is?"

"No. Should I?"

"Not unless you like country music."

"You mean like the Beatles?"

"No. Not like the Beatles. Country music . . . never mind."

"What did Mr. Waylon say?"

"Mr. Jennings," Robert corrected Fong.

Fong smiled. "You people still using the given name first? When will you learn?"

"Probably when we're as old and smart as you Chinese."

"Ah – could be a while." Robert nodded and allowed himself to smile. Fong asked, "So what did Waylon say?"

"He said that he was a success because he turned fifty and didn't own a single suit or tie."

"You're older than fifty, aren't you?"

"Fifty-two."

"You own a suit and tie."

"Seventeen suits and more ties than I can count."

"So you're not a success then?"

"But I am."

"Then perhaps Mr. Waylon is wrong."

To Fong's surprise Robert looked out the window. Then he adjusted his tie despite the fact that it didn't need adjusting. When he looked up Fong was staring at him. "I don't know Fong . . . I really don't know."

Fong clearly caught the note of hurt in Robert's voice. He noted the man's pallor. It wasn't good. How sick had he been – or was he?

"By the by – you owe me a thank you."

"I do?"

"Yep. I arranged to have your Beijing watcher picked up for loitering."

"Loitering?"

"Kananaskis is a very tight little community – they're not big on strangers. He should be out by now. I left a message for him to meet you in Calgary." Robert giggled. It was a strange sound.

"What?" Fong demanded.

"Have you ever tried to find an address in Calgary?"

"No. I've yet to have the pleasure."

"Actually the city is laid out in a very orderly fashion. Whole areas of streets have the same name like Crowfoot."

"Isn't that confusing?"

"In theory, no, because there is a Crowfoot Road, a Crowfoot Terrace, a Crowfoot Boulevard, a Crowfoot Crescent, a Crowfoot Circle and many more Crowsfeet than there are on an old man's face."

Fong didn't follow that but he smiled anyway – it seemed to be what Robert wanted.

"The problem is that each of these Crowfeet roads feed into and out of each other. So once you are in Crowfeet land you should be able to find any Crowfeet address. That's the theory."

"And the practice?"

"Not always so simple. For example, I gave your Beijing handler 1249 Crowfoot – no road, boulevard, crescent et al. I wouldn't be the least bit surprised if he's still looking for you."

"He'll find me quickly enough. He's no doubt already reported me at large."

Robert shrugged.

Anxiously, Fong asked, "He's not hurt, is he?"

"No, Fong. I'm a lawyer not a terrorist."

"That is a kind of terrorist in some people's eyes."

"In yours?"

Fong paused. He stirred his coffee. "Terrorism takes many forms – hope, but a few."

Robert didn't know what Fong meant. Suddenly he wasn't completely sure what much of anything meant. Why had he come first to Calgary and now to Banff? What the fuck was he doing altogether? But all he said was, "Huh?"

Fong looked Robert straight in the eyes. "If you stood at the top of a building whose lower floors were on fire – what would you do?"

"Wait for help?"

"And if the building was tall enough that you knew no help could get to you?"

"No way down?" Robert was suddenly fully engaged.

"None."

"I'd wait until the heat got to me then I'd jump, I guess."

Fong looked at Robert with something akin to wonder in his eyes. "Would you?"

"Jump? Would I jump, yes."

"Would you?"

"Yes. Fong?"

Fong didn't answer. He looked out the window at the mountains – snow-covered crests, trees clinging to life at every jutting. Then he shook his head.

"What, Fong?"

"Agnes's special coffee tastes like dark water."

"Ah, New York City coffee has come to the great Canadian West." Fong looked back at him, a question rising to his lips. Robert beat him to it, "Never mind. So, would you jump, Fong?"

"No, Robert — I'd fly." He almost added: like the guy from the Trade Towers but didn't because he wasn't sure either of Robert's reaction – or his own.

Robert nodded. A path of perception opened and Robert in a simple synapsal flash knew why he was in Banff, Alberta, wearing a suit, a tie and an overcoat, and he knew that he had one thing left to do in his life – fly. Fly fly fly at the end of the day.

The old assassin waited patiently. He'd made himself wait all day, so waiting for a few more minutes didn't bother him. In front of him in the line were a young American couple with two children. One was asleep in the arms of her mother; the other was pulling hard at the coat of her father. She had clearly had enough for one day.

"Now what?"

"You'll like this, Beth."

"I won't. I didn't like the other stuff we did today, why should I like this?"

Because it's like candy, the old assassin said to himself as he felt the tug of his own desire for something sweet. That "tug" was now very much like an addiction, he knew. How odd to have an addiction at this point in one's life. He'd heard that Brezhnev, the former Soviet leader, had had a serious smoking habit and that he had been given a silver cigarette case with a timer in it as a present by the Swiss ambassador. The timer was set so that Brezhnev, at that time the second most powerful man in the world, could only open the case and get to his cigarettes on the hour and the half-hour. Those who were in the know realized that if they wished to get anything from the old bear they had to schedule their meetings either just after the hour or just after the half-hour. If not, Brezhnev hardly followed the conversation because his concentration was fully on when he could get his next cigarette. An image leapt into the assassin's head. A desperate military man rushes into Brezhnev's office screaming: "Missiles are heading our way, Premier, what should we do?" But Brezhnev doesn't answer. It's seven minutes to the hour. All his concentration is on getting through those seven minutes to his next smoke. Missiles be damned, I need that smoke.

The assassin smiled. When he met Premier Brezhnev he had been sure to have his conference set for just past the half-hour. It had been a very successful meeting. The Bear had been smoking, happily. He had listened carefully as the old assassin had laid out the conditions upon which the Guild would accept work from the Russian. Brezhnev had commissioned two assassinations through the haze of his smelly Ossetian tobacco. The old assassin had bowed shallowly and replied that he would present the opportunity to the Guild. He did nothing of the sort. The Russians were the enemy – always had been and always would be.

Now he too had a habit, the old assassin thought. Sweets. He craved sweets – like this BeaverTail concoction for which he was waiting in line. He'd first seen a ski-jacket-clad woman eating one on the street. He had stopped and stared, then tracked down the source of the sticky Canadian delicacy, and now he waited patiently for his turn.

"In the car and out of the car and in the car and out of the car and in the car and out of the car . . ." the girl sang quietly as if to comfort herself – although it occurred to the old assassin that the child was commenting on the trip she had had with her parents. He looked at the parents. They didn't seem to be having much fun either; maybe a BeaverTail would perk them up.

The BeaverTail was a disappointment. Although sweet, it was a wheat pastry. And wheat, though now popular in the New China, was not something that he had ever developed a taste for. So he picked the syrupy parts and the hard candy off the flat dough and sucked on them as he watched the sun set over the mountains that encircle Banff. I hope Fong is enjoying his time with the sick Long Nose, he thought as he watched the fading of the light. Quickly, he was surrounded by the darkness and the cold. He cast aside the remainder of the BeaverTail, purposefully missing the municipally supplied garbage can. Several passersby stared at him. One was about to comment then thought better of it. This overconcern with cleanliness reminded him of Japan. He hated Japan. A little filth was only human. It stopped obscenity like he had seen as a boy in Nanking during the war.

His training had not been completed when the word came to the school that they were all needed in the old capital. By then the Japanese had controlled most of China for almost a decade. The Manchu emperor was a contemptuous joke and the Japanese were bleeding China for all it was worth to support their war effort against the Americans. The Japanese soldiers who had invaded China were cruel but well trained. They were committed occupiers – Japanese descendents of the Samurai. In their own way honourable. But as the war wore on and China was no longer a military concern, the Japanese rotated their troops. These new soldiers were conscripts, often illiterate country people, who hated the Chinese with a passion that only a child can have for a powerful parent. The hatred had come to a boil when Nanking refused to surrender. A brief battle ensued and the much-underarmed Chinese were quickly defeated.

Then the Japanese soldiers were let loose on the populace. Thousands of women were dragged from their homes, stripped naked and gang-raped. Old men were nailed to walls, young men castrated, whole ancient inner-courtyard compounds were sealed shut with all their generations locked inside while the buildings were set alight.

Then the Guild of Assassins had arrived. They were not large in numbers, but they were trained to kill. His first night in Nanking the old assassin had killed seven Japanese soldiers as they sat by their guard post and told stories of Chinese women crying beneath them as they had their way. Of course he was not an *old* assassin then.

As a result of that night, the next day the Japanese executed hundreds of people in the marketplaces. But this did not deter the Guild. Every night the streets ran with Japanese blood. Every day Chinese blood flooded the ancient sewers. But eventually the Japanese backed off. They retreated to their safe zones and left the rest of the city to fend for itself.

And so Nanking had stayed, until Japanese imperial ambitions were atom-bombed to an end.

The old assassin sighed. He preferred a little litter – it was more Chinese.

After Fong told Robert everything he knew about the blood trade, and Robert told Fong about his contacts in Vancouver, they ate dinner at a small Chinese restaurant upstairs from a chic clothing shop. Fong looked at the menu – pages and pages of it. "This is a Chinese restaurant?"

"So it claims."

"Why don't I recognize any of the dishes? Who's General Tso and how does he rate a chicken? And what's chicken and pineapple?"

"Chicken with pineapple, no doubt."

"Why would anyone put chicken with pineapple?"

"Maybe because it tastes good."

"Maybe because they aren't really Chinese and just fooling you people that they are."

"Counterfeit Chinese restaurant, you think? Should report them to the authorities. But we're in Alberta. They don't actually have government ministries here. Of course if we were in Ontario there is a ministry of restaurants and rest rooms that might take an active interest. Maybe the heritage ministry? Defaming of multicultural food practices may be a federal offence . . . I'll have to look into that."

A Chinese family came in – mom, dad, grandma, all the brothers and sisters. They spoke Cantonese to the proprietor. Fong looked at them — so many children. So many children for a Chinese family. He couldn't put that together. He was about to dismiss them as not being really Chinese when the grandmother flipped over her plate and read the manufacturer's insignia there – tinked it hard on the table to test its durability and then announced with stunning finality: "Cheap." So they were Chinese after all.

Across the way two young blonde-haired women spoke loudly to each other. "Are they speaking English?" Fong asked.

"Sort of English. They're Australians."

Fong listened to their conversation. They laughed like men. They were loud and aggressive like men and seemed to think the entire restaurant really ought to be privy to their conversation. "Why are they like that?" Fong asked.

Robert looked at them for a moment. "They're faraway from home. They've got to prove they belong. That they have a right to be here. That they are young and alive."

That sad note again. Fong noticed that Robert had moved more food around his plate than he had eaten. He had also taken two tablets of something before they began.

Robert noticed Fong examining him. "Don't."

Fong's head snapped back as if he'd been caught looking in a woman's open window. "Sorry."

"Where to next?"

"Calgary, then we fly to Vancouver."

"Your handler might pick you up in Calgary."

"I want him to. It's safer if Beijing is watching." He paused, then said to himself, "I think."

The old assassin moved slowly down the snow-covered street and turned into an alley that he had scouted earlier. He sat on the cold pavement and drew his knees up to his chin. Then he allowed his mind to float.

"I hurt him, Master," Loa Wei Fen had said to him.

He smiled and canted his head slightly.

"But Master, he's hurt."

Slowly he had nodded then turned to Loa Wei Fen, noting how his skin shone with sweat, his hair matted – his eyes so, so beautiful. He nodded again. "You only hurt him, Loa Wei Fen."

"Yes, but he's . . ."

". . . the enemy. We are not here to hurt an enemy. We are here to eliminate them."

"Master . . ."

"Kill him, Loa Wei Fen. Do what you've been trained to do. Kill him."

The boy on the ground began to beg. To claim that they were both students. Friends. Loa Wei Fen had turned to him for advice, but he had remained very still. This was a choice that every member of the Guild faced. If Loa Wei Fen failed to vault this hurdle then he would have to be "put down" and the obligation would fall to him as the failed boy's master.

But Loa Wei Fen did not fail. Later that night the boy had, for the first time, come to his master's bed.

Robert drove and Fong took it all in. They followed the road as it made a wide left-hand curve around a river. Across the way, deep in a valley, was a huge factory with seven massive chimneys bellowing plumes of white smoke into the cold clear air. Fong looked at Robert. "Lime. It refines lime."

"For cement?"

"Cement and cleaning drains, I guess."

As they passed it, Fong turned to get another look. The scale of it was so large, yet it was made tiny by the surrounding mountain.

They snaked their way with craggy peaks on either side. But it wasn't the peaks that fascinated Fong. It was the trees that somehow had gained a purchase on the barren rock.

"Hope," he said aloud.

"What?" asked Robert.

But Fong didn't respond. Life from rock was hope. A thing in short supply these days.

The sun began to set as they left the foothills heading east towards Calgary. Fong reached up and tilted the rearview mirror towards him so he could watch the mountains retreat behind him.

"You like mountains?"

"I don't know."

"You don't know?"

"Yes, as I said, I don't know. Their scale worries me. But their scale is also exciting." He wasn't sure he could talk about trees growing out of rocks with Robert Cowens. What would lawyers understand about such things?

Robert nodded and continued to drive.

In the rear-view mirror Fong saw the mountains rising out of the plains as if someone had said, "Start here. This is a good spot." He wasn't anxious to think who that someone might be so he turned the rear-view mirror back towards Robert. Through the front windshield he saw the moon rising over the far reaches of the highway. As if in Canada you could actually drive to the moon. Yes. This road leads you to the moon.

The traffic thickened as they passed Canmore. SUVs and vans were everywhere. Was that about big families too, Fong wondered. A few kilometres past Canmore, Fong yelled at Robert to stop.

Robert pulled the car over to the shoulder and hit the brakes. Fong was out before the car came to a full stop. Before Robert was out of the car, Fong had raced across the highway and was running back up the wide, grass, highway divide. Robert finally caught up to Fong. In the fading light at first he couldn't make out what had caught Fong's eye. Then he stepped a little closer and he saw.

Fong was standing over a full-grown male wolf that had been hit by a car while it must have been trying to cross the highway.

Fong knelt and touched the fur. A coarseness met his hand and a thick musk odour filled his nostrils. He sunk both his hands into the fur and touched the hot skin.

It was only then that Fong felt the pulse.

The animal's great head lifted from the ground and

turned towards Fong. Fong was within the reach of the savage teeth. The lips pulled back as if to snarl, then the jaws opened wide. A spray of blood shot from its mouth. And a sound, low, like a woman's moan, filled the cold night. The animal momentarily was lit by the headlights of an oncoming car then thrown back into darkness. Every passing light drew the great animal's amber eyes. A lull in the traffic brought a moment of rest and the wolf's eyes turned up to the night sky. A low growl came from the beast and the animal turned its massive head and looked right into Fong's eyes. Fong met the animal's gaze. A car roared by. In the strafing headlights, Fong saw the retreat in the wolf's eyes – a glaze slowly sealing in his life. Fong leaned in close to the animal and whispered in his upturned ear, "Fly. Fly to your new life."

The ancient animal exhaled deeply. The dank earthiness of his breath filled Fong's nostrils. Fong breathed in the animal's breath. He realized that he was the last thing this great beast would ever see. He reached towards the face. The animal's mouth opened and closed twice. Then a calm filled the animal's eyes. The immense head came slowly to the ground. And he lay still. So very, very still.

It was only then that Fong realized that Robert was at his side.

"He's dead?"

Fong stood. Behind Robert was a huge billboard for ski goggles.

"Will someone bury it?"

"The hawks will get to it first."

"Hawks." Fong nodded and thought again of flight in the presence of death.

When they were back in the car, Robert asked, "Why did we need to go to Banff to meet?"

Fong shrugged. "I've never been to Banff. I wanted to

see it. Besides it's very highly thought of by the Japanese."

Memories of his own early kills flooded the old assassin, but it was always the image of Loa Wei Fen that kept floating to the surface. Just before dawn the image of the boy turned to him and said in a child's voice, "If you loved me you will kill the man who took my life."

"I promise," he said to the cold dawn as he rose and walked towards the bus station as fully refreshed as anyone who had just risen from a full night's rest in a featherbed in the Fairmont Hotel.

CHAPTER FIVE

CALGARY

The French tourist sat in Captain Chen's office at Special Investigations on the Bund. She was anxious to register her report and cause as much trouble as possible. She had already contacted a French doctor and was anxiously awaiting the results of a battery of tests that cost more than most Chinese workers made in a year. The man across from her, this Captain Chen, was as ugly a human as she had ever seen. He smiled. Or at least that's what the French tourist assumed that curvature of his lips intended. She sat. He sat. They both waited. Captain Chen spoke only country-accented Mandarin. And the French tourist, naturally enough, spoke only French. So they waited. The office was dingy. The officer was ugly. The French tourist was as angry as . . . as a French tourist can get.

The knock on Fong's Calgary hotel-room door surprised him. He opened the door. There standing politely in the hallway were three modestly dressed Chinese men. One elderly, one in advanced middle age and one in his early twenties. They were all the exact same size and their facial features were comically similar. Only their eyes varied. The eldest had deep sadness buried there, the middle-aged one had controlled anger and the youngster had rage. "Inspector Zhong," began the young man, "we wonder if we could have a moment of your valuable time." The voice was controlled, the English clearly that of a native speaker. Fong ignored the young man and bowed slightly to the elderly man. "Can I be of assistance, Grandpa?" he said in Mandarin.

"If you would be so kind," replied the old man with remarkable dignity.

"Have you been in the Golden Mountain a long time, Grandpa?"

"Forever."

Fong stepped aside and the three men entered his room. Fong glanced into the corridor before he closed the door. He might have been wrong but he was pretty sure that he saw a figure duck back into a doorway some way down the hallway.

The French tourist lit her third cigarette as she completed her tale of woe. The translator slowly related the woman's story to Captain Chen. He nodded. The basics of the story were pretty straightforward – and troubling. A tourist out for a walk in one of the several crowded street markets in one of Shanghai's many densely packed alleyways had been assaulted by someone with a hypodermic needle.

Through the interpreter Chen asked to see the wound. The French tourist hesitated for an instant, then pulled her blouse aside far enough to reveal a rather large, already infected hole, just below her navel.

Chen turned to the interpreter, "Tell her thank you and ask her if she has seen a doctor."

Her response was quick and angry. "Of course I've seen a doctor and not a ridiculous Chinese doctor. A real doctor. A French doctor."

"I want her to see Lily," Chen told the interpreter.

After a flurry of angry protests, the Frenchwoman threw up her hands, then followed the interpreter in the direction of the Special Investigations forensic labs that were still located above the abortion clinics in the Hua Shan Hospital, just down the road on Jiang An Lu.

Robert picked up the phone in his hotel room and dialed. A familiar voice from his past said, "Balderson." Polite, although gruff, Canadian – Western Canadian.

"Evan, is that you?"

"Yes. Who's this?"

For a moment Robert hesitated. He hadn't been in touch with his old college RA for almost five years. "It's Robert Cowens."

Without a moment's hesitation Evan replied, "You haven't called for five years and over six months and then all of a sudden, up you pop."

"Has it been that long?"

"How the fuck would I know? You think I have nothing better to do with my time than keep track of your comings and goings, like the stupid girl with the candle in the window in *Moonfleet*?"

Evan taught English literature and assumed that everyone he spoke to had read the same books he had. He'd almost lured Robert into graduate work in literature but the clarion call of money had led Robert to the law instead. Evan had never really forgiven him.

"Foreclosed on any widows lately?"

"No, I'm trying to cut back."

"Good idea." Evan evidently still had a beard, the sound of which scraping across the mouthpiece was clear in Robert's ear.

"How's Meredith?"

The sigh from Evan was enough to tell Robert that Meredith, the love of Evan's life, had sunk deeper into the veils that MS had looped around her consciousness.

"Sorry."

"Yeah," said Evan, then added, "She has her good days – her vehement days."

Robert didn't know what to say about "vehement" days. Meredith came from very old Family Compact money. She could be very tough, Robert knew, but "vehement"? About that he didn't know much, so he ignored the comment and said, "I need your help, Evan."

"You finally finished that novel you started at my insistence and need a publisher?"

"No, I need an entree."

"To what?"

"This'll sound strange, but I need access to the business establishment of Vancouver."

"You're a fuckin' lawyer, surely you know . . ."

"I don't – not in Vancouver."

Evan laughed. "This couldn't have to do with your religious affiliation, could it?"

"In a town where we're often referred to as Hebrews and the phrase 'he jewed me' is in common parlance, what do you think?"

"I think you'd need the help of a guy like me whose last name is Balderson. Care to tell me what this is all about?"

Robert surprised himself when he answered, "Business, just business."

A few more clever quips from both and Robert hung up the phone. Then he stood very still and asked himself a very simple question: "Why didn't I tell Evan what I needed from him?"

"As I said," Fong reiterated, careful to avoid the young one's angry eyes, "I can be of real service in this regard but ultimately the foreign office will have to pursue the Canadian government to get you an official apology."

There was a brief pause and then the middle-aged man said, "As a Communist you should be more practised at lying. Hence, you should be able to lie better than that."

The grandfather snapped a look at his son and the man retreated. Fong glanced at the younger man.

"Are you married, Inspector Zhong?" asked the old man.

"Not now."

"But you have been?" the grandfather persisted.

"Twice. My first wife died."

"And your second?"

Fong wasn't thrilled with this line of questioning but decided to get through it as quickly as he could. "We're divorced. We share custody of our five-year-old daughter."

"Xiao Ming," stated the father. With a sneer he added, "We have our sources too, Inspector."

The grandfather stepped in front of his son and said softly, "Swear. Swear on the love of Xiao Ming that you'll give every effort to get Beijing to force Ottawa to formally apologize to the Chinese community of this country."

"And if I so swear?"

"We'll give you all the contacts you need to complete your work here," the son said. Fong noted how carefully that was phrased.

"It might interest you to know, Inspector Zhong," said the grandfather "that the Chiang family has had dealings in this country for a long time."

So their sources were good enough in the Middle Kingdom to interest them in the Chiangs, Fong thought.

The old man continued, "The Chiangs were, in fact,

the official agent of the Canadian Pacific Railway in China. They lured coolies to this country. They made money as those men died. They made money from their deaths. They even invented the name 'coolie.'"

Fong bowed slightly.

"So do we have your word?"

Fong bowed again and said, "On the love of my daughter, Xiao Ming."

Then the young man handed over a thick sheaf of paper. "Every sin they committed against the Black Haired People is documented here."

The sins were vast. The document's introduction read:

Between 1881 and 1885 fifteen thousand Chinese males, virtual slaves, were brought over from China by the central government of Canada to build a railway so that the renegade province of British Columbia wouldn't join the United States. Ironically an American railway engineer, Andrew Onderdonk, was put in charge of the project. He wanted Chinese workers because they were cheap and "If they could build the Great Wall of China they could build a railway." The Ching dynasty permitted Onderdonk to venture up the Zhuijiang River delta and take workers from the poor villages there.

The Chinese were shipped to Canada in such tight quarters that they had to intertwine legs to find a place to sit. Four hundred grams of rice were served up to sustain ten men. Many starved to death on the long voyage. When they finally arrived in British Columbia they were divided into groups of thirty men and put through a long forced march over mountains, with heavy packs on their backs, to get to the site of the work. It was winter and few had anything more than the clothing they wore in the subtropical villages from which they came. Waking to frozen bodies was a part of a coolie's life. The Chinese workers carved thirteen tunnels through the mountains with only pick and shovel as tools. They moved over 11 million square metres of rock and gravel. From Yale to Lytton they built six hundred bridges, hauled a thousand tons of steel and 40 million boards. Scurvy took many. Starvation took more. Over a thousand Chinese workers died in the Fraser Canyon section of the railway alone. In total over six thousand Chinese died in the building of the railway – more than one a mile. The workers were charged fifteen US dollars to ship their dead home to the waiting burial grounds in Xinhui.

The Chinese workers were never supplied with gloves, coats, helmets or shoes and they received less than seventy-five cents a day for their efforts. When the railway was finally completed no transportation was supplied to the Chinese workers. Wherever the Chinese workers were when the "golden spike" joined the tracks from the east with the tracks from the west they were simply left – to fend for themselves – and by the way, to get out of Canada. In 1885 Canada increased the incentive to go by introducing a head tax for any Chinese man who wanted to bring in his wife and children - fifty dollars a Chinese soul. In 1900 the Canadian government got annoyed with the number of industrious Chinese men who could afford the head tax and raised it first to one hundred dollars a Chinese head, then three years later to five hundred dollars. To put that figure in context: in 1903, five hundred dollars in Canada could buy two hundred acres of prime farm land. By the end of 1923 it is estimated that the Chinese had paid $26 million in head tax. The cost to build the railway was only $25 million. In 1923 Canada had had enough of the Chinese altogether and passed the Chinese Exclusion Act that stated, "With the exception of diplomatic personnel, business people and students, no Chinese may enter Canada. No Chinese are allowed to bring their family to Canada. This ruling applies to Chinese only." Nice of them to clarify that.

But still the hatred lingered. In 1907 riots broke out in Vancouver's Chinatown. In 1908 Vancouver and Victoria passed *laws excluding Chinese students from attending the same schools as white children.*

Finally, in 1947 the Chinese Exclusion Act *was repealed. The act was in place for just under twenty-four years. For that time Chinese people living in Canada had virtually no legal status. Yet, many fought – and some died – for Canada in the Second World War.*

Things have changed. In 1957 the first Chinese man was elected to Parliament. In 1965 a Chinese man was elected mayor of a major city. And now we have a Governor General who is Chinese. But there is still something missing. An apology – an official apology from the government of Canada to the Chinese people of this country who had a lot to do with making this a great nation.

Fong put the document aside. He didn't need to read the sixty pages of supporting material to know that the opening statement was true.

"Where are you folks from?" Fong asked.

"Here now."

"Right. But where originally?"

"Anhui Province."

The phone rang in Robert's Calgary hotel room. Robert picked it up, but before he could say anything he heard Evan's gruff voice say, "I teach a course in Philosophy."

"So this would be helpful because . . ."

"Because I teach it downtown, at night . . . to businesspeople. They love it. I'm very in, very happening, starlike, if you will."

"Really?"

"Really. You're coming to town, I assume."

"Yeah."

"When?"

"Should be there tomorrow."

"Call me the day after. At the very least I'll have someone for you to talk to. But Robert . . ."

"What, Evan?"

"Do behave yourself – no talking with your hands."

"I promise. Ham and Swiss on white bread with butter."

"I like a bit of mayo on mine."

"Evan?"

"What?"

"It's late."

"So it is."

"See you in two days."

"Looking forward to it."

"Good." Robert hung up the phone and looked at the bedside clock – just past two in the morning. Only one in the morning in Vancouver but clearly Evan was alone. The love of his life, Meredith, had insisted on living on her own as the disease grew in and around her. It was her way of saying that she was free – even from MS. She had at one time been a highly respected political power broker, a real behind-the-scenes operator. But not anymore.

Robert thought of Evan. A bear of a man – roaming the darkness of his house, once their house – but now, his alone.

CHAPTER SIX

A FIRE SCENE

Joan Shui wasn't happy. The preliminary report from the fire scene that unfurled from the fax machine in her Hong Kong condo struck her as cursory at best. But she hesitated to make a fuss. She was new to the Shanghai police force and all her years on the Hong Kong constabulary as a chief arson inspector meant squat to the Shanghanese. If anything, those years counted against her. Years of steady propaganda had instilled a deep loathing for Hong Kong in the Shanghanese, despite the fact that Shanghai was actively trying to out "Hong Kong" Hong Kong in every conceivable way. As well, her sponsor and lover Zhong Fong was off in the West at a counterterrorism conference. "That's why I'm hesitating to respond to this bullshit fax," she thought, then cast aside the thought.

She reread the faxed report. Claptrap about a kitchen fire that got out of control. She was in Hong Kong finalizing the sale of her condo when she'd gotten the first call. The men in charge of the investigation were none too happy when she told them to fax their report to her. They were none too keen on taking orders of any sort from a woman, especially a woman who they thought of as a

Westerner. She'd done her best to hold her temper when she spoke to them on the phone.

"It was what?"

"A simple kitchen fire. You know these people, they have kitchens now and they don't know how to use them properly."

Joan knew that since the last "great leap forward" the entire population of Shanghai had basically eaten from communal kitchens – they had little choice because most Shanghanese had to melt down their kitchen utensils to meet the Beijing Government's ludicrous demands for steel that they were supposed to produce in backyard blast furnaces. So it was possible that finally having a kitchen could pose issues. But it didn't sound right.

"All three are dead?" she asked.

"Mom, pop and kid," the cop said.

His cell phone crackled for a few seconds – unusual in China where cell phone communication was first rate. Without the advent of cell-phone technology China could never have had the extraordinary economic growth of the past decade. There was no way to wire 1.3 billion people. But with cell phones there was obviously no need for tele-phone poles and trillions of kilometres of wires. Besides, cell phones were made in Chinese prisons and therefore were cheap. In fact, because cell phones came into China when they did, China never went through the early woes of cell-phone technology. In New York or London or Rome, cell phones regularly cacked out. Not in China. So the crackling sound on the man's cell phone raised alarm bells in her head.

"All dead. How?"

"Fire."

She took a breath and told herself to keep her cool. "From burning or suffocation or body injury?"

"I don't know."

"Find that out for me. Then notify Lily that after I take a look, three bodies will be coming her way and we need cause of death on each. What about time?"

"Well, the neighbour heard the boom around two in the morning."

An odd time to be using the kitchen, Joan thought. "How many rooms were in the apartment?"

"Three." The man's voice was flat, angry.

Naturally, she thought. He probably lived in half a room with another family on the other side of sheets strung on clotheslines to divide the place, so three rooms would strike him as offensive. "Were they rich?"

"Recently from HK." This time his voice wasn't flat. The anger was open. "Oh, yeah, he worked for the department."

"What?"

"He had one of those English names . . ."

Joan held the phone away from her ear. Kenneth Lo – it could only have been Kenneth Lo and his wife and daughter. She looked out at the twinkle of lights across the bay in Macau. "They seemed to say: Kenneth is gone – an omen. Stay away from Shanghai!"

"Three rooms, you said?"

"Yeah."

"Bedroom, kitchen and what?"

"Sort of an office, I guess. A desk, a couch that pulls out into a bed, a TV and dinner table and lounge chair and lots of electronic stuff, paintings, kids' toys – stuff. What kind of room would you call that?"

A room where you shoved together what you used to have in four or five rooms, she thought. Kenneth had moved his family from their six-room apartment in Hong Kong's fancy Causeway Bay district to three rooms in

Shanghai's upscale, but modest, embassy district.

"Was the desk destroyed?"

"Yep."

"And his computers?"

"Melted junk."

"Inform Captain Chen that after I take a look the computer equipment will be brought over to him." She wondered briefly how well Chen knew Kenneth Lo. Probably pretty well. She needed Chen's expertise; he was the only other technical expert in Special Investigations. "Tape the scene. Clear out the apartments on both sides and above and below. This is a homicide scene."

"What . . ."

"Just do it. And no one but no one is to touch anything until I get there. Is that clear?"

She hung up and called her lawyer. It was late but he agreed to meet her and they quickly settled the final arrangements for the sale of her condo. At first light she was at the airport, and by the end of rush hour she was heading towards the fire scene – towards Shanghai, towards a life with Fong. For a moment she recalled her first trip to Shanghai – six days dressed as a peasant working as a Dalong Fada courier and a troubling night when she slept with a peasant's animals and awoke unable to catch her breath. But that was behind her, she hoped.

Joan stood very still looking at the scorched little girl with the plastic doll melted to her tiny chest. The smell of barbecued human flesh still lingered in the room but she knew it was not as overpowering now as it would have been the day before when the fire ate this place. Now the smell lurked in the charred drywall, hid in the carpets, hung from the ceiling tiles. Just a fire scene she told herself. Just like so many she'd seen before.

It was only when she went to take out her notebook that she realized she was crying.

She checked to make sure that the gas outlets were turned off and that all the electrical appliances were unhooked. She wasn't surprised to see that the food in the small refrigerator had been cleaned out. "Cop's privilege," she thought. What did surprise her were three sweet confections called Hostess Cup Cakes that for some reason had been left. They had been torn from their wrappers and the centre squiggle of white icing removed. Aside from some rotting tofu, they were the sole occupants of the icebox. The refrigerator itself was dented but unharmed. It was clearly not in the line of the blast.

Once she was sure that the place wasn't going to blow up a second time – something not unheard of in arson circles – she photographed the site in a practised manner. Slow, exact, meticulous. Then she began to go through drawers – and she came across another shock – there were baby clothes.

"Oh, Kenneth, you didn't." But she knew he must have. No one keeps baby clothes without a baby. She recalled that Kenneth had taken six months to arrive in Shanghai claiming that he had business to complete in Xian – or somewhere. What she remembered was how angry Fong had been when Kenneth finally sauntered into Fong's office, six-plus months late for work.

She slammed the dresser drawer with the baby clothes shut and spun around. Where? She wanted to scream. They had only found the one child. Kenneth and his wife must have had a second child and hid it for fear of retribution for breaking the second child policy.

"Oh, Kenneth, once a cheat, always a cheat," she mumbled and then turned slowly, with real trepidation, to examine the walls of the room. Joan touched the wall and felt the heat still in it. She forced herself to make the palm of her hand move slowly along the wall about three feet above the baseboards. She circumnavigated the kitchen and the bedroom but found nothing.

Then she took a deep breath and entered the room with the desk and the couch. She slowly pulled the burnt furniture away from the wallpapered wall. The design was badly scorched but it was a complex pattern of light vertical and horizontal lines on a dark field, with what seemed to be black dots wherever a vertical intersected a horizontal line.

Joan ran her hand over one of the "dots." It wasn't a dot – it was a hole. Every dot was a hole! An air hole!

For a moment she wanted to run. To get far away from here. But she didn't. Instead she got down on her hands and knees and examined the baseboards. It was hard to tell – there had been so much damage from the fire. She stood and placed her hand flat against the wallpaper and slowly began to walk.

Halfway across the second wall, which backed onto the bedroom, she felt a ridge. Right on a vertical line. She traced the line down to the floor and up about four feet, then horizontally for about three feet, then down to the floor. She tried to pry her fingers into the ridge but it wouldn't budge.

She stood back and looked at the rectangle she'd traced. The design on the wallpaper looked the same as the rest of the paper in the room. But then she noticed smudge marks in the very centre of the rectangle. She put her hand on the smudge marks and pushed.

She heard a latch give before anything moved. Then the rectangle slid out on straight wheel casters. For a split second Joan wanted to laugh – a safe.

Then her breath caught in her throat.

And the smell of charred human flesh assaulted her.

A tiny, once ornate, metal crib bent from the heat.

A synthetic blanket melted to a tiny body.

It had been a long time since she'd vomited at a crime scene but she was on her knees retching before she took another breath – and she stayed there for a long, long moment before she got to her feet and staggered to the door.

CHAPTER SEVEN

VANCOUVER, BRITISH COLUMBIA

"It's beautiful," Fong said as Robert guided their rental car towards Vancouver from the international airport.

"Rumour has it that we are under the visitor's umbrella. Once you rent a place, the umbrella is removed and the rain starts – and never stops."

Fong turned in his seat to face Robert. "That's an awful thing to say."

"Yeah, I guess," Robert replied.

"Why don't you like Vancouver, Robert? The air seems clean. There are mountains and the ocean and sunshine and space – look at all the space."

"If you like space, you'd love Saskatchewan," Robert mumbled with a distinctly nasty edge in his voice.

"I don't understand, Robert."

"Fine, Fong. Vancouver's paradise," Robert said as he switched lanes to avoid the cars waiting to make left-hand turns off Granville Street.

"You don't like paradise, Robert?"

"It's just one of those things, Fong – let it be – fine. I don't like paradise."

Fong considered replying then thought better of it

and turned his attention to the road. Large single-family homes sat on both sides of the four-lane street. Some were hunched behind dense hedges; others were obscured by tall slender trees planted unnaturally close together. There were extravagant homes like this in the new outer reaches of Shanghai, although these houses were of an older vintage. Straight ahead, on the other side of what Fong assumed was the city centre, were snow-covered mountains. But here in the city the temperature was moderate and the sun was shining – and many pretty women in spring dresses strolled the sidewalks – paradise of a sort, surely.

"Where are you going to start, Robert?"

Robert allowed a car to pass him then changed lanes. "I have two contacts in Vancouver. One is actually from Toronto but he happens to be here now, but he's a loose cannon, a really odd kind of guy. I know how to find him here but I haven't gotten in touch. My other contact I called from Calgary. He's an old teacher of mine who can introduce me to people who can perhaps introduce me to people. If this blood business is really big stuff then someone will know someone who will know someone – I hope."

Something occurred to Fong and he hissed, "*Tian na.*"

"Sorry, but my Mandarin's a bit rusty."

"*Tian na*, it means 'golly.'"

"I doubt it means golly – nothing has meant golly since the fifties." He waited for a response; none was forthcoming. "Golly what, Fong?"

"I don't know why, but it never crossed my mind. But is it even illegal to import blood into Canada?"

"I'm happy to tell you that for the first time in this little venture I'm a step ahead of you. I used my Ontario law licence and logged into the law library in Calgary. It's debatable, Fong. Raw blood is most probably illegal, but treated blood products, like those coming on that ship, are probably not illegal to import. Sorry."

"Not illegal?" Fong shook his head.

"Probably not illegal," Robert corrected him.

"*Cao ni ma de, cao ni, feng zi, bian tai, chu sheng, nao zi you mao bing!*"

"I assume those are charming home-grown cuss phrases of some sort. But I wouldn't throw in the towel just yet. This is Canada, after all, and the province we're in is called British Columbia – accent on the British. And with the British, shame works. Britain was shamed out of India. Can you imagine the French being shamed out of their colonial holdings – or the Germans or the Dutch or the fucking Belgians? But the British were shamed out of the crown jewel of all colonies, India. And there is enough vestigial British guilt here that, even though it may be legal, those who profit from the importation of Chinese blood could be 'outed.' Vancouver's a social place, Fong – pariah status doesn't get the missus an invite to the good parties."

"So you think . . ."

"Embarrassment could work, Fong. In Montana or Texas or Alberta – no – but here, it's worth a shot . . . as long as you have a good hook."

"Hook?"

"The newspapers and television will need a personal angle on the blood story to get them interested. Articles in the press are a good beginning in shaming people."

"So I would need something personal about the blood importer?"

"Better if it's something about a blood victim. Something personal. Name and shame the money man with the name and story of the victim. Then we've got a chance."

"That sounds straightforward."

"Straightforward and difficult."

"Find the money man; find a victim's story and get it published."

"That sounds easy to you?"

"No. But even the longest journey begins with a single step."

"Yeah, Fong, and life is what happens while you're busy making other plans."

"Who said that?"

"The same guy who said even the longest journey begins with a single step – John Lennon."

"Really? John Lennon quoted Chairman Mao." Fong smiled. "I never would have guessed."

Robert slid a CD out of its jewel case and into the player on the dashboard. He hit play and the whisky-soaked tones of Tom Waits filled the car. "Is he trying to sing?" Fong asked.

"He's singing, Fong."

"Is he in pain?"

"Most probably. This song is 'Kentucky Avenue.' Open your ears and you'll learn something."

And Fong did – and he did. On the other side of the scratchy voice were lyrics in stark contradiction to the melody. The song told the story of a boy breaking into a hospital to see his quadriplegic friend in the middle of the night and the friend's request to be wheeled on his gurney bed out into the hall and launched through the plate-glass window – "slide down the drain pipe all the way to New Orleans in the fall."

Robert sang the final lyrics with Mr. Waits then hit the repeat button and "Kentucky Avenue's" agony once again filled the car.

"And this is a popular song?" Fong asked.

"It is with me. It didn't used to be, but it's a fave of

mine now. I heard it maybe twice in the last three decades but it stayed with me. So when I saw it in the Toronto airport I couldn't resist. You know Fong, despite the fact I haven't heard it for years, I know every word of this – every word. Isn't that odd?"

Fong was going to reply that it didn't strike him as odd that at certain moments of our lives pieces of art fall into place – begin to make sense – but before he could speak, a cop swung his motorcycle out in front of them, its siren blaring, and signalled them to pull over to the curb. The smile changed on Fong's face – still a smile, but different. "Were you speeding, Robert?"

"Not unless everyone else on this street was."

"Is it common in your country to be detained by a police officer for no reason. It seems somewhat dictatorial. Now, where exactly are your human rights in a situation like this?"

"Are you done being a smart ass, Fong?"

"No, I'm actually enjoying this."

"Don't. If the cops in this town know about our little mission then everything, but everything, will get complicated."

It turned out that the rental car had a broken taillight. The police officer, a young man with mirrored sunglasses, kept looking across Robert to Fong – as if he were checking something – perhaps a likeness.

Fong looked too. He looked at the two small holes on the breast pocket of the officer's shirt – holes that were left after the man had removed his name tag.

"Is there anything else, Officer?" Robert asked as he put his driver's licence back into his wallet.

"No. But I need you to get that light looked after."

"I'll call the rental company right away and give them holy hell."

This was clearly intended as a joke on Robert's part, but the young cop didn't take it that way. The police officer lifted his sunglasses to reveal the lightest pair of blue eyes that Fong had ever seen. "There is nothing holy in hell, sir."

Fong saw the vein on Robert's forehead suddenly pulse. He leaned across Robert seemingly to speak to the police officer but in fact to watch the blue-eyed cop's right hand that rested casually on the rental car's side-view mirror. "No offence was intended, Officer," Fong said.

"Is that so?" The officer's voice was frosty.

"It is, Officer."

"And what is your name, sir?"

Fong was tempted to ask the officer for his badge number but after looking more closely into the hatred in those watery blue eyes thought better of it. "Zhong Fong."

"And are you a Canadian citizen, sir?"

"No. I am here . . ."

". . . you have no right to question him about that," Robert said. "You have no just cause. He has done nothing wrong. I was driving. I rented the car with the broken tail-light, not him. Customs and Immigration Canada both cleared his entrance to our country. He does not have to answer your questions or present any form of identification to you, Officer."

"You're a lawyer, Mr. Cowens?" He emphasized the "cow" part of the name.

"Yes, but that has nothing . . ."

Before Robert could complete his statement the officer flipped down his sunglasses, returned to his motorcycle and zoomed away. Fong was not sorry to be done with those watery blue eyes, but he was surprised to see how rattled Robert was. At first Fong assumed that Robert was angry because the police officer planted a tiny metallic bug behind the driver's side outside mirror of the rental car, then he realized that Robert had not noticed. Fong wasn't upset by this, in fact he thought of it as a potential weapon – a way to lead the trackers rather than be followed by them.

"Can I . . ."

"Drive? No. You don't have a driver's licence, Fong, and even if you did, I didn't put you on the rental agreement. So even if I wanted you to drive, which I don't – you can't."

"I don't want to drive, Robert."

"Good."

"Ah . . ." Fong said, although he wasn't exactly sure what he was "ahing" about.

"Where to, Fong?"

"Let me out here. Go to your hotel and arrange to meet your contact – the good one. While you're at it, at least get in touch with the oddball. Who knows when we might need his oddness. Let's at least gather together the weapons we have. Contact me tomorrow and we'll compare notes. We have at least forty-eight hours before anything really happens."

"Why's that?"

"The blood shipment isn't due to arrive in port for at least two more days." He didn't bother mentioning the other "little surprises" he'd put in place in Shanghai before he left.

"And what are you going to do til then, Fong?"

"Understand Vancouver."

"How do you plan to understand Vancouver in two days, Fong?"

"By walking and talking and following my instincts. Places have essences, Robert, that are not that difficult to sense when you are an outsider. Foreigners can often tell me things about Shanghai that I didn't know, despite the fact that I've lived there my whole life. Outsider's eyes are not tainted by preconception."

"Fair enough. How do I get hold of you?"

"You have my cell-phone number."

"It's a Chinese local number, Fong."

"You can afford the long-distance charges, Robert. Go to your hotel, meet your old teacher and see who he can introduce you to who might introduce you to someone who might introduce you to someone, etc., etc."

"Very funny, Fong. Where will you be?"

"It's better that you don't know that, Robert. Call me to tell me where to meet. We'll have dinner together tomorrow."

Fong got out of the car and Robert pulled away from the curb. Fong noted the broken taillight. The splay lines of the glass suggested it had been hit with a hammer. Hardly an accident. So they were ready for them even before they landed in Vancouver. Fine. He was ready too.

He put his hand up to hail the cab coming up the road and got in. "Where to, boss?" asked the cabbie – who just happened to be the angry young man who had been with his father and grandfather in Fong's hotel room in Calgary.

"It's your town – you pick."

"Are your people in place?" Fong asked.

"The timeline you gave me was tight but, yes, we managed it," replied the young man as he swung the cab out into traffic.

"And your father doesn't know?"

The man didn't answer.

"Stop the cab and let me out," Fong demanded.

The young man continued to drive. He swung the cab west and headed parallel to the city centre which could now be clearly seen out of the right side of the cab. Finally the young man spoke, "No, my father doesn't know, Inspector. But are you sure about him?"

"I'm sorry but, yes, I'm sure that your father is at least peripherally involved in this. He sits on the board of an investment company that has heavy stock positions in the International Exchange Institute's holding company." It had taken Kenneth Lo a long time to explain this idea to him. "Now answer my question."

"Yes. I mean my father doesn't know. He thinks we are out gathering information to bring to the Chinese government for them to use as leverage to get the Canadian government to apologize."

Fong studied the young man's face in the rear-view mirror. Finally he said, "Why are you doing this. . . . I'm sorry, but I don't know your given name?"

"Matthew. Middle name Mark. My mother wanted to cover as many apostles as possible."

Although Lily had already answered Fong's question, Fong was anxious for Matthew Mark to answer it. "Well, Matthew Mark, why are you helping me with this?"

"As a gay man I have seen what AIDS can do." He took a deep breath then added, "Up close. We all have."

So that's who his people are, Fong thought. It answered a host of Fong's other questions. "I did not mean to invade into your privacy."

Matthew pointed to his right. "Down there is Kitsilano – once all hippies, now upscale condos, most of which leak every time it rains, and it rains a lot. The street we're on leads out to the university lands at the end of Point Grey."

"The university has one of the postal codes I sent you, right?"

"Yes. The other postal code is for Vancouver's largest hospital."

Fong thought about that as he watched the foot traffic on West Fourth. Young people and baby carriages – fruit stands and open bars – and space – everywhere excess space. "Drive me to the university."

The traffic thinned as they drove along and then swung north on Macdonald and travelled along the south bank of the harbour estuary. After passing through a forested area, they finally approached the university lands.

Several young people gathered at the side of the road and then disappeared in single file down a path in the woods. They all held bath towels, but none wore bathing suits and none carried bathing suits.

"What's down there?"

"First an open area called the meadows, then Wreck Beach. It has the only warm water in the entire area and, oh yeah, it's a nude beach." The young man was smiling, clearly interested to see Fong's response to that.

For some reason the thought, Robert would like this, popped into his head. He filed it away.

Seeing that he wasn't going to get any noticeable response from Fong, Matthew said, "The university lands begin in earnest farther up the road."

Fong was not prepared for the wealth and privilege – students, many Chinese, lounging in expensive clothing enjoying the sun. The place had a museum of its own and, according to the signs, a golf course. Finally he said, "Are there scientific labs on campus?"

"To the right behind this large building."

"And is there a medical school?"

"It's part of the science faculty. It's very exclusive and expensive."

Fong nodded, thinking, No kidding. The buildings themselves screamed expensive and exclusive – as no doubt was their intention. For a second Fong thought of

Robert in his overcoat out here – the picture didn't sit easily.

The young man handed him a map of the campus. Fong took it and noted the buildings that the young man had pointed out. "Okay, take me into town. Is this place always like this?"

"The university?"

"Yes."

"It's a bit sterile, I agree."

"The Chinese kids look English."

"American actually. If you think that's bad, you should see the South Asians – Indian Indians as they're sometimes called out here."

Fong nodded as the young man swung the cab in a wide U-turn.

They travelled through the wealth of the British Properties, Shaughnessy and Kerrisdale, then out towards the other major university in Burnaby. The wealth quickly backed off and was replaced by an almost surly poverty. Fong recognized what was now common in China after the "economic miracle": the anger of exclusion.

The car took the steep inclines up to Simon Fraser University without any strain. Fong looked at the young man who simply smiled, "It looks like a cab but there's real guts in this thing. I have a friend who's a mechanic; he thought we might need the extra power."

Fong nodded and sat back. The university appeared all at once as the cab took a long steep curve. It sat atop a smallish mountain. The columns and porticos gave it a mildly Mussolini/Aztec fascist look. Fong found it bleak.

Matthew circled the campus and pulled into a dirt lot. Immediately, a well-dressed Han Chinese male and a Chinese man who was as wide as he was tall, clearly the muscle, climbed in back with Fong. Without prompting,

Fong held up his hands and the muscle frisked him. He almost laughed when the man announced, "He's not carrying." Would these guys be able to speak if it wasn't for John Woo?

Matthew swung the cab onto the campus's perimeter road and drove the speed limit. Fong looked at the new passengers. Dalong Fada, the pseudo-religious political party, was outlawed in China. But it was very strong in Vancouver and had been enlisted by Matthew to back up his people. The Dalong Fada members had insisted on meeting Fong – first, because he was a powerful Mainland Chinese cop, and second, because they were aware of his connection with Joan Shui, who had at one time been a Dalong Fada operative.

Fong turned to the well-dressed Dalong Fada leader and said, "I appreciate any help I can get in this matter, but what does Dalong Fada have to gain by assisting me?"

"We repay our debts."

"You owe me nothing."

"True. Our debt is to your lover, Joan Shui."

Fong didn't know what to do with that bit of information so he forged into the upcoming plans. The Dalong Fada leader listened closely and added a few suggestions then ended their conversation quickly and slid out of the car just before Matthew finished their second loop around the campus. Fong stuck out his hand, "Thanks."

The Dalong Fada leader didn't take his hand. He leaned into the car and said, "Don't underestimate your enemies. I don't underestimate mine." Then he added, "By the by, you're being followed."

Fong had known that for some time, but Matthew was shocked. "They're good, that's why you didn't see them," Fong said. "It looks like a four-car surveillance – two off-white Fords, a blue Subaru Outback and a black Passat."

"What should I do?"

"Just drive. We're not going anywhere secret, just touring this fine city."

Fong glanced in the rear-view mirror. The Subaru pulled over and made a left as the black Passat pulled out ahead of them and seemingly sped away. Matthew turned around to face Fong. "The road's in front of you, not behind. Is your restaurant ready?"

"Yes."

"Good. Then just drive."

Taking the Second Narrows Bridge, they travelled through the upscale suburbs of North Vancouver. They took the Capilano Road exit and headed north up a deep gorge. "What's up this way?" Fong asked.

"The Capilano suspension bridge. It's a big tourist thing."

"I'm not a tourist, Matthew."

"I know that. But I wanted to show you what Canada looks like racially. Everywhere in the city we drive you'll think that this is a big multiracial city. Lots of Asians. But in the tourist spots it's old Canada – white, white, white."

To Matthew's surprise Fong ordered him to stop the car and he got out. "Stay here," Fong said and began to walk up the steep incline. Such Zhong Fong "walks" had become legendary in the offices of Special Investigations, Shanghai District. No one ever accompanied him and he often returned with unusual insights.

He headed back through the woods. Quickly he was surrounded by astounding trees that soared straight up seemingly a hundred metres into the sky. There were indeed tourists here, and in fact they were all Caucasians. Farther on, he paid the fee and entered the park. He stepped past the tourist shop, with its wide and active picnic area, and once again headed into what he learned from a pamphlet were Douglas Fir woods. A few kilometres farther he saw a more private camping spot where a few brave picnickers had brought their lunch this far up the gorge. Not much farther was a fish-hatchery complex and beyond that the famous Capilano suspension bridge that was built in the late 1890s by early settlers, with the help of local natives.

Fong found the suspension bridge, with the river thundering over boulders beneath it, more than a little treacherous. A bit of rain and getting across would be a real challenge. The boards of the bridge were bolted into place but still seemed flimsy. And the thing constantly swayed! At the very centre of the bridge he leaned over and spotted a six-stone figure on the riverbank below. Each stone was balanced atop other stones and formed a semblance of a human shape – more importantly, each captured some sense of human movement itself. He looked back and started his return. Every time he approached an oncoming tourist, one of them would have to turn sideways to let the other pass. The word "defensible" popped into his head.

Back at the cab Matthew put away his cell phone and asked, "Do you think we lost them? No one's come this way?"

Fong looked up the road. "How much farther north does this road go?"

"A kilometre or two."

Fong shook his head, "Then we haven't lost them. They know there's nowhere for us to go up here. Let's go back. I need to see more."

They drove out of the gorge, continued past the entrance to the web of roads that lead to the Lions Gate Bridge and entered West Vancouver, which literally climbed the side of the mountain. "At home rice paddies climb mountains, here it's rich homes."

The young man grunted a yes to that – what else was he to say. He lived there too.

On one of the upper-level streets Matthew pulled the cab to the side of the road and Fong got out again. The air here was cooler. They were higher up the mountain. The high-rise section of the city was now below them, across the water, to the south. He looked at the manicured gardens and the carefully painted house fronts. A weird word came to mind as he looked at them – "geegaw." He remembered it as having something to do with gingerbread houses but couldn't remember exactly what. A few grownups on bicycles, complete with helmets and wearing what Fong assumed were bicycle-riding clothes, passed him. Then a skateboarder took a tight corner behind him and whizzed by. Fong began to trot to keep the boarder in his line of vision. The boy took a second corner at terrific speed then flipped the board over and landed flat on its top and continued down the hill. Flew down the hill. Flying. The boy was flying, Fong thought as he walked back to the cab. When he approached Matthew, he asked, "Are they common?"

"The skateboarders?"

"If that's what they are called."

"Yes, there are lots of skateboarders."

"Is it just for wealthy people?"

"No. Why?"

"I don't know why," he said, but it was a lie. Fong never distrusted his instincts. He knew that there was no such thing as coincidence – just meaning forcing itself upon our consciousness. Things that fly were now important to him. "I want to see more of them."

Matthew drove across the Lions Gate Bridge and through Stanley Park. Fong marvelled at the open green space and the brightly coloured rollerbladers all going in the same direction. When they passed a police officer on Rollerblades evidently giving a rollerblader a ticket for going in the wrong direction, Fong thought he had fallen asleep and had awakened in some silly dream. He mentioned it.

Matthew's retort surprised him, "It makes sense. This is Western Canada, Inspector, not the East. Westerners are pretty practical people. Any law that doesn't make sense has a tendency to be ignored and quickly removed from the law books. People out here aren't crazy about government intruding on their lives – except when it makes sense."

Fong watched the skaters. So many, and such a narrow path. He nodded – yes it made sense to all go in one direction.

Matthew drove along the north side of the city centre and swung south again crossing the Burrard Street Bridge. On Sixth he stopped the cab and pointed at a series of stores. "Skateboarders," he said.

Fong got out and approached the shops. He was immediately assaulted by the alternative language and nuance of the place. Equipment covered every inch of every wall. The music, if it was music, was shrill and played very loudly. The salespeople – all young, all pierced, all tattooed – were a bit suspicious of a middle-aged Chinese man in their midst. One salesperson flicked back the long hair from his face and approached Fong. "Are you looking for something particular, sir?"

Fong thought about that – he certainly was. "Is it hard to do this skateboarding?"

The clerk laughed a clear unapologetic guffaw, "I wouldn't suggest it for someone of your age."

"That isn't what I asked. Is it hard to do this skateboarding?"

A little put off by the harshness of Fong's response, the clerk took a beat before he spoke, "At first it's very hard to even stand on it. Then it gets easier for a bit. But to get any sort of real proficiency – to be good at it – is extremely hard and takes real practice and dedication."

Fong was pleased with the answer and a bit surprised that the long-haired salesperson was so well spoken, "Does it have a big following?"

"Do you mean do lots of people skateboard?"

"Yes, that's what I mean."

"Lots of young people – no one your age – that I know of."

"Is there a place where they do this?"

"Well, there are a few skateboard parks." He gave Fong directions.

The skateboard park was a revelation to Fong. A marvel of poured concrete ramps and metal rails and boys on boards – seemingly attached to boards and wheels – no, *of* boards and wheels – and glory. Fong watched in amazement as they whizzed past him, then up ramps and flipping and turning, baggy pants, hats backwards – and smiles, understanding that they were as alive as they would ever be in their lives – that they were flying.

And somehow they took Fong with them. He was there as over and over the boys flew, committing sins against both gravity and self-preservation on their boards. A young boy, maybe twelve or thirteen, slides on a metal rail then flips the board and takes a moulded curve with grace – like the wind slewing down a mountain valley. A lanky older boy nose slides a board down, over and around a hill with the ease of a cat's tail rubbing a pant leg. A bare-chested boy leaps a metal rail and lands on his moving board with no more concern than a man opening a door for a lady. A rollerblader draws the ire of several skateboarders – this flying is for boarders, not skaters. Over and over again a young teen in a brown T-shirt lands his skateboard on a raised, bent metal pipe, stays there then flips himself and his board back to the pavement. Fong assumed there were names for all the apparatus and the manoeuvres, but they didn't concern him. The names were just an attempt to make rational the flying. A heavy Pakistani boy's skinny father yells, "Done yet!" "No," the boy says and the vastly more slender and more talented white boys around him applaud his pluck. A teenage girl, the only female present, brings a new elegance to the moves – a real sexiness. A teenager – a Rasta-curled black youth flips his board over the iron rail and lands on it smoothly with both feet. The board never varies its speed, the boy's head stays perfectly level – eyes and mouth wide open – swallowing large gulps of the air – in flight – and tasting God.

Fong pulled himself away from the vision before him. He got up and noticed a jean-clad man in his mid-thirties sitting across the way, who seemed as entranced by the boarders as he had been. He thought of smiling at the man, then decided against it and headed back to the cab.

They drove in silence back across the Granville Street Bridge and into the city centre. They turned west up Robson and Fong hopped out again. The street was filled with tourists. Lots of Japanese. And coffee shops. One intersection actually had three corners with coffee shops selling the same brand of expensive coffee. Fong spotted the followers who were now on foot. He stopped in front of the large plate-glass window of a store that evidently sold shoes for running.

Deep in the reflection of the window Fong caught a

fleeting glimpse of a pair of almost black eyes staring at him. He whirled around. Was it a face from the plane from Shanghai? He forced his mind to track back. He felt sweat accumulate between his shoulder blades. Slowly he walked towards the entrance of the store, making himself try to remember the faces on the plane. Then something else caught his eye.

One of the running shoes in the window was tilted up off its plastic podium. The light from beneath it caused the bottom to reflect off the shiny metallic backdrop. Fong's mouth dropped open and rage filled him as he crashed into the store.

The teenager trying on a pair of shoes was surprised – no amazed – when Fong reached down and pulled the new sneaker from his foot. He was just sitting there trying to find a new pair of kicks and this wiry Chinese dude reaches over and snatches the kick off his foot – what the fuck!

Fong flipped the shoe over and there on the bottom was a prison ID mark he'd never forget. "Hey!"

"Shut up." Fong whirled on the paunchy store manager who was moving quickly towards him.

"Is there a problem here, sir?"

Fong was amazed that this piece of blubber thought he was powerful. "How much does your store charge for these shoes?"

Every eye in the store turned to Fong.

"Hey man, give me back my fuckin' . . ."

"Sir, I've already called security . . ."

"I really don't care if you called your prime minister with the funny name."

That stopped everyone – which prime minister with the funny name – except for John Turner they'd all had funny names as far as the clientele of this store was concerned. "Tell me how much and I'll leave this store."

"The price tag's right on it, sir. A hundred and twenty-nine dollars and fifty-nine cents."

Fong flipped the shoe back to the boy, who caught it and bent forward to slip it onto his foot. Fong put his foot on the boy's back and pressed hard. Then he addressed the whole store. "These shoes were made in a Chinese prison by prisoners, often political prisoners, who make no money whatsoever to manufacture them. This is the product of slave labour. Your store, sir, makes money off slave labour. And the purchases you people make support slave labour. Think about that."

And to Fong's surprise the good shoppers of Vancouver not only listened to him but they also heard and began to put the shoes aside and head towards the door.

The boy shoved Fong's foot from his back and stood. The boy was more a man than a boy – he towered over Fong. "Tough luck, fella. These are solid kicks. So fuck you very much for the info."

As the boy turned and headed to the front desk to pay for his shoes, Fong was tempted to run after him and tell him that he had been in that prison for almost three years. That he had made shoes for this same company. That his imprimatur was only one digit different from that of the prisoner who had made the boys shoes: 99chi11203 had been his prison number. The boy's shoe had been made by 97chi11203 – the man had been incarcerated two years earlier than Fong – and he was probably still there. Still in Ti Lan Chou Prison, just up the Yangtze from Shanghai – the world's largest political prison and supplier of running shoes for rich kids in the West. Then he remembered the black eyes he'd seen reflected in the window of the shop and he felt as if his heart had stopped.

Back on the street, the cab moved quickly to pick him up. Fong was breathing heavily.

"What happened in there?" Matthew demanded.

"We need to use your escape plan – and quickly. Do you have a backup?"

"Yes, you asked us to . . ."

"Good. Then we use both. I don't think I'm just scaring myself. I think someone other than the police is following me."

Matthew hit the accelerator and the car roared forward. They headed momentarily west then took a hard right. Instantly they were in a residential neighbourhood. Fong had never seen such a drastic change in an urban landscape happen so quickly. The streets became one-way. The cab zigzagged its way north, then crossed a major street and careened to a halt in front of a small restaurant. "This is it?" Fong asked.

"They're friends and ready for you. Go in. Order. Take the insults and follow their directions."

"Take the what?"

"Go!" Matthew yelled as he revved the cab.

Fong hopped out and entered the small, crowded restaurant. Before he could do or say anything, a tall flowery headwaiter yelled at him in a voice that could cut cheese at forty paces, "You need a written invitation, jeez, take a seat." So Fong did.

The draperies in the place were closed. Not a beam of natural light entered. One of the waiters noticed Fong taking note of that and called out, "Twilight is for lovers and it's always twilight here." Fong blushed. All the waiters swished. All the waiters wore pants that were too tight. All the waiters insulted him – and everyone else in the small place. Then suddenly the lights went out.

Fong felt a hand, a strong hand, grab his arm and pull him towards the back of the restaurant. In a brief moment they were through the kitchen and out the back door. A small sedan waited for them. The restaurant's headwaiter was behind the wheel. As soon as Fong was inside, the man hit the accelerator and the small car skidded into a turn that took them eastward.

"You okay?" the waiter asked.

"Yes. Thanks."

"No. Thanks to you. We're all rooting for you, Inspector Zhong. The entire gay community is behind you on this one."

"Good," Fong said, since he didn't have any idea what else to say. "Where to?"

"My instructions were to bring you to Pender Street and they're going to set you free there."

Fong sat back and tried to collect his thoughts. They were going to use the backup scenario he had requested in case of emergencies. "Already an emergency," he thought, "and I was just getting the lay of the land."

Pender Street in Vancouver's East Side was a revelation to Fong. Opium was the drug of choice in Shanghai, but here on these dark blocks it was heroin that left its indelible marks on the citizenry. Vacant eyes and open mouths followed his progress down the dank concourse. There were sudden erratic movements in the alleyways. Fong had seen and been in many complicated places but this place – this open sore – spooked him in a way that no other had.

In a shadowed doorway a young addict slaps at the veins in his arm trying to get something to rise to offer passage for his already blood-tipped needle. Behind the man Fong saw the outline of a middle-aged female addict on her knees making the money needed for her next fix.

This is a place of howls, he thought.

Of open maws.

Fong instinctively reached to his breast pocket in search of his pack of Kent cigarettes – but he had not smoked since he ended the life of the assassin Loa Wei Fen in the deep construction pit in the heart of the Pudong almost nine years ago.

A bag of filthy clothes encasing a man approached Fong, "Got a light, ol' Chinky?"

Fong recognized the insult but let it pass and went to step past the rag man.

"Turn left at the next corner," said the alcohol-laden breath. "There's a car there waiting for you. Get in when it flashes its lights."

"Thanks . . ."

"Don't. You be careful now, ol' Chinky, another dead Chinaman don't mean nothin' to these bastards. On that you can trust me." Then he spoke louder, "You got a ten-dollar bill for little me? All you Chinks are stinking rich." Suddenly he was shouting. "You don't own this country yet, you fuckin' wog."

Fong almost stumbled under the verbal assault, it was so sudden. Then he glanced across the street. A window curtain was still swaying – as if it had been held aside then suddenly let back to its original position. The rag man turned as the door across the way flew open.

Fong raced to the corner, saw the lights flash and ran to the car.

Fong was shown a basement door. He pushed it open and was immediately met by two young, clearly gay, Chinese men. They ushered him quickly down a narrow corridor, through a large Chinese kitchen and into a small parti-tioned-off section of a vast dim sum parlour. When he entered, the two Dalong Fada men, the restaurant head-waiter and six expensively dressed Chinese men stood. There was tea on the table and Fong helped himself.

Matthew came in and closed the door behind him. "You know most of these people, Inspector Zhong."

"True, all but the six thugs dressed like Pudong pimps," Fong said, not looking up from his tea.

One of the men stepped forward. The others fell in behind him. "We are not in the Middle Kingdom here."

Fong still concerned himself more with the tea than the man. "Yes, but a Tong leader is a Tong leader wherever he happens to be." Fong rose to face the man.

Matthew stepped between the two. Turning to Fong he said, "None of this could be made to happen without their help."

"And what do they want in exchange for their 'help'?"

"Nothing," the Tong leader said.

"And why would that be?" Fong demanded.

"Because my family comes from Anhui Province."

Fong sat and drank the rest of his tea.

"Are we done with the nonsense?" the Tong leader demanded.

Fong looked at his "troops." "Where's the rag man from Pender Street?"

"He's supposed to be here," said Matthew. "He's late."

Fong felt an old shiver of fear work its way up his spine. "Find him. Okay, what else do we have?"

Quickly, notebooks were opened and copies of computer documents were handed around. Fong read his quickly.

"So you have people placed with the Chiangs?"

"A driver, a cook, the granddaughter's personal trainer, and all their phones are tapped."

"And their cell phones?"

The Tong leader smiled and said, "It's easy to eavesdrop on cell phones, just tell us when you want us to start."

"Might as well start now. But in two days when the ship arrives with their spoiled blood they will begin to scurry – and to make their phone calls. We have to know who they call. Understood?"

Nods all round.

"What about the International Exchange Institute's Vancouver legal counsel? Have you found them yet?"

"No."

"Damn."

"We're out of leads on that. Surely you folks have more access over there than we do," the Dalong Fada leader said.

"We don't – yet," said Fong as he rose to leave.

The Tong leader stepped forward, blocking Fong's exit, "Who was following you today, Inspector?" With a forced nonchalance he added, "It wasn't your Beijing watcher who, by the by, is finally on his way to Vancouver from Calgary, or the police. So who else is out there, Inspector?" The man's voice was etched with an odd fear.

"I don't know," Fong replied. "Probably no one."

That sat in the air like something big and fat.

"Where will you stay tonight, Inspector?" asked Matthew.

"You're welcome to stay in one of our fine establishments," said the Tong leader with a smile.

"Thanks, but whorehouses . . ."

The head of the Tongs took a step forward.

Fong backed off a pace and canted his head in a simple apology. The Tong leader accepted by bowing in like style.

Finally Fong said, "I have to have time to myself. I

thank you for your offer. You all know how to contact me and I know how to contact you." He turned on his heel and left.

Fong found his way to Jericho Beach across from West Vancouver. There, arrayed before him, were the great ships of many nations awaiting off-loading in the Port of Vancouver. Far up the estuary huge cranes swung and gripped and off-loaded the cargo of the world – the Pacific world.

The beach lay before Fong. Several campfires dotted the wide arc of sand welcoming the dying of the sun.

And lovers.

Many lovers – kissing.

Fong found himself thinking of the women that he had known in his life. If there was a god, women were certainly his gift to Fong. His first wife Fu Tsong, Lily and now Joan Shui, whose information he was now awaiting.

To one side, a couple stopped and, seeking the privacy of the side of a large tree, kissed and fondled and entwined. Fong couldn't help himself. He watched like an old man in a window remembering the glory of the touch of mouths – the awe of kissing. It occurred to him that as sex entered his relationships, kissing faded away. Yet there was something so intimate about kissing. So volitional. So much a choice.

He tasted the salt air on his tongue and forced himself to move farther down the beach. Then his cell phone rang.

The connection was bad.

Fong had never spoken long distance across an ocean before. He had images of wires going beneath the sea – the idea of signals bouncing off satellites simply didn't enter his way of thinking.

"Hold on to your hat, if you're wearing a hat, Fong."

Joan's voice was suddenly clear, as if she were sitting beside him on Jericho Beach watching the lovers stroll and touch and caress.

"Fong, I said hold onto your hat."

"I heard you the first time."

"So answer, jeez."

"So I'm holding onto my proverbial hat. What have you found?"

"Kenneth Lo and his whole family are dead."

"What?"

"Their apartment was firebombed – a cheap but effective timing device that could have been set days ahead, then plastique with a planche. Not exquisite but a pro for sure."

"When?"

"Last night."

Fong held the phone to his chest and tried to calm his breathing. Joan heard the sound of his heart and she was suddenly afraid. Finally Fong spoke into the phone. "Are you sure? I'm sorry Joan. I'm not questioning you, I'm just . . ."

". . . upset, Fong? This was arson. I actually found bits of the timer and there was evidence of directionality. It was set to go while they were asleep. All four died . . ."

"Four!"

Joan explained. Fong cursed his own stupidity – six months to complete business in Xian – and Fong had agreed. As if a man like Kenneth Lo would have business of any kind to finish up in Xian of all places. But he said none of this. What he said was, "Go through it slowly for me, Joan." She talked him through her findings. He asked a few questions about the wallpaper, the baby crib, the icing pulled off the cupcakes in the refrigerator and the condition of the computer.

"I got the hard drive over to Captain Chen, but between the inferno and the water they used to put out the blaze . . ."

"Yeah," Fong said, cutting her off more abruptly than he intended. "I needed the International Exchange Institute's computer to tell us who their lawyer was. The Vancouver Tongs haven't been able to find the lawyer either. Fuck, I need the name of that lawyer, Joan." He paused. "Joan, do you remember the woman who murdered the man she loved?"

"The Chinese woman who put an itty-bitty gun to the temple of her Long Nose lover?" she asked. What she thought was, Who could forget?

"So do you remember or not, Joan?"

"I remember."

Fong slowed his breathing again. Joan was the smartest, most intuitive woman he'd ever known. And she was a cop – and he didn't want her to put all the pieces together. Specifically that he had insisted that Kenneth Lo return to his office a second time in the middle of the day, carrying the International Exchange Institute's computer. Fong had virtually paraded Kenneth around with that damn computer. Fong knew there were snitches in the department and was sure that Kenneth's visit with the computer would be reported to someone who knew someone. And the word would be out: Fong's on your trail. It was the only way he knew to get the blood traders to track him, not Kenneth Lo, but him, and maybe, by doing so – show their hand.

"Fong!" her voice was strong and angry in his ear. "Fong!"

He let out a long line of breath. He had known from Kenneth's first visit, late at night, that there was a connection between the International Exchange Institute and the blood trade. He'd needed the blood traders to make a move, put prints in the dust, scurry, and he'd used Kenneth's second visit in broad daylight to set all this in motion, and now Kenneth and his wife and his two children were dead. "Joan, I need the name of that law firm." He spoke quickly. He didn't want her to interrupt him to accuse him of Kenneth's death. "Find the woman who killed the man she loved and press her for that."

"Will the prison let me talk to her, Fong?" Her voice was hard but not accusatory.

He let out a sigh of relief. "You're with Special Investigations. Cajole, threaten, do whatever you have to do, but get in to see her. Get hold of Chen and have him work on that computer. Maybe the fire didn't do as much damage as they wanted. Joan?"

"Yeah?"

He wanted to ask her if she understood what he had done. If she forgave him. But he couldn't ask. All he could think of doing was ask, "What's the time back there?"

"It's just before dawn."

"The sun's setting here."

Neither mentioned that they were also a day apart. It was Tuesday morning in Shanghai but only Monday evening in Vancouver. Long-distance silence descended on both of them.

"I'll go see the girl as soon as I can."

"Let me know what you find."

She didn't say anything. The click of the line disconnecting was the loneliest sound Fong had heard in a very long time.

Fong took a breath and watched a young woman silhouetted against the flames of a campfire remove her blouse and snuggle close to her boyfriend. He walked down the beach, and Kenneth's ghost walked beside him.

"It could get dangerous," Fong had warned Kenneth in their last meeting.

"Blood's like that, Fong – life-giving, life-taking – dangerous," Kenneth had responded with that confidence that was so common to Hong Kongers.

Fong looked past Kenneth. He had purposefully left his office door open and insisted that Kenneth bring the CPU from the International Exchange Institute with him. And as he had known, eyes from the other rooms had snuck peaks at the man from Hong Kong and the computer he carried. Shrug and Knock, the party-hack assistant who had been forced on Fong, went so far as to actually come into the office and hand over a sheaf of papers to Fong with a terse, "Signatures needed."

"What's he looking at?" Kenneth asked jauntily.

"You," Fong wanted to say but only managed to mumble something about fucking party political appointments.

"Well, be that as it may," Kenneth began and launched into a twenty-minute explanation of holding companies, shares in public companies and, finally, end users.

"End users? You mean the buyers of the blood?"

"Not really, Fong. The buyers are like wholesalers. They sell to retailers who then sell to the end users."

"You mean clients then?"

"Yes, Fong. We have the beginning in Anhui Province. We have the retailers in the two Vancouver postal codes – both hospitals. The clients are the ones who actually pay for the blood products."

"Fine, Kenneth, but I'm not interested in arresting the peasants in Anhui Province who gave the blood or some sick old lady in Vancouver who needs a blood transfusion. I want to get to the money behind all this."

"I know, Fong. But maybe the only way to do that is

to work from both the end and the beginning towards the middle where the money is."

Fong made a face as he thought his way through that. He'd chosen to work directly from the middle – the money. That's why he'd insisted that Kenneth appear openly, at midday in his office with the computer.

"Smile, Fong – things could be worse. At least we have an end and a beginning – and we have something else."

"What's that?"

"Me and whatever else I can find on this CPU," Kenneth announced as yet another cop invented a reason for walking past his open office door, "and all the secrets I can release from this little ol' CPU."

Fong looked out the window.

Kenneth got up to leave but stopped at Fong's office door, "Question?"

Oh, shit, don't ask me, Kenneth – don't ask me why I ordered you to come to my office with that fucking CPU in broad daylight, Fong thought. But what he said was, "Ask."

"Do you know a good school? My daughter's almost ready to start school."

Fong put on his best smile, "I'll ask Lily. How's your family settling in? Business all done in Xian?"

"All done," Kenneth said, then something dark crossed his features and disappeared as quickly as it arose. "We all love Shanghai." Then he quickly added, "All three of us love it. What's not to love, huh?"

And he was gone.

And Fong was alone walking on a Vancouver beach seeking the darkness and a way to forget Kenneth Lo and how he had used him and his family. He wanted a place to rest and renew himself for tomorrow's terrors.

He looked across the water, and a huge freighter made its way slowly into harbour. An oceangoing freighter – perhaps one very like the one carrying the spoiled blood.

Robert looked out the window of Evan's classroom. Across the way was the new offices of EA – Electronic Arts – which specialized in computer sports games. In the other direction was an obscenely expensive hotel that specialized in layovers for tourists about to get onto the Alaska-bound cruise ships that boarded just up the estuary. Farther east was the T-shirt mecca of Gastown, with its inexplicably popular steam-run clock in the midst of overpriced ice-cream shops and questionable sushi joints. Just up the way from there was Vancouver's tender underbelly, the complication of Pender Street.

"Is our wealth predicated upon their poverty? Or is their wealth, no matter how limited, a function of our economic success?" Evan spoke without referring to his notes. His audience was some sixty strong and an interesting mix. The men were older than the women. All were well dressed. All were well scrubbed, coiffed and manicured. Almost all were white aside from two Han Chinese males, one Japanese female and two fully veiled females – or at least Robert assumed they were females. Evan was lecturing on the ethics of business as seen through the eyes of several different philosophers. Few people took notes but everyone seemed to be following the arguments. References to particular texts elicited head nods all round. These folks were hardly your basic Philosophy 101 students. These were business elite types who thought a little philosophy could spice up their boardroom chatter or maybe their bedrooms.

Evan went through the standard arguments about the creation of wealth – *The Wealth of Nations*; the Sam Adams argument; the Keynesian approaches; early Marx and Engel's writing – pretty standard stuff although worth rehearing since all of them had influenced the nature of the present, if limited, economic debate in the West.

Then Evan cranked up the rhetoric. "If our wealth is indeed predicated on their poverty, then they have every right to bomb those institutions that continue to enslave them. Like the World Trade Center."

The response was interesting. This was a group of businesspeople, so Fong assumed that they would have vociferously objected, but these are Western businesspeople. They too, in their own way, felt a form of enslavement to the works coming out of buildings in the East like the World Trade Center. So the objections were loud but not as loud as Fong would have thought.

Evan answered a few brief questions. Made a joke about a son of his who runs an ethical mutual fund that only invests in companies that do not take advantage of non-unionized labour and dedicate themselves to the preservation of the environment. Someone asked, "How's the fund doing?" Evan ducked the question and assigned next week's readings. It was an odd assortment – Thomas Aquinas, Immanuel Kant and *The Spy Who Came in from the Cold.*

The familiar sound of students packing up to go followed. A few people approached Evan with questions or excuses – "my stock portfolio ate my homework" or maybe "my Jaguar died" or some such.

Back at his office overlooking the harbour, Evan tossed his battered leather briefcase onto a wine-coloured Windsor chair. The satchel more resembled something the Scots would use to make Haggis than an article meant to carry a professor's books.

Beside the chair was a new top-of-the-line Apple computer with a WATCHDOG button on its side.

"So what do you think, Robert?"

"Of?"

"My lecture, my office, life, Vancouver?"

"I thought your lecture a bit pat, your office the fanciest I've ever seen for a university professor, life on the whole sucks and Vancouver is looking wonderful."

"It is, Robert. Vancouver is wonderful. It's a privilege to live here. Drink, Robert?" Evan asked.

"No, thanks."

"As much as I'd love to believe that you called me because you miss my fine company and sparkling repartee, I can only assume you called because you wanted my help with something. And since I agreed to see you, I tacitly agreed to offer whatever help you want – so ask?"

Robert paused for a beat, then asked, "Did you know that there is an AIDS epidemic in China?" Evan poured himself a modest amount of a single malt scotch into an elegant crystal snifter and sat. He listened as Robert told him the details of the blood industry in China. Robert ended his recitation with the fact, "The money behind all this comes from Vancouver."

Evan got to his feet and looked out the floor-to-ceiling plate-glass window that looked west up the estuary to . . . well, to Japan. Finally he turned back to Robert. "Do you have any idea how much money I make teaching for the university?"

Robert had no idea why Evan had brought up this subject, but he responded, "You've been at it for most of forever so I assume you make reasonable coin."

"Wrong. I make a dollar a year. I've always made a dollar a year. My father and father-in-law before me taught for the university for the same wage."

"Why would . . ."

"Because we come from old money, Robert. Something you might not know much about. With that money comes an obligation to give back. We all gave back the same way by teaching for a dollar a year." Evan turned away from Robert. The moonlight silhouetted him, like Alfred Hitchcock at the beginning of his old television show. It was hard to be sure, but it seemed to Robert that Evan let out a very long silent sigh. Before Robert could think that through, Evan turned back to him.

"How can I help?"

Before Robert could answer, the phone on Evan's desk buzzed. "Yes. Yes, I'm here. Fine, it went fine. Do you need anything? I'll be right up." He hung up the phone and turned to Robert, "Meredith." He paused and seemed to be contemplating something. Then he said, "She's very brave. Some days she's more herself than ever – others . . ." He lifted his hands then let them fall as if their actions were beyond his meagre control.

"He was frightened near the end."

Joan Shui listened carefully to the woman across the Ti Lan Chou Prison table from her. She'd last seen the woman about ten months ago. Those ten months had changed the woman who killed the man she loved. There was a pastiness about her skin and her muscle tone was already beginning to deteriorate. Her beautiful hair had been shorn and her scalp exhibited fine examples of prison bug bites. There was a jagged scar across her left cheek running diagonally from the bottom of her nose to her ear. But her eyes still shone, although with wariness now, not joy.

"Why was that?" Joan asked.

Ignoring Joan's question the prisoner asked, "Where's that cute little squeeze of yours. The one that locked me up.

I think about him sometimes. Well, not him, his hands. I think about his hands and what they could be doin' for me."

Joan permitted the whore act to continue for a bit longer then said, "Answer my question. Why was your boss frightened at the end?"

"Mr. Clayton had some pretty powerful business partners. And they pressed him. Squeezed him to get more and more."

"More and more blood?"

The woman who killed the man she loved looked away as if suddenly something on the dark cinder-block wall was of interest. Joan lit a cigarette and held it out to her. The woman's head swivelled towards the smoke. Her nostrils flared. For a moment she looked straight into Joan's eyes then said, "Thanks." She took a long pull on the cigarette. Her posture changed and just for an instant she was beautiful again – and she knew it. She raised her head, showing her long elegant neck, and let the smoke out in a long line of pleasure. "Can I keep this?"

Joan nodded.

"Yeah, more blood. He was being pressured to get more . . ."

"Blood, and in doing so spread AIDS through an entire province." Joan's voice was sharp. It brooked no simple response. She reached over and took the cigarette from the prisoner.

"Hey, you said . . ."

"Yeah, well I changed my mind." Joan crushed the cigarette on the cold concrete floor.

Anger flared on the prisoner's face then slunk back into its cave. "You don't understand," she said.

"No. I understand perfectly. You slept with a man who murdered other men so he could make money to buy you fancy clothes or . . ."

"No."

"No? Really? What else exactly would you call it? You get off and they get dead."

The woman who murdered the man she loved looked away – towards the cinder-block wall again. Finally she said, "This is a hard place."

Joan nodded.

"I didn't have a lot of choices back then."

"Bullshit. You were the best-looking woman I'd ever seen and I'm not exactly hard to look at myself."

The prisoner locked eyes with Joan. Then she reached up and pulled on a patch of hair. "Not so beautiful now, am I?"

"Hair will grow back. You aren't sick – yet. But much longer in here and no one'll even know that at one time men threw money at you."

"Yeah, I see that."

"So tell me."

"Tell you what?"

"Who were your boss's business partners?"

The woman who killed the man she loved stared at Joan for a second. The voice-activated audio recorders deep within the cinder blocks paused. The cameras pivoted and the woman put out her hand towards Joan.

Joan looked at the proffered hand – its once French-manicured nails, its still beautifully shaped fingers – then noticed the shred of toilet paper balled up between the woman's middle and index finger. Joan took the hand and allowed her eyes to roam the prisoner's face. The woman who killed the man she loved released the ball of tissue into Joan's fingers then she withdrew her hand. "If you want me to touch you with that hand it'll put you back ten thousand yuan. Want me to touch me it'll cost you double that. You look like the kind that likes to watch." Then her voice lowered and in a whisper barely louder than the movement of the air in the room breathed, "Get me out of here – please get me out of here." Then the woman who murdered the man she loved pursed her lips as if she were ready to be kissed and laughed – or what passed for a laugh in this awful place.

Once Joan was back in her car she carefully unravelled the piece of tissue and spread it with her palm on the dashboard. The woman who killed the man she loved had printed ten words there in a precise, beautifully drawn hand: *Henderson, Millet, Cavender and Barton, Attorneys at Law, Vancouver, Canada.*

CHAPTER EIGHT

AN ANHUI STORY

The BlackBerry device beeped and, as Fong had been instructed, he punched the receive button. Up came Mandarin the character text:

"Fong I think this is important. I wrote it down as I remembered it – as it happened. I've faxed the complete document to the agreed-upon number. Go get it – and read it – just in case you are considering giving up on this whole thing. Once you read that fax you won't. I want you to get those bastards, Fong. Get them. If not for me, then for that poor man. Your ex Lily."

Fong hurried back to the agreed-upon fax pickup, a small convenience store owned by a Chinese family who had recently emigrated from Shanghai. He got the lengthy document that Lily had sent then returned to Jericho Beach. He wanted privacy to read it.

It began:

"I'm sorry," I said to the square-shouldered peasant who had arrived unannounced almost a week ago at my office door, "but she died last night while you were asleep up here." I was going to add that I didn't wake him because it was the first time that I'd seen him sleep since he had arrived. But I didn't. I didn't know what to say or do for this unfortunate man, Fong.

The Hua Shan Hospital had refused to help him and in desperation he'd banged at every door in the building. I was in the forensic labs running a final check on a hair analysis when he hammered on my door. "My wife," he'd said. The woman that he carried in his arms was terribly sick. He was clearly beyond exhaustion. I'd taken them in and bullied the hospital into admitting the sick woman. As you know, Fong, a cop can do that to a doctor, you taught me how. At any rate for five days he'd stayed in my office. I'd brought him food and news of his wife. He never left. He slept on the floor. He was always gentle. Always thankful. Always still.

Now I brought him news of her death.

He sat awkwardly on my swivel chair, his large calloused hands on my desk. A grimace worked its way across his heavy features. For an instant I thought he was going to hit me.

But he didn't.

He pushed down on the desktop and stood. His head nodded to the rhythm of some interior logic – as if he were finally agreeing to something that he had resisted for a very long time. He took three strides towards the door, then stopped. He turned, looked at me then down at his feet.

I rushed towards him but I was too late.

His legs gave out under him and he crashed to the floor – and he stayed there, his left cheek pressed flush to the cold tiles.

I knelt down and looked closely at his face for signs of a seizure. There were none. "Sir?" I wanted to touch him but didn't know what his response would be to a woman's touch. His breath was coming in tight sharp gasps. "Do you need a glass of water or tea, something else?"

He didn't move. He didn't look like he'd heard me. He just lay there with his face against the floor - his cheek a mere two storeys above the now very cold cheek of his wife whose body had been transferred to the morgue two floors below.

I looked away to give him a little privacy. When I looked back he was on his feet and striding forcefully towards the door. "Sir" I called but he didn't stop. He pulled on my office door but it needed to be pushed, not pulled, to open. He pulled again, harder this time. Again the door resisted. He gave it one last mighty heave - to no result. Then he turned to me and his large peasant hands came up, one holding his cap, and he criss-crossed the air with his palms. Then he took a single deep breath, a shudder - even the door had betrayed him - and began to cry.

There was a knock at the door.

"Dui." My husband, Chen, was there with a haughty white woman and her translator. The Long Nose snarled in a foreign language. French I guessed, more from attitude than any knowledge of that language. No one on CNN or Jerry Springer speaks French. Her translator mumbled something about a needle and a marketplace, I couldn't follow it. I held up my hand for silence. The French woman continued to fill the air with screeching but her translator had the good sense to shut his trap.

"Speak English, you?" I asked the translator in my very best English. He nodded. "Her English talk?" He shook his head. "Good. What fuck happen to stupid lady?"

The translator looked at me the way you used to Fong on occasions when I put the odd English word out of order. Who cared? What's the difference? Who could remember all those English rules? The rain's a pain when Spain is plain - who fuck give?

Finally the French translator began to nod his head. You used to do that too as if he was in the process of decoding what I was saying. At first I found it cute then I found it irritating, Fong. Very irritating. My English is just fine, thank you and fuck you very much.

The translator finished with the nodding and told me about the needle puncture and the pending test results from the French doctor. "French she?"

"Yes."

I looked carefully at her. Her clothes were beautifully cut. Her makeup was exquisite. Even from a distance I could tell she smelled good. Very impressive haircut as well. Then I looked back at the peasant man in my office and swore in Shanghanese. Then I said, "This woman has no real problem. Send her home."

He said something in French to the woman who threw her arms up in the air, muttered something that was no doubt a slander against the Middle Kingdom and everyone of its 1.3 billion inhabitants then turned on one of the heels of her expensive black pumps and left. I found myself breathless. This kind of woman takes all the oxygen from a room.

My husband stepped forward to apologize for bothering me with this creature but I waved it aside. "Come in, husband. I need your help."

Chen shut the door as a final exclamation of fury floated up the stairway from the angry French woman. I find the phrase "Angry Frenchwoman" redundant. Chen

stepped into the outer office of the forensic lab. He
nodded to the peasant man who stood against the far
wall, his hat now held by both hands in front of his
mid section. The man did not respond to Chen and
retreated to the inner office.

"Is his wife okay?" Chen asked.

I shook my head. And shook it a second time trying to stop the tears but they wouldn't be stopped.
Chen held out his arms and I allowed him to hold me.
Finally I stepped back and indicated the inner office
where the newly widowed peasant stood. Once again his
back was against a wall.

"Has he spoken yet?" Chen asked.

"Not since that day he arrived with his wife."

"He needs someone to hear his story." That would
never have occurred to me. You and me were born and
raised in Shanghai. Our city has a story not each
individual. But my husband was born in rural China and
he knew their ways. He understood the importance of
being heard and the silencing that happens to those
from the country when they come to the city. He also
understood the huge risk taken by peasants who make
their way to Shanghai - especially if one of those
people was an active AIDS victim.

Chen poured steaming *cha* from a Thermos into two
glass jars that used to contain Tang. He held one
out to the man. "You can still taste the orange in
the glass if you're lucky," he said. The man's face
lifted.

I stood to one side, an outsider in my own
office. This was going to be a conversation between
two men. Two countrymen.

The man took the offered *cha* and slouched down

the wall so that he was in a full squat. Was he twenty
or forty - I couldn't tell. Chen squatted down opposite
the man making sure that he wasn't any taller than the
peasant. "What's your name?"

The man looked at my husband then looked again.
My husband is a very kind man. A very good father. But
he has not been blessed by the gods when it comes to
appearance. I hardly notice anymore but most people
when they first see him need to take a second look to
be sure that their eyes have not deceived them. I'm
trying to say that the American actor Bread Pit need
not fear for his job from my husband. Does bread have
pits in America?

The peasant took a second look then took a long
sip of the hot *cha*. Chen sipped his after the man had
begun to drink. He asked again, "What is your name,
sir?"

Finally the peasant spoke, "You talk better than
most of the people around here."

Chen smiled. "I'm from the country too. Lake
Ching, around Xian."

The man nodded, noting that although Chen clearly
had power, he was not so different than himself. "Is
she really dead?" The question came out with a bit of
spittle.

"What's your name, sir?" Chen asked as if he hadn't
heard the man's question.

"Dong Zhu Houng," said the man.

"Hello, Mr. Dong. My name is Chen Liu Chi." The
man nodded. "And how did you meet your wife, Mr. Dong?"

I couldn't have been more shocked by Chen's question. I shot him a look. He ignored me.

"Was it at a festival? Was she from your village?
At a market perhaps? How exactly did you two meet?"

```
     I thought the man was going to attack Chen - but he
didn't. He took a huge breath . . . and began his story.
```

The ancient assassin removed his shoes and crouched, allowing his toes to knead the sand. He could see Fong down the beach. The assassin pushed the heel of his right foot down into the cold dark sand and rose up on the leg – and stayed there. He began his internal checks – just as he had been taught to do all those years ago as a student at the academy – internal checks that were necessary before every kill.

To Fong's right the small campfire was little more than smoke. The lovers were hidden from sight behind a large log. Before him the oceangoing freighters were silhouetted against the twinkle of North Vancouver's lights. To his left an old man was completing his pre-sleep exercises.

It was beautiful here. He lifted the fax and returned to Lily's tale:

```
     "Chen smiled. "She must have been very beautiful,"
he said.
     The man nodded. "The most beautiful in all Anhui
Province."
     My god! Anhui! Anhui is so far from Shanghai. How
had they managed to get all the way to the coast? If
they came from the west side of the province just get-
ting to the Yangtze River was a feat. If they lived in
the east around the Yellow Mountains there was at
least easy access to the great river that could, if
they were lucky and resourceful, get them within
striking distance of Shanghai.
     "The most beautiful," the peasant repeated. Was
that a smile on his lips?
     Yes.
```

The man's smile lightened the air in the room. Chen stepped forward and prompted him to continue his story, "So you two got married?"

"Yes. On the third day of the fourth new moon. We moved in with my parents. It was not easy. There was so little space and my mother did not approve of . . ."

He never said her name. In fact I didn't know her name. The tag on her toe in the morgue two floors below simply said: Han Chinese Female. The doctors had been too distressed with the extent of the disease to bother with niceties like names. The tag on her arm was a less neutral. It said simply: AIDS. BODY TO BE INCINERATED WITH ALL HASTE.

"Did she work the fields with you?"

"No."

That surprised Chen. "You couldn't use an extra set of hands in the rice paddies?"

At this suggestion the peasant just looked away. Chen knew perfectly well that there was always a need for more hands in the paddies.

"No, she was more helpful in other ways. She knew plants. Everything about plants. No one could find the valuable medicinal herbs in the mountains like her. She was so smart. She dried and saved them. We were close to having enough to raise the money necessary to begin to build a home of our own when . . ." His voice slacked off as if all moisture had left his system. He bowed his head. Silence enveloped the three of us just as the winter fog wraps its arms around the junks late at night down by the Su Zu Creek.

Chen waited for a moment then stood and looked out the window at the interior courtyard in which the arsonist Angel Michael had stored his grisly messages. Chen tapped the windowpane sharply. Dong Zhu Houng looked up as if he were a schoolboy frightened of being reprimanded for dozing off during a lesson.

"Tell me about the herbs she collected."

"We lived outside a small village west of the Da Bie Mountains."

I almost gasped. The Da Bie Mountains were in the severe west of Anhui Province. A totally isolated area. The region is deeply impoverished, colder than most of China in the winter and hotter in the summer. At least if they had lived near the famous Yellow Mountains, the Huang Shan, they would have been exposed to some of modern China's advances. But in the west - nothing much reached that far inland. Yet somehow these two had managed to get all the way to Shanghai!

"We took the herbs she collected to the nearest town, Luo Tian, which is the county . . ."

"Seat?" Chen suggested.

He nodded. "She was so clever with the merchants there. She never sold more than a small sample. She made them hungry for more. Much more. When they asked for further quantities, she insisted on a contract. They always resisted but always gave in when they realized that no one else had these special herbs from deep in the mountains. They always gave in, signed the contracts and gave her money to collect more."

No doubt they got five times over what they paid her when they sold the herbs in bigger cities. Picked by hand, sold from hand to hand from smaller to larger and finally to a rich man in a city.

"She could read. Did you know that?" he asked me.

I shook my head. "No, I'm sorry I didn't know that, sir." I was shocked by his direct address.

"City people always think we from the country are all fools."

"It is a common error," said Chen, "that people like yourself must help us correct." Dong Zhu Houng shifted his weight in his squat. A distinct odour came from him. Not a body odour. More the smell of dark earth after a rain.

My husband's next question surprised me again, although it shouldn't have

"What herbs did she collect?"

There was no hurry. Dong Zhu Houng's wife was dead and he was probably infected himself. As well, his home was far far away. His trek home would be like the great Peking Opera, a full Journey to the West.

"She was fast on her feet. Others tried to follow her to her special places in the mountains but she was like a goat. She'd go up sheer cliffs and double back to her secret places. Always deeper. Always deeper."

"Deeper?"

"Into the mountains. The valuable herbs are far-thest from the paths. Those that were easy to find have been taken long ago. But the ones deep in the mountains have had the longest time to grow and are most potent. The most expensive. And she was collecting. We were saving."

"For a house."

"Of our own." Suddenly his voice grew angry. "If I hadn't wanted . . ."

"She wanted the house too, didn't she?" Chen said. The man looked right into Chen's eyes. Chen held his gaze. "She wanted to be alone in the house with you as much as you wanted to be alone in the house with her, didn't she?"

Slowly he nodded.

Chen looked at me and smiled. I've grown used to

his smile. I see well beyond the bones and skin – all the way to the very fine man beneath.

"But we still needed more money for the house and the season for herbs was quickly ending. It would be a full six months before the herbs would sprout again. And we were short." He turned to me as if pleading for my understanding. "We were so close but we were short. We were short so she . . ."

"She sold her blood?" Chen prompted gently.

Again the man's heavy head nodded. "To a blood head. Those men were always coming through our village. Always with money. How do men like that have money and men like me never have any?"

Chen avoided the man's eyes.

"Did she get re-injected after she gave her blood?" I asked.

"Of course, how else would she get her blood back?"

I nodded. It was the common belief in the country. No amount of effort could convince peasants that in time their own systems would regenerate the blood they needed. So the blood heads took the peasants' blood, removed the most valuable components, sold them to the West and a week or two later returned to the village and re-injected the peasants with diluted blood drawn from a common pool – an AIDS-infected pool this time.

Chen looked at Dong Zhu Houng, "Was the money she got for her blood enough?"

Again the man's hands fluttered up in the air like two exhausted pigeons that had flown far out to sea and now could find no place to land, no place of rest. Finally he said one simple, flat word: "No."

"How soon after she sold her blood did she get sick?"

The peasant looked at his hands as if somewhere

in the grime-encrusted crevices of his palms was the answer to a riddle that would take it all away – make it yesterday, when his wife was still alive. "I don't know for sure. She hid it from me. At first I thought she was pregnant. She vomited so much and when I checked the privy after she used it, her stool was so soft, like dark water. She began to clean her clothes every day. Sometimes twice a day. 'What are you doing?' I asked her. 'Trying to stay pretty for you,' she said. 'I wish I had a new dress for you to see me in.' I told her, 'I don't need anything like that.'

"Then I said something to her that I've never said before. Now I'm happy that I said it. At the time it made me feel . . . I don't know the word for what it made me feel."

"What did you say to your wife?"

"I said, 'You are more beautiful than anything I've ever seen. I wake up at night to watch you sleep. I'm frightened that in the night you will vanish, like a dream.' Then she touched my face."

He paused for a moment and then smacked his calloused hand hard against the wall. "I should have seen it then. Her skin had begun to change colour. To be almost clear like glass."

Chen looked at me. I nodded. It was an earlier indicator in certain Han Chinese.

"She was like that for two, maybe three months. I was worried but didn't know what to do. She wasn't pregnant. She began to cry in her sleep, and cling to me. So tight. So tiny. I begged her to tell me what was happening to her. She told me it was nothing. Just woman's things. Why would she do that? She told me everything else – everything else. Why wouldn't she talk to me about this?"

"She was ashamed," I said. He looked at me as if for the first time seeing that I was a woman.

"Why would a woman be ashamed to be sick?"

"She wanted to be perfect for you."

I caught Chen's glance. This was important but threatened to derail the man's story. I retreated a step and pretended to busy myself with a report on my desk. Chen knew what he was doing.

"Things got worse?" Chen prompted.

"Yes. One day near the second harvest she came into the paddies with me. I was surprised but pleased. We were pulling shoots near the eel pens. I looked over at her. Her jacket had ridden up her back. There was a large black leech on her spine. I called to her and she came over to me. I smiled, turned her around and pulled hard at the leech."

He took a deep breath, trapping a sob in his throat.

"She screamed."

Silence filled the room. He looked up at Chen then at me as if he was looking for forgiveness from us. Then he spoke quickly.

"I thought she had suddenly become squeamish about the foul things but it was not that. I had hurt her trying to pull the thing from her. I hurt her. These hands hurt her."

Chen said gently, "But it wasn't a leech, was it?"

The peasant looked at Chen as if in wonder that this city cop understood. "No. No, it wasn't a leech."

"A lesion?"

"I don't know that word."

"A cut that scabbed over."

"Yes. A lesion." He said the word as if it had no meaning. "I wanted to bring her to the village clinic but she wouldn't let me. That night after she was asleep I awoke and lit a candle. I pulled back her sleeping clothes. There were more of these marks down her front. Three were very big and blood seeped from some of them. I picked her up and brought her out into the moonlight. She whimpered but she didn't wake. I took off her top and lifted her in my arms. I carried her out into the deepest paddy then held her up over my head to allow the moon's rays to cleanse her skin.

"I don't know how long I held her. The frogs sang and there was a gentle wind from the mountains. The moon was almost full. I held her and held her and held her. She was so light. She was always tiny but now she seemed to weigh almost nothing. Finally I held her to my chest and walked out of the paddy. She rolled over in my arms and whispered, 'Tell no one. No one must know my shame.'

"The next day I promised to seed our neighbour's farthest paddy if he lent me his cart. He agreed after I agreed to also seed his near paddy. I put my wife in the cart and took her to the clinic in Luo Tien. We travelled from before dawn so that we could be seen first. But there were many people from Luo Tien already in the outer room when we arrived. The people of Luo Tien looked at us as if we were grubs that had gotten into their beds. Like cockroaches in their rice. The sun was already high in the sky before it was our turn.

"We went into the inner office. The old lady there smiled at us as we came in, as if we were there because I could not get my wife pregnant or something. Her smile vanished when my wife removed her jacket. The old lady stared at the sores then backed off a pace. She did not touch. 'Do you have fever?' she asked. My wife nodded. 'How long?' the old lady's voice was becoming like stone. 'A month perhaps.' 'What village are you from?'

"I wondered why she needed to know that, but wasn't sure I was allowed to ask. My wife gave her the name of our village. She jotted it down carefully. Then she nodded and said, 'You go back there now.' 'No medicine?' I blurted out. 'No. You go. You go now.' 'What are these sores? What makes them come? Will they go away?' I was too frightened to ask if the sores were serious. But it didn't matter what I did or didn't ask. The old lady ignored me and yelled for her assistant. Then I saw her eyes. They were examining me. Every inch of my exposed flesh. I took my wife by the hand and we headed out of that office.

"Before her assistant closed the clinic door I saw the old lady reach for a cell phone. My wife was exhausted and very frightened. We headed towards the building's main entrance then I stopped. 'What?' asked my wife. 'Nothing. But let's go out the side door, okay?' She gave me a little smile as if it were some kind of game. I led her down a long corridor. At the end there was a locked door with a sign. I asked my wife what it said. She told me it said that this door must remain shut. I pushed on it but it was locked. I kicked it open. It was the first rule that I ever broke. The very first."

He looked at Chen as if perhaps he was going to be punished. Chen said, "How long ago was that?"

"Over seven moons ago."

My god, had they been travelling for seven months?

"Were there soldiers waiting for you in the front of the clinic?" Chen asked.

"Yes. We slipped out the side door and I peeked

around the corner. There were four soldiers with rifles on the steps. We waited for dark in the basement of a laundry on the edge of Luo Tien. Then we headed home."

"Weren't soldiers waiting for you there too?"

"Yes."

"Then why go?"

"We needed the bags of dried herbs my wife had collected. They were the only kind of money we had and Beng Pu was a long way away."

"You were heading towards Beng Pu?"

"Yes. There's a big hospital there and I thought . . ." Again his voice dried out.

Beng Pu is a city of 9 million people whose sole claim to fame as far as people from Shanghai are concerned is that it is the only stop on the express train from Shanghai to Beijing. No one is allowed to get on. No one ever wants to get off. The place seems like one large factory with holes for people to sleep in. It's one of the old Soviet cities. Practical. Sterile. Idiotic. Like Beijing Lu in Shanghai. Miles and miles of hardware stores side by side. Only a Russian could think this made any sense. I assume the train stopped in Beng Pu to restock. I never asked. No one ever asked.

"Were there soldiers at your parent's house?"

"Yes. My parents were serving them tea. My wife and I made a plan. She hid while I walked right into the house. Before anyone could speak I cursed my wife. 'You were right, Mama, she's a whore. I am sorry I brought such a person into your home.' I really can't believe I was able to say those things. But I did. You understand that I had to?"

Chen nodded.

"'Where's she now?' my father asked. 'I don't care. I threw her off the cart just outside of Luo Tien.' The soldiers all looked at me and nodded their approval but wanted to know exactly where. I made up a story. They began to pack up to go. I thought my mother was going to hug me. Over their shoulders I saw my wife dart from behind the neighbour's hut and race towards ours. I saw her duck down and enter the crawl space beneath our home where we hid the dried herbs in three canvas bags.

"I went to bed that night alone. Just past moonset I crept out of the house and raced across the highest of our rice paddies to the forest where we had arranged to meet. She held me and drew me to the ground and we . . ."

Chen looked at me. I knew we had to test him before he left. Then he said the most surprising thing. This rough man. This man who couldn't even say the word "sex" or "love." This man who never used his wife's name said, "It was so sweet, so very, very sweet."

"The next morning we set off through the woods and into the mountains. She knew the way from her times spent there searching for herbs. We travelled in the early morning while the mist kept us safe and then rested deep in the forest until dusk. Then we set out again. The mountains at night catch the moonlight. Did you know that? I didn't. We ate berries and mushrooms. We used the bags of herbs as pillows at night. By the third morning we were very high up. It was cold. I had trouble waking her that morning. She seemed locked in her dreams. She had vomited on her clothes."

He stopped. He was sweating. For a moment I

wondered if he was going to vomit too.

"You cleaned her clothes," said Chen.

"Yes. In a cold stream. I tried to bath her but she didn't want me to see her body. I carried her for several miles. We moved that whole day in the light. We were high up. If the army had sent out patrols looking for us I hoped they wouldn't have come this far. Around noon she was regaining a little of her strength and she slid out of my arms and began to walk. And she talked, talked, talked. She talked about her childhood and her friends. The monk who had taught her how to read despite her parents objections. She talked about wanting children. 'Hundreds and hundreds of them. All over the place. All over the grass. All over you and all over me.' Just before sunset I heard something in the brambles at the side of the path. I signalled for my wife to move back and hide in the trees. She did. I carefully walked towards the sound. The bamboo was thick here. There was a scuffling sound. Then a moan or a cry I couldn't tell which. I pulled aside a thick stand of bamboo and a small deer was there. Caught in the thicket.

"Its huge eyes looked right at me. It was crying. Its right foreleg had snapped cleanly between its knee and its hoof."

He looked at Chen carefully as if he wasn't sure if he should tell him what happened next. He needn't have worried. "Deer meat is very healthy," Chen said.

"Yes. I made a fire. For the first time since we left our village we were warm. I put chunks of the flesh on sticks and heated them over the flames. I burnt most of them but I don't think I ever tasted any-thing as good as that meat – ever, in my whole life."

"Did your wife like it?"

He looked away then said, "She cried for the thing. She said it was just a baby that it had its whole life ahead of it and all the lives it would help make. I looked at her. So sick. Yet she was concerned for this deer. 'Its leg was broken,' I said to her. 'It would have died in the bamboo even if I had not found it.' She looked at me. Her eyes were like the deer's but angry. 'Do not lie to me.' 'It is no lie. It would have died with me or without me. Animals would have eaten it, not us.'"

"Only then did she eat a little of the flesh. I begged her to eat more. She wouldn't. She did help me cut the remaining flesh into thin strips and put it over the branches I'd spread by the side of the fire to start the drying.

"The next morning we packed our meat and began our descent. It was harder going down than up. The heavy mist clung to the rocks and I slid and fell many times. She, even that sick, had extraordinary balance and moved from one rock to the next like the jugglers that came through our village. No, that's not right. She was more graceful. More beautiful. She was like a ghost in a dream.

"That night, our sixth, we lit no fire. We were closer to the east end of the mountains. The mouth to a large valley was to our east. There a small village at the end of the valley. I put my jacket around her and told her to rest. I needed to go ahead and see what was what. I couldn't imagine that the soldiers would have come this far. But they may well have called ahead. Besides small villages are suspicious places. Dangerous places for outsiders. Outsiders are not welcomed and when they do arrive the Party official is notified right away. I waited until the darkest time

of night then approached from across their rice paddies.
The night had gotten very cold. There was smoke coming
from the chimneys of several of the larger huts. I
moved from one to the next, avoiding the windows, then
stepped into the mud street. At the far end of the row
of huts was a wooden sign hung from the curved eaves.
I can't read but I recognized the character. An
apothecary.

"The next morning we buried most of our herbs
under a pile of rocks. Then we waited until the sun
was high in the sky and entered the village. Wary eyes
followed us as we made our way to the apothecary's
shop. Inside an old man was surrounded by dozens of
jars of herbal medicines. The man looked away. He did-
n't say a thing. 'We have ylang-ylang for sale,' my
wife said. The man spat. 'No, this is the real ylang-
ylang.'

"He looked at us for the first time. His right
eye was clouded and milky. He tilted his head to get
us in focus with his left eye which was dark and very
very clear. He held out an ancient claw. My wife
reached into her pocket and pulled out a small piece
of cloth. She unfolded it on the counter and put the
small portion of ylang-ylang in the old apothecary's
hand. He held it, as if weighing it in his palm. Then
he took one bud and crushed it between a yellowed
thumbnail and his index finger. He brought his hand to
his nose and sniffed. A surprised look crossed his
face. 'Ylang-ylang.' 'Ylang-ylang,' my wife agreed.
'How much?'

"Twenty minutes later we had agreed on a price.
We returned to our hiding place. Took out the agreed-
upon amount of ylang-ylang that we were going to sell
to the apothecary. Put the rest of the herb inside my

wife's jacket - it made her look fat. It made me
smile. My wife fat. How odd. An hour after that we had
given the apothecary the amount of the ylang-ylang he
had wanted and he gave us both the information about
bus service to Beng Pu and more than enough money to
buy two bus tickets."

"We sat at the very back of the bus. My wife kept
the bags of ylang-ylang safely inside her clothing.
She slept. I watched. I'd never been east of the mountains before. There are great flat fields planted in
wheat. Flat fields. No need to make paddies! And great
temple gates outside some of the cities we passed.
Have you seen them?"

These were common enough features in the country
but he had evidently not seen them before, Fong. They
were stone structures often four or five storeys in
height. Usually three or stone four pillars supported
a large slab crosspiece. On the crosspiece there was
often an inscription honouring a person of signifi-
cance from the region. The Red Army often had the
tributes rewritten so that they praised the army or
peasants in general but some of the original inscrip-
tions still remain. Some are quite ancient. Many have
been restored recently. These free-standing tributes to
special people from the towns were often as close to
shrines as China now has. Few were very impressive to
us from Shanghai but to this man they were plainly
special.

"Yes," said Chen. "My village has one honouring a
fisherman from long ago who taught us all how to fish
with cormorants."

The man smiled. "The bus passed many wonders. A
huge raised bridge across farmland. Not across water.

A bridge with no water beneath. Just fields down below."

He was referring to one of the many viaducts that
stretch across the best of our farmlands. A wise
thing. China needs every available field to feed our
population so the roads are lifted up over the most
fertile farmland and the fields are planted in and
around the posts of the raised roadway. That way very
little arable farmland is wasted to road ways. But you
know this already, Fong.

"Then we came to a great dam that holds back a
river. I'd never seen anything so big. A huge lake was
held back by the dam."

As you know, Fong, that's only true sometimes.
Flooding in the interior plain is still common and
deadly. But the dams are impressive. I hoped they had-
n't thought that the water being held back by the dam
would lead them to the Yangtze because this water
flows into the southern basin, not north to the
Yangtze that would at least get them close to
Shanghai. Then something occurred to me.

"Why go to Beng Pu?"

"There is a hospital there."

I looked at Chen. He signalled me to continue.

"But there's got to be a hospital in He Fei, and
it's the capital of your province, isn't it? And it's
closer to you."

Dong Zhu Houng stamped his feet, shuffled back and
forth, then looked away from me. "It was the train,
wasn't it?" Chen said.

Chen was talking about the express train to
Shanghai that stopped in Beng Pu.

Dong Zhu Houng stood. Chen came to him and put a
hand on his shoulder. "It was good thinking."

Dong Zhu Houng looked at Chen. "Beng Pu has the

hospital and the train. He Fei has only the hospital."

Classic peasant thinking. Good thinking. Chinese thinking. If you are going to have to travel, travel to the place where you have as many choices as possible. This kind of thinking is part of the strength of the whole country. Chinese. Very Chinese.

"What happened when you got to Beng Pu?" Chen asked.

The peasant didn't answer.

Chen tried again, "How long was the bus ride to Beng Pu?"

"A full day and most of the night."

Probably just over sixteen hours.

"We arrived in a drizzling rain in the biggest place I have ever seen."

No doubt.

"There were so many people. Some not Han Chinese."

There was a small but quite visible Muslim population in Beng Pu. They were closely monitored and had to this point caused no trouble, unlike their Western cousins.

"We asked directions to the hospital but people either ignored us or spoke so quickly that we couldn't understand what they were saying. We were concerned because we didn't have residency passes and there were many police officers. So we walked. And walked. We went through the markets that only sold straw mats. Some blue and some wheat-coloured. But so many and just mats. Then we came upon the ox- and cow-trading market. People shouted numbers and . . . it's funny but the thing I remember most is the thousands and thousands of bicycles that were all parked together in one place. I couldn't help wondering how you ever found your own bicycle in all that. What if you took the wrong one? And none of them were locked. And they were all basically the same colour. Isn't it funny, but that's what I remember most about the markets in Beng Pu."

"Then what happened?" Chen asked.

"We found Hao Zhou."

The herbal medicine market.

"All day my wife had been walking like she was in a fog. She bumped into things. Sometimes I had to almost carry her. I couldn't actually lift her and carry her in the city or some police officer would have seen so I held her up by her arm. But even that attracted attention. I noticed that none of the other couples touched. So I had to let her sort of stagger along beside me. She hadn't spoken since we got to Beng Pu. I was hoping that the bus ride would allow her time to regain her strength but I was afraid it hadn't. In fact something new seemed to be happening to her. I couldn't say what. But something new . . . something bad."

"What happened when you got to the herbal medicine market?"

"My wife seemed to wake up. Her eyes got a little clearer and she looked with real interest at the products that were being sold there from tables and burlap bags on the ground. About halfway through the market she tugged on my sleeve, 'Ours is much finer than anything here.' 'Shall we try to sell some of our herb here?' 'No. These are sellers not buyers. We need to know who they sell to.' I pointed to all the people here. 'No,' she said. 'These are regular people looking to buy small quantities for themselves or their families. We need to know what stores buy here then resell the herbs.'

"I looked at her in wonder again. I have no idea how she knew things like that. She approached a woman a little older than herself who had a white hospital hat on her head. 'Are you a nurse?' my wife asked. 'No, sweetie, but the hat is good for business.' I didn't understand this but my wife evidently did. 'Gonna buy something? You look a wee bit peckish.'

"My wife smiled and moved away. I followed her. She approached several different dealers. Most sold medicinal herbs. Some sold spices. She ignored the spice sellers but watched closely as the biggest of the vendors plied their trade. About an hour after we arrived something caught her eye. 'What?' I asked. 'That man,' she said, pointing to a very ordinary-look- ing man who, like most of the others in the market, was dressed in a blue Mao jacket with a blue cap on his head and dark blue pants. 'What about that man?' I was worried that this might be a police officer. 'He has a notebook.' I hadn't noticed that. 'And he's been at almost all of the biggest stands. He talks to the sell- ers then jots down something in his book.' 'The price?' I asked. 'Probably and the quantity available. He also touches the herbs in the right way. He must be a buyer for a shop.' 'Maybe his own shop?' 'Maybe.'

"I followed the man with my eyes and sure enough he approached another large stall and did just as my wife had said. 'So what do we do?' I asked. 'We follow him until he goes back to his shop.'

"And that is what we did. It wasn't until late in the afternoon that he finally left the market. We fol- lowed him. 'What if he goes home and not to his shop?' I asked. 'Then we sleep outside his home and follow him the next day.'

"I couldn't believe how strong she was. But fortune was with us. We followed him down several back alleys, through a courtyard and finally to a small door with a

sign over top. It was not an apothecary sign. I looked
from the sign to my wife. She was ghostly pale. 'What
does the sign say?' 'Nothing.' 'What do you mean it
says nothing?' 'This man is not allowed to say what it
is he does, so the sign says Medical Help.' 'That's
good, isn't it?' 'No, husband. He's an abortionist.'

"I was shocked. I had only heard of such things
but never imagined in my life I would ever meet such a
man. 'What kind of herbs was he looking for then?'
'Those to put people to sleep. Those to stop bleeding.
Those to produce heat.' 'But I thought he was also
noting our ylang-ylang.' 'He was.' 'But what would an
abortionist want with a plant that helps men stay
strong.' 'I don't know. Let's ask.'

"Before I could do anything, she had knocked on
the door and pushed it open. The place was small and
dank. A single bare light hung from a ceiling. A table
that smelled of bleach was in the centre of the room.
Around it were counters with herbs and plants in bot-
tles. The man threw aside a leather curtain and walked
into the room. Without any introduction he came right
up to my wife and reached for her. She allowed him to
touch her – rather to touch the bags of herbs she wore
around her body.

"'What's this?' His voice was thin and there was
a slyness in his eyes that I really didn't like. He
reached up and turned her face into the light. 'What
do you two want?' He pushed her aside and noted exactly where his hands had touched her. 'You sell ylang-
ylang,' she said. He looked at me; a nasty smile was
on his lips. 'He's a little young to have the droops.'
Before I could say anything, my wife said, 'He does
not droop. He is strong like a young horse. And ready
any time I call.' The man backed off a step. 'Then

what are you here for. You're not pregnant. You're
sick somehow, but not pregnant.' 'I'm not sick,' my
wife said, with so much strength it astonished me.

"Then she opened one side of her Mao jacket to
reveal one of our three bags of herbs tied to her
side. 'Ylang-ylang,' she said, 'directly from the high
valleys of Da Bie Shan.' 'All the way from the mountains? You wouldn't be lying about that, would you?'
'No.' 'You wouldn't by any chance have a government
licence to sell ylang-ylang, would you?' 'You wouldn't
by any chance have a licence to perform abortions,
would you?' my wife fired back. The man permitted a
small smile to his lips. 'So is it real ylang-ylang?'

"My wife nodded and held out two perfectly intact
dried yellowish-green flowers. The man looked at them,
then reached out and plucked one from her palm. He
turned it slowly in the light and allowed himself to
nod. 'Ylang-ylang.' 'Ylang-ylang.' 'Wild ylang-ylang.'
'Wild ylang-ylang.' Then he looked at her more carefully. 'How much of this do you have?' 'How much money
do you have?'"

"We spent that night in a room that we paid for.
I have never been in such a place. The bed smelled
bad, but it was a bed. The water ran brown from the
tap, but there was water. Down the hall was a place
for my wife to clean herself. I think she suffered
most because in our travels she couldn't relieve herself whenever she needed to. Here she could. As well,
for a few more grams of the herb the man told us the
name of both a hospital and a traditional healer and
how to get to both."

He looked up at me. "Finally there was a way to
get my wife some help. But that night she was very

sick. She called out all night long and the people in the next rooms complained. Well before daylight the proprietor had thrown us out of the room. He also charged us much more than we had agreed upon. But I could not fight. I needed to find help for my wife.

"It was hard in Beng Pu to know when the sun was up. The whole place seemed surrounded in clouds but not like in the mountains. There were smoke clouds from the factories. The walls and streets were slick with wet ash. We both held our noses as we made our way towards the traditional healer's shop.

"We bought some food from a ten-spice egg seller. I ate mine in almost one swallow but my wife only took a tiny bite from the top of her egg. 'Please, eat.' 'I can't.'

"When we arrived at the traditional healer's shop, he was finishing his morning porridge. He smiled at me. He had no teeth. He turned to my wife. He allowed his old head to nod up and down several times and pointed to a chair. My wife sat and he indicated that she should remove her jacket. I stepped to one side when she did. The scars were much more numerous now and several of them bled. Again the old man let his head nod up and down several times. 'Have you been sick long, child?' 'Months.' 'Did you give blood?' It hurt me deeply to see her cry. 'Yes.' 'Put your jacket back on.'

"He turned to me. 'Take her to the hospital but be careful. They may deport you to one of the compounds. Do the authorities at your home village know about this?' I nodded. 'Well, then, I wouldn't be surprised if your entire village is already under quarantine or moved to the camp.' He went to his jars of medicines and began to put bits of this and that together into a stone bowl. Then with a large pestle he mashed the ingredients together. When they were fully mixed, he took small amounts of it and put them into each of twelve small paper packets, which he folded shut. 'Make her a tea out of this. Boil the water fully then let it sit until it is just too hot to put your hand in. Then put one packet of this into the hot water. Swirl it around until the mixture is basically dissolved. Then she must drink it right away. And she must drink it all. It will not get rid of the sores but it will help her system fight the infection that is causing them. She can only take the medicine for twelve days. It is very strong and can kill her if she takes too much. Bring her to the hospital. See what they can do. But be careful. Do you know what this disease is called?'

"It hadn't occurred to me until that moment that my wife had a disease. I just thought she was sick. I know that sounds stupid."

"It doesn't. You are not a doctor. You are just a man with a sick wife." I shot Chen a look. His use of the present tense bothered me. This man's wife was dead, not sick. "What did he tell you the disease was called."

"AIDS."

"Had you heard of this disease?"

"No."

Chen nodded. "How did she take to the tea."

"I'd never seen her so sick. So terrified. I had begged an outdoor stall to let me brew the tea. I couldn't believe how much money they charged me to boil water. I prepared the tea as I had been instructed. My wife sat at the end of the alley with her back against a wall. I think she was delirious. I brought the tea back to her. At first she pulled her head away from the smell of the drink. Then she opened her mouth and allowed me to put some in her mouth. She spat it out. I begged her to drink it. She finally did, then threw away the bowl. It crashed against the cold stone wall of the building on the other side of the narrow alley. Then she burped. It made her smile. Then her smile disappeared and she grabbed her stomach and cried out in pain. She was like that for hours. I held her and rocked her. And cleaned her when she shat in her pants. Finally she slept on my lap. We stayed like that all night. I just hoped we were far enough back in the alley not to be seen and reported.

"The next morning she had a little strength and we made our way to the hospital. I tried to figure out if it was safe for her but I really didn't know how. I discovered where you had to go to get to see a doctor but saw quickly that you had to present a residency card for Beng Pu. So I waited and watched. A young doctor was looking after those checking in. Several nurses worked for him and were efficiently dividing up the incoming patients. The flow of patients continued without let up until just before noon. Then things began to slow down. I watched a patient being led through the doors by the doctor. I let a little time pass then followed them. I went down several hallways and then saw an open door. This young doctor was tapping the patient's back with his hands. Words were exchanged between the two then a nurse stepped forward and talked to the patient. As she did the young doctor slipped out of the room and headed down a corridor. I followed him. He left the hospital by a side door and travelled quickly for several blocks then went down a series of steps into an eating place. Once I saw him take his seat I

rushed back to the hospital and got my wife who had
been sitting on a bench in the sun at the east side of
the building. For a moment when she saw me, I don't
think she knew who I was. Then she smiled, 'Let's go
home,' she said. 'No, let's go see the doctor.'"

"The young doctor was very surprised when I sat
down beside him in the restaurant. 'I mean you no
harm, doctor.' 'You're the one who was in the waiting
room all morning but never registered to be seen,
aren't you?'

"I really didn't understand what he meant, but I
nodded my head. 'You are a good doctor,' I said. The
young man smiled a little and said, 'Thank you.' 'My
wife is sick.' 'I'm eating my lunch here. Bring her to
the hospital and I will see her there.' 'I can't do
that.' The young doctor put down the chopsticks he
held in his right hand and asked, 'Why is that?' 'I
think she has AIDS.'

"I was looking for a backing off from him but I
saw none. He picked up his chopsticks and swirled some
noodles around them and put them in his mouth. He must
have noticed me watching him. 'Hungry?' I nodded. He
ordered me some noodles with pork then asked, 'Where
is your wife now?' I pointed out the window. She was
leaning against a building across the street.

"The young doctor shouted to the waiter to put
the food in a bag, got up and crossed the street to my
wife. 'Can you walk with me a little?' he asked her.
She nodded. They walked. I couldn't overhear their
talking. At one point she took out one of the eleven
remaining packets we had gotten from the traditional
healer. The young doctor opened it and took a pinch of
the mixture up to his nose. Then he returned the mixture

to the paper, carefully refolded it and handed it back to my wife. Shortly it became clear that they were walking back towards the hospital. My wife kept looking back to make sure that I was following. I was.

"They entered the hospital from one of the back courtyards. Around the open space, the only green I'd seen in this entire city, sat elderly patients taking in a little sun. The young doctor led my wife into the basement of the building and down a long dim hallway. Just before I followed them I thought I noticed one of the old patients get up from his bench and walk fast towards another entrance to the hospital. But I had no time to check this.

"At a heavy door the young doctor stopped and knocked. No one responded. He knocked again. Still no response. He slipped a key out of his pocket and opened the door. She went in and he signalled for me to follow. The place was a cold open room with a cement floor and a table made of iron, slightly tilted with a bathtub drain at the bottom end.

"The young doctor turned to my wife. 'Take off your clothes.' Then he turned to me. 'Do you know what room this is?' I shook my head. 'The temporary morgue,' he said. Before I could question him, he said, 'It's the only place I could think of that would be safe to examine your wife. If one of the nurses were to find out about this you would be reported and I don't even know what they would do to me.'"

Probably he'd be sent west of the Wall. Internal exile was an effective way of keeping people silent but productive - as well you know, Fong. Beijing has not admitted that there is a single case of AIDS in the whole country, let alone an outbreak in the far reaches of rural, peasant China. No doubt they want to control the dissemination of such volatile information.

"My wife stood on the cold floor with her clothes off but pressed hard against her body. I could see lesion marks down her legs. And she was so thin. With the bags of the ylang-ylang wrapped around her I had forgotten how thin she was. She was shaking violently. 'Help her up onto the table,' the doctor said to me. Then to her, 'I'm sorry but it is going to be cold.'

"His examination of her was not long. She cried out several times when he touched her or pressed his fingers against her. Finally he told her to get dressed and waved me over to one side. 'The herbs you got from the healer may well deal with the infection that is causing the sores. But her lungs are badly infected. She has pneumonia and I think there is a growth beneath her breastbone and another behind her left knee. Both may not be life-threatening but the infection in her lungs could kill her.' He reached into his pocket and extracted a bottle of pills. 'These are a very strong general antibiotic. It's hard to tell, but these may help. Give her two every time you give her the tea.' He stopped and looked away. Then he turned back, 'This is just the beginning of this. If you manage to stop the infection in her lungs she may get better for a while but she will get infected again with something else. Probably much worse and most probably fatal.' 'What do I . . . ?' 'Do? Get her to Beijing or Shanghai. Try to get her treated there. There is a thing called a cocktail that if she is not too far gone could save her life for a while.' 'Don't you have . . . ?' 'No. This is China, remember. There's not suppose to be any AIDS in China so why would there be a need for this cocktail here?' 'But why in Shanghai or . . . ?' 'Because the powerful

are there. And when their wives or sons get sick, they
want them treated.'

"Before I could nod, there was a loud knock on
the door and a command to open it. I saw the young
doctor's face grow pale. I looked around the room.
There was a storage room in the back. I grabbed my
wife's hand and we ran in there and hid behind the
boxes. From the next room we heard hard voices questioning the doctor. Why was he here? 'To check on our
autopsy facilities.' 'Why, are you a forensic doctor
now too?' 'No. I'm just trying to familiarize myself
with the hospital's capabilities.' Then an old man's
voice said, 'He came in with a young girl.'

"So that was it. The old man thought the young
doctor had dragged my wife into the hospital's basement for some illicit reason. I looked at my wife. Her
face was stained with tears. She whispered in my ear,
'I don't want them to hurt him.' Then I heard a dull
thud and the sound of a body crashing to a concrete
floor . . . then the sound of it being dragged out the
door and down the hallway."

"Two hours later we snuck out of that room and
out of the hospital. Beijing or Shanghai? We made our
way that night all the way across the city and in the
cold morning finally got to the train station. We
waited until well after sunrise before I went into the
depot. I thought, I have money, I'll just buy tickets
to Shanghai. I looked carefully at the soldiers around
the station. If they were looking for someone it would
be a couple, not just an ordinary countryman like me.
I stood in a line that was surprisingly short. When I
got to the window I asked for two tickets hard seat to
Shanghai. The man laughed at me. 'What?' I asked. 'The

train stops here to refuel but no one gets on or off.' 'Where's the train from?' 'Depends on the direction. Going south it starts in Beijing and ends in Shanghai. Going north, the reverse.' 'Are there other trains?' Going west, yes, but nothing going east, to the coast or north. You want to go west, give me your money, otherwise step aside.'

"I stepped aside. No wonder there really wasn't much of a line for tickets. This station sold tickets to go west back into the countryside, not east to the city. I went back out and told my wife. She nodded but seemed almost in a daze. I put my coat around her and hid her back behind a row of parked railway cars. Then I went towards the platform and watched.

"The trains heading west were small, with three, four, five cars. The first trains from Beijing amazed me. More cars on one train than I'd ever seen. The train came just before noon. As it approached I saw many men running towards the platform with carrying rods and baskets on their backs. They all had the same kind of shirt with a crest on the right sleeve. I guessed it identified them as train personnel. As I watched, the train stopped and the men with the train shirts filled their baskets and headed onto the train. As soon as they entered the first car I began to count. I was up to just over nine hundred counts when they began to leave the train from the rear cars. Their baskets were empty and already the train was beginning to pull out of the station heading towards Shanghai.

"Two hours later the process was repeated on a train coming from Shanghai and heading towards Beijing. This time the porters were off in just over eight hundred and fifty counts and the train was already picking up speed as it headed out of the station. Neither time did any passengers get off the train.

"I watched two more trains, one in each direction. The last one pulled out just before sundown. For those last two times I wasn't counting. I was watching the porters. Finally I found what I wanted. A thin young man with an angry face. As he left the last train I fell in beside him and offered him a cigarette.

"He took it, but said, 'What do you want, old man.' He called me an old man."

I could see that being called an old man really hurt him, Fong.

"At first I didn't say anything to him, just walked by his side. 'You not able to talk, old man, or what?' 'I can talk,' I said. 'Good. Talk.'

"I told him I wanted to buy his shirt. He didn't act surprised. The first price he named made me laugh out loud. My counteroffer made him cry out loud. Eventually we settled on a price and he gave me his shirt. I had never spent so much money for anything ever before in my life. I returned to the railway car and wrapped my wife in my arms and sang to her. It was all I could think to do. I sang. She cried.

"The dawn was even colder than the night. It was hard to rouse my wife. I finally did and we went to the platform. I told her the plan and made her repeat it to me several times. We watched the early-morning train heading to Beijing, then the late-morning train heading to Shanghai. Both times we talked through what we would do. Then we retreated to the railway yard and waited for the last train. I figured that the later train would be in the most hurry. The least likely to scrutinize things. We didn't sleep well. I dreamed of lightning in the sky. Large forks of lightning, hit-ting the land and ancient trees sparking into fire.

"At sundown we moved carefully towards the railway platform. As the huge train blew its whistle to announce its arrival I slipped behind the train sta-tion and put on my porter's shirt. The other porters were already running towards the platform. I kept my head down as I picked up my carrying basket from the far side of the train station.

"The huge train squealed on the tracks as its brakes began to slow. It was getting cold quickly. As I passed by her, I noticed that my wife was shivering violently. Our plan was for me to go on board the train as a porter carrying supplies, then make my way to the back of the train and open a carriage door for my wife.

"I stepped into line with the dozens of porters who were ready to carry their supplies onto the train through one of the forward doors. It was already get-ting dark when the train finally pulled to a full stop and the front door was flung open.

"Inside, the train's lights were off. Many of the passengers were asleep. I followed the line of porters through the front three cars then into a fourth car that was free of seats. Boxes and sacks were piled high on both sides. I placed the supplies I was carrying beside the goods that the porter ahead of me placed on the floor but didn't turn and follow him back to the front of the train to pick up more supplies. I knelt down and pretended to roll up my pant leg. Finally the guard in charge of the storeroom stepped out onto the platform to have a smoke. I snuck out the back of the car and ran as fast as I could through the train cars filled with sleep-ing city people. I had counted the cars as they came into the station. There had been thirty-seven. I counted as I ran. I was trying to get to one of the last five cars. That's what we had agreed on. That I would open a door in one of the last five cars for her - my wife."

He went silent as if that choice of the last five cars had somehow caused his wife's death. I looked at Chen. He nodded and prompted, "What happened next?"

The peasant looked up at Chen and stared at him for a long moment as if he couldn't place his face. Then he smiled. He was missing a front tooth. Why hadn't I noticed that before?

He sighed deeply then spoke. "I was running through the cars trying not to trip and wake people. Some were still awake, especially in the hard seat compartments. They were drinking and smoking and playing cards. They yelled at me. Things they thought were smart, I guess. 'Got to pee bad, buddy?' 'Lose your girlfriend?' 'Where's the fire?' Some said things I couldn't understand.

Those would be the Shanghanese, I think, Fong. Our dialect is so filled with clichés and idiomatic expressions that many outsiders haven't got a clue what we are saying. It's the way we like it, isn't it, Fong?

"I ignored them but their yelling made me lose count which car I was in. I knew I was somewhere in the twenties when the train began to move. I couldn't believe it. The thing clanked and rattled then began to pick up speed. I raced to the nearest door and flung it open. My wife was the only person on the platform - she was already twenty yards behind the last car of the train. Even from that distance I could see her tears. I jumped off the train. I hit my head. A tooth came out."

He said it all so simply. He jumped. He hit his head. A tooth came out. When I was young my mother came home with a small dog. I loved that dog nearly to

death. I squeezed him all the time. Do you know that
it's a law in Shanghai now that you have to have an
electronic implant for your dog or they can take him
and kill him. There are over 100,000 dogs in Shanghai
– that's a lot of implants. I bet some city official
owns the lab that implants the stupid things. At any
rate I thought of that dog of mine because it got run
over by a pedal bike on the sidewalk. It mangled one
of his front legs. He cried and did a lot of lying in
my lap for several days then he just got up and began
to walk – with a limp. But he was the same as before,
just that now he was a dog with a limp. He never
regretted that he couldn't run fast anymore. That was
before. Now he was a dog who limped. This man was a
man who bumped his head and now was missing a tooth.
No regret, just moving forward. I wish I could live my
life that way, Fong, I really do. Just looking forward, never back at what could have been or what was.

   "That night I found an abandoned railway car and
we slept. Before sunrise they came."
   "Who?"
   "Bandits. They robbed us of all the money we had.
They beat me up and two of them dragged me to the corner of the car and sat on me."
   He stopped talking. Dear God they didn't rape his
wife, did they? I didn't even know how to broach the
question.
   Chen did. "Was your wife attacked?"
   Dong Zhu Houng looked away. After a long silence
he said, "They ripped off her clothes but a train
pulled in, and in the train's front light, they saw
the sores on her body. They cursed her and ran away.
But not before I saw one of their faces in the light.

"It was the porter who sold you his shirt, wasn't it?"

The peasant nodded.

A silence fell on us all. Dawn was beginning to lighten the eastern horizon.

"So what happened next?" asked Chen.

"We went back to the Beng Pu market and sold more of the herb, then took the money and bought train tickets south, towards the Yangtze."

"Why not just sell all the herb and buy first-class bus tickets all the way to Shanghai?"

"We didn't know if we could get onto a bus with her being so sick. At least on a train we could get on at night and go hard seat. Everyone looks awful in hard seat. Besides we didn't know how much money we'd need to get her treated in Shanghai and that herb was the only source of money we had. We couldn't spend it all before we got her treated."

Chen nodded. "So you headed south?" The man nodded. "How was that train ride?"

"Lonely."

I didn't expect that - hard, boring, painful - sure, but lonely?

As if he could read my thoughts he said, "She slept the whole way. And so deeply. I couldn't wake her even to feed her."

"But you finally got to the river - the Yangtze?"

"Yes."

"Where?"

"At Chungking. I wanted to rent a place for us so she could stay in a bed for a bit. Until she was at least a little stronger. I thought she was dying."

He looked up at us. Both Chen and I nodded.

"I found a very long alley and put her in the

darkness at the end of it, then covered her with both our coats. I couldn't have her with me when I went to find a place. People would look at her and close the door on us. I needed to find a place that didn't have an old lady with the keys sitting in the front. A place where they wouldn't report us. We had no papers allowing us to travel, let alone to be in Chungking.

"There were building projects down by the river. Lights on tall towers lit up these huge pits where hundreds and hundreds of men lifted and toted heavy muck on their backs. I stood and watched. I'd never seen anything like it. It was raining and the men were the same colour as the mud. It was as if the ground itself was lifting up and moving up the walls of the pit. But even as I watched, I saw that the men working were being replaced by newer workers. I looked in the direction from which they had come. There were many low huts made from that wavy metal."

"Corrugated iron," Chen said.

The peasant looked at Chen, grateful that Chen had supplied this bit of information but also surprised that anyone would need more explanation than "wavy metal."

"I went there. The man at the door was from Anhui Province. I told him I was looking for work and needed a place to stay for me and my wife. He shrugged. I offered him money. He found me a place in the back."

There it was again. Simple facts. No judgment.

"Just before sunrise I settled my wife into the bed and fell asleep on the floor beside her. I don't know how long I slept but I awoke like someone falling off a cart. It felt like I had rolled over on a large stone or something. Then I felt the pain in my side again but sharper this time. This time I also knew it wasn't a stone – it was a boot. A heavy boot was kicking me in the ribs. I jumped to my feet and immediately stood between my attacker and my wife. 'Morning, princess. No work for the princess this morning?'

"At first I thought he was talking to my wife. Then I looked at her bed. It was empty. He was talking to me! I was princess. 'No work, no pay. No pay, no place to stay, princess.'

"It was raining and cold. I had only my sandals."

Fong, he looked us straight in the eyes. A kind of pride blooming there.

"I have worked in the fields every day from dawn until sometimes late into the night since I was a little boy but I have never been forced to work like that. Been punished by work like that. And I was desperate to find my wife. Where was she? Why was the bed empty?

"When my shift finally ended I ran back to the hut. My wife was sitting on the side of the bed. She had made tea somehow. She stood as I approached. 'You have worked hard, husband, you rest now,' she said to me. I don't remember falling asleep. But I think she held me and rocked me. She, so sick, did that for me.

"I worked there three more days. I wanted her to get as well as she could because we had a long journey ahead of us. Before sunrise on the fourth day she awakened me and we snuck out of the hut and headed towards the river, the Yangtze."

He looked up at us. "Have you seen it?" I almost laughed, but then I saw the awe in his eyes and swallowed my giggles. "Is it not magnificent? All the way from the Yellow Mountains to the sea." He was looking at the rising dawn out the window. The first day he would spend without his wife – on this earth. A shudder began at the base of his spine and worked its way up his back.

Chen crossed over to him and put his hand on his shoulder. I assumed that Chen was going to offer sympathy to the poor man, but I was wrong.

Chen turned him away from the window and asked, "With your money situation you couldn't have taken a riverboat. So how did you get down the Yangtze all the way to Shanghai?"

"On a raft."

A raft! Like Huckleberry Hound? Chinese people don't use rafts.

"Just short of four moons."

They had been on a raft for almost four months!

"We floated and stopped. Sold some of the herb for food, then got back on the raft. I built a small shelter on it to keep out the rain. In the second week we spent a lot of money and bought a small brazier and some coal. I brewed her tea and she drank the last of her medicine. We watched the great ships pass us by and we floated. We floated. Until finally we came here. She was weaker every week but we were together and we were safe and we were floating as if we were already in the other world."

"Finally, you landed in Shanghai?" Chen asked.

"At the mouth of the Huangpo River. That was the hardest part. Landing the raft and walking to Shanghai. And we had no money left. None."

"Had you sold all the herb?"

"No. We were not foolish. Not foolish." He was suddenly vehement.

"Then why did you have no money?"

"Because no one here would buy it."

For the first time, Chen was confused - but I wasn't, Fong. Generic Viagra is cheap and plentiful in Shanghai. Their herb's value was totally supplanted by modern medical research. The carefully stored and lovingly picked source of their wealth was no more. I didn't need to hear the rest. I already knew, Fong. They must have wandered desperately in Shanghai and eventually found their way here to the Hua Shan Hospital, where they were turned aside until they knocked on my office door and I got her admitted.

He ended his story and stood very still. Chen approached him and put a hand on his shoulder, "Thank you, sir, for the honour of telling me your story."

The peasant grunted.

"Where will you go now?"

For a moment, Fong, I thought he was going to ask to stay in my office, but again I was wrong.

"Home," he said. "I will go home."

With that he left the room and took the first of thousands upon thousands of steps in his journey to the west.

Fong stared at the last words of Lily's missive on the flimsy pages. A few digital who-knows-whats was all that remained of this poor man's story.

Then some of those last words blurred as if a piece of flawed glass had been put in front of them. Fong tilted the pages – and the flawed glass moved and finally dripped over the edge of the sheet.

Tears do that.

Fong very slowly reached for his cell phone and pressed the speed-dial key. Then he paused, knowing full well that if he set things into motion neither he nor anyone else would know where they would lead. "Fuck it," he mumbled and hit speed-dial selection nine. With lightning speed the thing dialed seventeen numbers – three for overseas long distance, three for China's country code, three for Shanghai's city code and the eight digits of the local Shanghai phone number that connected him with the two young officers he brought to the late night meeting he had convened just before he left for the Golden Mountain.

"*Wei.*"

"You know who this is?" Fong asked.

"Yes, sir," the young cop answered, the tension clear in his voice.

"Good. Be ready to execute the plan that I gave you before I left."

Fong heard the young man take a deep breath and finally he said, "We'll be ready, sir."

The phone disconnected without the usual thunk. Down the beach the old man was still standing on one leg. Momentarily, Fong wondered if the chaos his plan would set in motion in China would make the ground here on Jericho Beach tremble enough to unbalance the old man.

That night on the sands of Jericho Beach beneath a breathtakingly beautiful Vancouver starscape, Fong dreamt of climbing ladders into the sky. When he reached the top he took off his coat, folded it carefully and laid it on the top rung – then he hurled himself earthward – flying – his arms open ready to embrace his end only to find himself on the bottom rung of the ladder climbing skyward again.

Once in the night he awoke. His shirt was open and he had the strong feeling that ancient hands had touched his bare chest, their rice-paper dryness tracing the circumference of his heart. He redid the buttons of his shirt and looked up at the heavens. Then he smelt it. Something sweet – like chocolate.

As Fong dreamt – or believed he dreamt – Robert stared at the massive crimson mess he had just extruded into the toilet bowl. His doctor had told him that it would begin this way. "Will there be much pain?" he'd asked. The doctor had reached into his desk and taken out a bottle of pills and handed them to Robert. "These will help with the pain initially but once things begin in earnest nothing but a strong morphine drip will bring you any relief. But, remember Robert, once you start that you won't leave it. You won't remember much. What life you live will be in a haze – you'll die in that haze as in time the ravages of the cancer will take you."

Robert thought about that – about ending his life in a Vancouver hospital bed – about maybe getting a transfusion of Asian blood to keep him alive. That stopped him. He had done many wrong things in his life but he wasn't about to add Asian blood to his list of sins.

He unscrewed the lid from the bottle of pills and swallowed three – although the dosage was clearly marked as "One every six hours – do not exceed prescribed dosage." Then he remembered his doctor's final warning, "If you take too many of those pills they'll make you feel like you're flying – but when you feel like that your vital systems are shutting down and the end will come fast."

Robert thought about that, then got dressed and turned to face the dawn.

* * *

Across the Pacific Ocean, in a Shanghai basement, four men from Anhui Province were bedding down for the night. Each had stuck a bloody syringe into the body of a

Caucasian that day. Each of them was committed – committed to getting their revenge against the West that had infected those they loved.

CHAPTER NINE

VANCOUVER DAY TWO

Fong stood beside the central monument halfway across the Burrard Street Bridge where he had agreed to meet Robert. He was looking west, to the East and thinking of all that he had left there.

He sensed them before he actually saw them. Then he heard their weirdly happy singing – then they appeared at the Kitsilano side of the bridge – hundreds of young people. Perhaps thousands, all with the same red-striped backpack slung over a shoulder, their faces all alight with smiles.

Fong found it troublingly reminiscent of the gibbering throngs of children who sang songs in praise of Chairman Mao at the same time as Mao's policies were sentencing millions of them to death by starvation in the Great Leap Forward.

Fong almost jumped when a hand landed on his shoulder. "So it gives you the creeps too, huh?"

Fong turned to look at Robert Cowens. "You're still wearing an overcoat. No one here wears an overcoat."

"Evidently no one west of Kenora even owns an overcoat."

Fong had no idea where or what a Kenora was but didn't bother asking for further details. He pointed at the happy singing throngs making their way across the bridge. "What are they?"

"The Pope's Romper Room graduates."

"I'm sure that means something to someone, but it doesn't mean anything to me. Could you just answer my question? Why are they all carrying the same backpack and why are they all singing . . . and . . ."

"Smiling? Yeah, it's the smiling part that always gets me."

"So?"

"Well, they're a bunch of happy Catholics – kiddy Catholics actually – but then again religions are always taken most to heart by the very young and the very old – like sweets."

Fong looked at Robert. "Are you completely incapable of answering a straight question?"

Robert smiled. "Try me again."

"Who or what are all these teenagers and what are they doing?"

Robert pretended to think for a moment then said, "They are young Catholics from all over the world who have landed in Vancouver because the Pope told them to show the world the depth of their faith."

Fong waited but there was no more information forthcoming. "That's it?"

"Yep," Robert said, "that's all she wrote."

"I heard that young people in the West gathered in large groups in order to get laid."

"It used to be that way back in the good old days. Now they gather in large groups to not get laid and to proclaim the beauty of keeping their pants on – and keeping their knees tight together."

"You people are perverse when it comes to sex."

"I don't deny that."

The song ended and there was a moment of blessed quiet, then a new song began. Somehow everyone knew what the next tune was going to be and just launched right in. Thousands of voices singing in sickeningly sweet unison. Many marchers carried guitars. The sun shone. The faces smiled.

Fong hated it.

"Amazing grace how sweet the sound that saved a wretch like me," they sang.

"Who's Grace?" Fong asked.

"Grace is a holy state of acceptance, not a person."

"But Grace is a person's name, isn't it?

"But not in this case."

"Couldn't this Grace be so amazing that she saved this wretch?"

"Are you done making fun, Fong?"

Fong nodded. "Is this a well-known song? Better known than Mr. Waits's 'Kentucky Avenue'?"

"Much better known, although it's little understood."

That interested Fong, "How so?"

"Well, it was written by an English ship captain who made his considerable fortune by transporting slaves from West Africa to the American South."

"Why would their god save such a wretch? That's obscene."

"I agree." A sudden wave of nausea swept through Robert. He couldn't tell whether it was the cancer or the smiling throngs that were making his stomach roil.

And as suddenly as it came, it left. Robert breathed deeply then said, "It's like a crusade, Fong. In the Third World people struggle to survive. It takes up most of the time of most of the people. In the West we don't spend our time on survival. We spend our time on finding meaning . . . or sex."

"Which could have some meaning if you weren't so perverse."

"True."

"Do you spend your time seeking meaning, Robert?"

"No, but I'm not– on a certain level I envy them, Fong."

Fong didn't respond. He just looked at the happy vacant faces and wondered if there were enough toilet facilities for so many young people. Then he looked over the edge of the bridge to the parklands beneath and wondered where the security was. Surely things like the Burrard Street Bridge were potential targets. Where were the police officers? Did these people really believe that their silly songs make them immune to the motions of the world?

The cream cheese squeezed out of the side of the bagel and adhered to Fong's upper lip.

"So what do ya' think?" Robert asked.

"It's too much cheese."

"Then you should have asked for a shmear."

"A what?"

"Never mind. Tastes good though, huh?"

"This red thing is fish, right?"

"Lox."

"Lox fish?"

"No, the fish is salmon."

"So why do you call it lox?"

Robert thought about that for a bit and even considered telling Fong about gefilte fish which really wasn't any particular fish at all but decided against it. Instead he said, "Because it's called lox. Don't be a pain in the tuchas. So do you like it or not?"

"It's good. A bit rich."

"Some delis now offer discounts for the local cardiologist with proof of purchase of their blintzes."

Discounts and cardiologists Fong knew, but delis, blintzes and proof of purchase remained part of the mystery of the Golden Mountain as far as he was concerned. Fong used his napkin to remove the cream cheese from his lip and said, "The food at this Benjamin's is very good."

"Benny's. The place is called Benny's."

"Yes, but Benny is a diminutive for Benjamin, isn't it?"

Robert nodded, "Yeah, but this place is called Benny's. If you got into a cab and asked him to drive you to Benjamin's he'd take you to a funeral parlour, but if you asked him to drive you to Benny's he'd take you here. Okay?"

"Fine, very fine, excellent."

Robert looked at Fong. "What?"

Fong pushed aside his plate. "The shipment of spoiled blood should arrive tomorrow. That's why I told you to leave the rental car at your hotel.

"I don't follow you."

"Didn't you notice that the cop who stopped us about the taillight put a bug on your outside mirror?"

"No," Robert almost shouted, "I didn't happen to notice that."

"Relax. We're safer if they think they know things."

"If who knows things?"

"That's a good question. Have you succeeded in your part of all this?"

"Yes, I guess. I let it be known that I represent a large syndicate of investors from the East who want into the blood-trading business. That they are prepared to offer upfront money in return for control of shipping the blood to the East."

"Good. And who did you 'let this be known' to?"

"The businessmen I was introduced to through my contact."

"And is the business community in Vancouver very large?"

"Not particularly. So the word should get out quickly." Robert took another bite of his bagel. "So, just for the record, let me get this straight. You don't mind them following me, you just don't want following you, which is why you hopped out of the rental car yesterday in the middle of Granville Street? Right?"

"Right. But Robert, why shouldn't they follow you? You've done nothing wrong."

"Just false representation is all."

"That's illegal in a business dealing? Really? How interesting."

Robert swallowed Fong's sarcasm with the last of his bagel. Then he waited for his stomach's reaction – nothing. He got up to get a coffee refill. As Robert moved away, Fong again watched him closely. The man laboured as if his legs were too heavy for him.

Robert returned with a steaming cup of coffee and took a long sip. "They do this great out here. He took another long pull clearly savouring the flavour and the heat of the beverage. Again his stomach offered no complaint. He glanced at the television set hung in the corner behind the counter. There was a retrospective of TV game shows playing silently on the screen. Robert pointed at it. "Do they have game shows in China, Fong?"

"Game shows?"

"On TV. Where people compete against each other for money or prizes."

Fong nodded, "Yes, we have American game shows."

"Which ones?"

"Jerry Springer is very popular and my ex-wife

watched this game show all the time. She learned much of her English by watching this show."

"That's frightening."

"Her English is somewhat short of perfect."

"With Jerry Springer as the model it's amazing that it even passes for English."

"Lily's English is, indeed, quite unique."

"Fong, the Jerry Springer show is not a game show."

"You are mistaken Robert, on the Jerry Springer show the people compete against each other to outdo each other . . ."

Robert chuckled and said under his breath, "A twenty-first–century Queen for a Day."

"They give out queenships on television in America?"

Robert shook his head, "Not even Americans do that. But that's not my point." For a moment Robert faltered, as if he didn't know if he should proceed, then he clearly made up his mind and continued, "Of late I've found that some moments in my life have begun to stand out. Do you find that? Insignificant moments really but they are indelible – bright, sharp, always in focus while important things fade back into the murk."

Fong nodded but didn't agree. Memories that stay in "focus" are bits of knowledge that shine like diamonds in the dirt. They are to be treasured. Only time tells you exactly what they really mean and why you continue to remember them. His first wife, Fu Tsong, had taught him that. "There are lines from some plays that I worked on years and years ago that are still fresh and alive in me, Fong. While there are lines that I will speak on stage this evening that are already fading into the past." "Like what?" Fong had asked. Fu Tsong had only smiled and touched his face with the tips of her elegant fingers and said, "Look at the way you are looking at me. I can't wait for you. You bowl me over. You knock me out. Your eyes kill me." Her delivery was so natural, so personal to him that Fong wondered momentarily if these were really lines from a play. But when she unbuttoned his shirt and put her palm on his chest he didn't care where the lines came from. The only thing that mattered was that his amazing wife had said them to him and meant them.

"Fong?"

"Yes. So what is it about an American TV game show?"

"Well, it's one of those memories. There was this show – this game show – this American game show on television when I was a kid. On this show couples were pitted against each other in various contests – sorting things, tossing balls into bins, figuring out puzzles – things like that. And every time you won a contest you gained five seconds on your clock."

"Five seconds on your clock?"

"Yeah, each couple had a clock and you earned five-second increments by winning contests. The couple who won the most seconds on their clocks got to try a final contest against the clock. If they had earned twenty seconds then they had twenty seconds to solve the problem, if they earned twenty-five, they had twenty-five. At any rate the final challenge had been the same for months and months because no couple could complete it. And if you didn't complete the final challenge all you got to bring home was a board-game version of the television show or a can of Coke or something. But if you completed the final challenge you won something significant, a car, a house – something big. Well, no one had won the prize for – well, what seemed like forever. As a kid every week I watched this show to see if some couple could win the final contest."

"What was the final contest?" Fong asked.

"Three wooden boxes each about a foot and a half tall and four inches wide – somewhat shaped like a two-litre milk carton – were set on a table like three small towers. The object was to stack the three towers, one on the next."

"This was the contest? Why was that difficult, were the boxes off balance with their bottoms all at different angles?"

"No. Nothing like that. The cardboard boxes were perfectly flat and completely normal."

"Then what was the problem in stacking the three boxes."

"The problem was that you weren't allowed to touch the boxes with your hands. Instead the husband and wife were each given a single piece of wood dowelling about three feet long. Only the wood dowellings were allowed to touch the boxes and you were only allowed to hold the dowelling by one end and only with one hand. Week after week the couples would put one dowelling on each side of a box and try to lift it and place it on top of another box. But every time, the lifted box would tilt and fall over. If you think about it, it would be very hard to keep the pressure exactly equal on either side of the carton – two people, two dowels. When they went to lift the carton the thing would flip over one way or the other. Only one time did a couple manage to get that middle box on top of the first one without knocking it over. The middle box, however, was so badly balanced that there was no possibility of putting the third box on top of the other two.

"Then one day a small, googly-looking couple won the introductory contests in twenty seconds to fifteen seconds. The host informed the couple that they would have only twenty seconds to complete the final contest to win the car or house or whatever it was. And that twenty seconds was a very little amount of time. When they came back from the commercial break the couple was standing in front of the table with the three carton towers on it. Both husband and wife held their piece of dowelling – and I'll never forget this – there was a shot of the two of them and they were completely calm, no hopping up and down, no nervous anxiety. The game show host asked if they were ready. The husband looked to the wife who nodded back at him.

"Set the clock at twenty seconds please!!! Get ready, get set – gooooooo!"

The clock ticked forward. The husband calmly took his piece of dowelling and tilted over the first of the three boxes onto its side. As he did this, his wife did the same for the second and then the third. Only four seconds had ticked by. Then the husband placed his dowelling on the bottom of the first carton while his wife placed hers on the top of the third carton. Then they gently pushed towards each other. Between their sticks, on the table, lay the three cartons perfectly arranged. The ninth second ticked by. But before the game show host could chime in with "Halfway!" The wife applied pressure to her end and the husband applied pressure back. Then the wife and husband lifted the entire tower of three cartons off the table and gave it a ninety-degree turn. The audience actually gasped. They lowered it to the table and slid away their dowels. There it was – the solution to the problem – puzzle solved." Robert seemed suddenly drained. His face flushed. "I don't know why I told you that."

"Because it is a precious memory," Fong said. He thought through what Robert had just told him. The winners didn't deal with the pieces of the puzzle but the puzzle in total. Then worked backwards. They analyzed the problem and the weapons they had and saw the solution in a new light. Very good. Important. Fong's mind suddenly put him back in Shanghai in his office on the Bund. His three columns of cards were in front of him on his desktop. The Lawyer, the Chiangs and the third column headed by a card with a large "?" on it. Each column – each tower – could lead to THE MONEY. Three columns, three towers. Fong looked back at Robert – it could just be the angle of the setting sun crossing the man's face – but Fong doubted it – this man looked ghastly.

"Look Fong, you can't try to attack Vancouver directly. It is often not what it seems. It is both more violent and more peaceful, more tolerant and more prejudiced, more paradise and more hell than you think at first glance. You have to figure out what weapons you have – dowels, if you will – then figure out how to use them to stand the blocks one upon the next. And it's not going to be successful if you try the way you first think. You've got to find a way to see the problem in a different light – a light specific to this place – or you won't solve it at all." Robert's face was a deep red. His throat stretched. A vein pulsed erratically in his forehead.

Fong changed the topic. "What did you think of that *Blood Trader* article I left for you to read?"

"Fucking Appleton, Wisconsin."

"You know this place?"

"Birth and final resting place of Joseph McCarthy."

"Who?"

"Just a dead American-style fascist."

"Is the information in that article public knowledge in your country?"

"Not really. I've heard a bit about this. The bigger scandal in Canada was about tainted blood bought from an Arkansas prison – some seven thousand Canadian hemophiliacs contracted AIDS when they were transfused. The guy running the Arkansas program denied that the blood he'd sold to Canada was tainted. According to this genius there was no homosexual activity in Arkansas prisons so there couldn't be any AIDS virus in the blood they sold. By the way, the guy was a Clinton appointee and confidante of both Bill and Hillary. Nothing's simple when it comes to blood."

Fong was happy to see that Robert's colour was returning to normal. "What's Monica up to these days?" he asked brightly.

"Who knows? You know Monica Lewinsky, but not Joseph McCarthy . . ."

"A free press is a recent development in the Middle Kingdom."

"Fine. Enough with the history lesson. Where to now, Fong?"

Fong shrugged but chose to ask a question rather than answer one, "What's your next move?"

"More schmoozing."

"What?"

"Schmoozing. Chatting with folks who don't want to talk to you – schmoozing – it's a verb and a noun and probably a gerund if I knew what that was."

Fong was happy that Robert was able to make jokes. He reached into his pocket and extracted a piece of paper with the name of the law firm that the woman who had killed the man she loved had given to Joan Shui. "Why not schmooze these folks?" Fong passed over the piece of paper.

Robert read the company name and blanched. "What does this lily white law firm have to do with all this?"

They are the name at the top of one of my columns that could lead me to The Money he thought, but what he said was, "They represented the blood-exporting company in China."

"Damn," Robert swore under his breath.

"What?" Fong asked.

"Nothing – it's just that these guys are the white heart of the darkness of this place."

Robert got up and despite the heat put on his over-coat.

Fong watched him, then asked, "What was the name of that game show, Robert?"

"*Beat the Clock*," he said and turned towards the door.

Fong watched Robert leave. The man shambled more than walked. Fong frowned. *Beat the Clock*. Now there was Western silliness. Surely the clock is the one thing that no living thing can beat. And the clock is running – sometimes faster, sometimes slower – but always running.

CHAPTER TEN

THE CHIANGS' SHIP LANDS

The ocean freighter tugged at its moorings, a restive wild thing straining at its tethers. Manifests were handed over. Three full containers were lifted from the hold by great cranes and set on the backs of three large flatbed trucks. A normal day in a normal port. Then something happened. A workman securing one of the containers removed his gloves to wipe the sweat out of his eyes and leaned against one of the containers. The metal container was hot to the touch. Refrigerated containers are not cold to the touch but they aren't warm either – and never hot – like the three huge shipments of blood products that sat on these three flatbed trucks at the Port of Vancouver.

The phone call was disturbing enough that the Chiang sons agreed to wake their father – a thing that needed careful doing. The eldest son took the lead.

The ancient liver-spotted eyelids slid back smoothly, revealing the coal black eyes of the patriarch of the Vancouver branch of the Chiang clan. Chiang's eyes were clear, aware. As if even in sleep he had been totally awake. He adjusted the plastic tubing in his nose, swung his legs out of the bed and breathed deeply. The portable oxygen tank obliged him with an invigorating funnel of almost pure oxygen. "Open the blinds," he said. His eldest son did as ordered.

The old man wheeled his oxygen canister to the window and stared at the mountains of North Vancouver – still so foreign even after all these years. He reached for his cigarettes only to find an empty pocket. Emphysema and cigarettes – the road to a hacking grave.

Then he thought of his beautiful granddaughter, the brilliant one who would take over all this, all that he had worked so hard to earn. He touched the cool glass of the window and examined his now-gnarled fingers as his eldest son reported the bad news from the docks. So much blood gone bad. So much money lost. But it was neither of those things that occupied his mind. He was thinking about timing. Blood goes bad. A new access to the Eastern marketplaces arrives out of nowhere. And a Shanghai cop walks the streets of Vancouver. He didn't like it. "Call Suzanne; have her meet me at the usual place." After the slightest of hesitations his eldest son flipped open his expensive cell phone and placed the call to Chiang's granddaughter. Chiang turned slowly away from the boy. The boy was closer to fifty than forty but he would always be a boy while Chiang was alive. A privileged boy with a very bad temper and a chaotic mind. He would have to advise Suzanne on how to deal with this problem too.

The "problem" son's call was immediately intercepted and orders were relayed. Tong members took their assigned places and a full-fledged surveillance swung into motion.

Forty-five minutes later a sleek black Mercedes pulled to a stop in front of a restaurant and Chiang got out. Before his foot hit the ground a doorman was there with an umbrella while the maître d'hotel offered a helping hand. Chiang permitted them to assist him into the backroom. This back-room had at one time been a sealed-off smoking room, but since the City of Vancouver had outlawed smoking in any public place, the restaurant had converted the sealed room to an oxygen-rich environment. Younger couples used its extra oxygen and privacy for their own ends. But the extra oxygen in the room was a different kind of boon to Chiang – it allowed him to unhook himself from his oxygen supply.

The enclosed space provided another advantage to Chiang – it was an easy room to sweep for unwelcome electronic intrusion.

The maître d' held open the door, and immediately Suzanne rose from the table and approached her grandfa-ther. They touched with a surprising intimacy and then she assisted him to a seat at the small table. The door wheezed shut. They were the only ones in the room. Tea and tradi-tional morning porridge were waiting on a side table.

Chiang sat and savoured the pleasure of unassisted breathing. She served him. It reminded him of being served by a class two geisha in Edo when he was young. He had found it highly erotic but had wondered at his own response to the ritual nature of every move, every tilt of the head; the almost theatrical approach to the simplest of acts – kneeling, speaking, pouring tea – the absolutely open acknowledgement of the façade. There was no attempt to make the client believe that the geisha was anything but a highly trained aberration of a female. It was in fact the linkage of that façade with eroticism that fascinated but confused him. Years later, after the war, he was in Paris completing a business transaction for his father when his host told him that they had been invited to a most exclusive soiree. Chiang had accepted the invitation and, once his people had cleared the security in the place, was happy to attend. There was a lot of fine food and drink and many people of great wealth and power milled about. But the centre of attention was a mad-eyed dishevelled French writer who repeatedly screamed the word "bourgeois" at the crowd. With each escalating scream of that word the crowd grew more and more attentive. Chiang found it perverse until he listened to the man. And here from the mouth of this uncouth artiste came the answer to the confusion he had felt in the presence of the geisha. "Sex is about an agreed-upon foolery. That's why whores call it turning a trick. The thing that starts sex is the acceptance of the fakery. The embracing of it. For example: it's not exciting for most grown men to be alone with a fourteen-year-old girl in a school uniform, no matter how high up she hikes her skirt. But for a grown woman to openly dress as a schoolgirl – no matter how little she rolls up her skirt – it's enticing. It's a trick. A folie à deux. She creates the portal of the masque and you both enter into the world of Eros together." He smiled.

"What, Grandfather?"

"Huh?"

"You were smiling."

"Was I? The porridge is very good."

"How would you know, you haven't tried it?" Then she smiled. He smiled back, then tasted the porridge. It was nothing special. His mother, Suzanne's great-grandmother, had made much better – and for far less. He put aside his spoon and laid out the problem they had before them at the Port of Vancouver.

She sat quietly and took it all in. When he finally finished, she reached for the teapot, then got up and crossed to his side of the table. With a practised dip she poured the hot liquid into his small cup. "We are sure that this was not an accident, Grandfather?"

"This was no accident, Suzanne." His voice was unusually sharp. "Three different, huge, shipping containers, each filled to overflowing with our blood products – the thermostats in all three fail – and the exterior monitors of all three containers just happen to be stuck exactly at the right temperature for preserving the blood products." He turned towards her. "That is some extraordinary accident, wouldn't you say, Suzanne?"

A darkness moved across her fine features.

He was pleased to see it – access to violence was necessary if one was going to lead.

When she spoke the darkness increased, "An extraordinary and perhaps very *personal* accident."

"I agree, Suzanne," he said, but the question in his head was *personal* against exactly whom?

"The blood trade is legal," she said.

He nodded but he didn't totally agree. He preferred doing business in the East or continental Europe. If a business transaction made money in those places, it was good. If it didn't, it was bad – simple. Money was the determinant of morality – of good and bad. But here in the moral hypocrisy of the Golden Mountain there existed what he thought of as theological capitalism that produced a grey area. If you steal a man's wallet at the opera it is theft. If you steal a man's wallet in a porno theatre or for that matter in a table-dancing club or, heaven forefend, in flagrante delicto with a whore, then you have entered the grey area. Fail to refrigerate sides of Kobi beef properly and there is culpable negligence. But – fail to refrigerate perfectly legal blood products and . . . grey area, damn the West's theological capitalism.

"What do we do, Grandfather?"

He thought about contacting their silent partner, then dismissed it. "Now we wait. We do nothing."

"And what exactly are we waiting for, Grandfather?"

He wanted to say, "For the other tower to fall," but instead chose to say, "for what happens next."

CHAPTER ELEVEN

THE LIE DETECTOR

Fong listened to the report on his cell phone as he looked at the overly ornate painted gate to Old Chinatown at the corner of Main and Cobalt. If this was Old Chinatown, what would these folks call places like Xian, he thought. Then he heard something on the phone that snapped him back to the task at hand. "That's it? No more calls to or from Chiang?"

"Not a peep, Inspector, except for the older son calling one of his mistresses," the Tong leader reported.

"And they know about the spoiled blood?" Fong pressed.

"They know, but just now they're doing nothing. We'll keep monitoring their phones."

"Good," Fong said but he was troubled. The spoiled-blood shipment should have sent the Chiangs into a flap of phone calling – hopefully leading him to the silent partner. "Keep me posted," he said, then hung up and turned to Robert. "So have you managed to pierce the heart of white darkness, Robert?"

"I did. My contact is very well connected. It didn't take too long before my story of representing an eastern syndicate that wants to invest in the blood trade got me the appropriate meeting."

"And it was at Henderson, Millet, Cavender and Barton, Attorneys at Law?"

"It certainly was."

"And what did you make of the lawyer you met there?"

Robert paused and did his best to put aside his natural prejudice but couldn't. "I hated him."

"Naturally, but what else?"

"He claimed that he represents the major investor behind the blood trade but that he has never met the man or his representative. That all his dealings are through blind trusts and Swiss bank accounts. Then, of course, he added that even if he could, he wouldn't reveal who his client was – lawyer/client privilege exists in this country, Fong."

"Do you believe him?"

"About not knowing who he represents? I don't know. It's possible but . . ."

"But what, Robert?"

"I can't tell. He pissed me off the moment I met him. So my judgment was clouded to say the least."

"Maybe he and his law firm are the source of the money behind the blood trade."

"I doubt it."

"Why?"

"Business – good business, bad business – all business takes balls. You've got to put something out – you've got to risk. Lawyers go to law school so they don't have to risk. They are risk-averse. The blood trade is dicey. These guys are lawyers. They make a killing without having to stick out their necks. It's just not in the genes of a lawyer to take a real chance. They've seen lots of businesses fuck up."

"But he might be lying to you. Robert, we have to know if he is lying." Fong's vehemence surprised Robert. "Listen to me. This lawyer could be our only access to the money behind all this." Robert turned away. "What?" Fong demanded.

"You remember I said I had a second contact out here?"

"Yes, but you weren't sure about him."

"I'm not. But he might be able to help us. But he's such a weird guy."

"How do you mean, weird?"

After a pause Robert looked Fong in the eyes and said, "He's a lie detector."

For a moment Fong didn't know if he'd heard Robert correctly. Robert nodded, "Yeah, you heard me right."

"He's a what?"

"A lie detector. We use him at my Toronto firm. He listens to tapes of final vettings of executives and then tells us if he thinks the guy is lying or not. He's better than a résumé-checking service and he's beaten every polygraph and eye-scan comparative study we've ever done. It's quite amazing. In fact, he's never been wrong in our experience and you can believe that we checked and then re-checked before we trusted him."

"And he's here in Vancouver, now?"

"He has a girlfriend who writes for a local paper so he takes any job out here he can get."

"What kind of jobs?"

"Theatre stuff mostly. He directs, whatever that means."

For a moment Fong didn't know what to do, then he asked, "Is he in rehearsal now?"

Because of his first wife, Fong knew a lot about the theatre. He'd seen a lot of plays and had heard endless hours of Fu

Tsong's tales from the rehearsal hall. But nothing prepared him for what he saw when Robert pushed open the door of the lower-level rehearsal hall of the Vancouver Theatre Centre.

Twelve men in business suits, extremely conservative business suits, were around a large table, some seated, others standing, with scripts in hand – nothing terribly unusual about that – but these men were clearly not actors – egotists yes, actors, no. One middle-aged balding man delivered a two-line speech without referring to his script, then actually stood to receive a "high five" from the man beside him.

"What is this?" Fong asked.

"A rehearsal for a benefit."

"A benefit for whom?"

"This theatre."

"But there already is a theatre here, why does it need a benefit?"

"Let's not go into that. Suffice it to say that arts institutions in this country have trouble carrying their own financial weight so they have to do things like this."

Fong watched a little more and made a face, "Like this? Really? Like this? But these are not actors."

"True, Fong. They're lawyers. Actually these men are the top lawyers in the city, four of them from the firm that handles the blood contracts out of China."

Fong watched a little more of the "performance." Finally he couldn't resist asking, "If they are lawyers, what are they doing on the stage?"

"Preening."

Fong gave him a look. "I don't know that word."

"Like a bird does when he puffs up its feathers."

Fong gave him an even stranger look. "These lawyers are doing some sort of sexual display for prospective mates?"

Robert thought about that and concluded that lawyers trying to be actors was pretty close to them being involved in some sort of sexual display. At least a notion of "mine's bigger than yours." So he said, "Close enough."

"And this theatre lets these lawyers do this on their stage?"

"Once a year. It is a performance for heavy hitters. Donors. Vancouver's social elite pay good money to come and see some of their own strut their stuff."

"In this play, is that what you mean?"

"Yeah, the audience'll have an expensive dinner with lots of wine and roll on over to the theatre all gussied up to eyeball their divorce lawyers and tax lawyers and bankruptcy lawyers make appropriate fools of themselves."

"And the audience pays for the privilege of seeing this?"

"Through the nose. It's actually one of the more successful benefits that theatres have found to do over the years. The lawyers themselves buy up the entire house and then resell the tickets."

"And can these lawyers do this play any justice?"

"Probably not, but at least it's a play about justice. It's called *Twelve Angry Men*."

The director, a curly-haired olive-skinned man in his middle to late thirties, was a real youngster in this crowd, although Fong noted his incredibly old eyes. He was trying to get one of the lawyers to make even basic sense of one of his lines, but the lawyer wasn't buying it.

"Henry Fonda didn't do it that way in the movie."

"This isn't the movie, it's the play," the director replied.

"Yeah, but the movie was great; why don't we use that script? I can make a call to Levine in Toronto right now," he said, whipping out a cell phone, "and he'll get us the rights, no trouble."

"Mr. McKintyre, can we please just do the play as it's written. We only have two rehearsals, then you guys are on."

"Park your ass, Mac," said another lawyer, "You ain't no Henry Fonda and I'm no Lee J. Cobb. Let's just do this."

"What's your hurry? Got a date?"

From the man's extensive girth Fong thought that unlikely.

An extremely thin, almost puny lawyer stepped forward and said, "Why do I have to play the E.G. Marshall role? He's such a dink."

The lawyer beside him said, "Dink? I haven't heard that word used in the new millennium. Actually I only heard it twice in the previous millennium."

"Was that in reference to your private parts?" asked another lawyer.

Fong couldn't believe it. These powerful, wealthy men were just boys trying to out-piss each other.

"I'll trade you for the Ed Begley role. I can be really mean."

"Yeah, like you were in that Pinson case, really mean," he said, putting up his hands in mock fear.

A tall blond-haired lawyer riffled through his script then tossed it on the table. "Hey, I hardly have anything to say in this play."

The oldest of the lawyers leaned close to the man beside him and said in a whisper loud enough to carry to the back of the rehearsal hall, "And who says there's no justice in the world?"

The razzing continued, but Fong wasn't watching the stage. He was examining the young director – Robert's lie detector. The young man was taking in the interaction of his would-be actors, deciphering codes and sorting out complex hierarchical structures. Then, suddenly, as if a page had turned, he smiled and forged into the piece with an accuracy that surprised Fong. As he did, the man's face lit with joy. The inherent old age in his eyes disappeared and was replaced by a surprisingly youthful glee. It was a joyousness that Fong had seen before but he couldn't recall where. As Fong watched, the young man lifted his head and tilted back – as if he were sniffing something above him.

It reminded Fong of the skateboard park. How exactly he didn't know. But for sure it reminded him of those talented boys flying on their boards.

Rehearsal continued. The young man's cadence was interesting. He found an instance of momentum and pursued it, then backed off when inertia set in. Then he shepherded his troops to a new section of the play. Before long they were waiting for him to guide them and the text took shape. The kid in the jeans was leading the twelve men in the expensive suits. Fong smiled.

"That's a miss," the young man said.

"A what?"

"A miss. The way you said that line was accurate to you but not to the character you spoke to. Look, if you were trying to get me to leave you alone, you would approach your line one way, but if you tried to get the man beside you to leave you alone you'd have to say the line another way. Truth is accurate to the person you're addressing, not to yourself."

"That's why it was a miss?"

"That's why."

"That's interesting."

"Yes it is, and if you're really interested in this, come on down and audit my master acting class – you might find that interesting too. Now, try the line again and be accurate to your acting partner, not to the words in the line itself."

Very impressive – almost Geoff-like, Fong thought. "What's your lie detector's name?" he asked.

"Charles Roeg," Robert said. "He specializes in doing these benefits. He's apparently raised substantial sums of money for the theatres in this country with this little parlour trick of his."

"He's teaching now."

"So he said. Why?"

"Just a thought."

Later that day Fong sat at the back of the open studio and watched Charles Roeg tear apart a scene on the video monitor. The packed room of actors hung on his every word.

The actors were clearly impressed with Charles. In fact, Fong might have been impressed as well but he found himself in the throes of an absolutely visceral response to this younger man.

"Because it's not in present tense," Charles said to the actress. The handsome woman made a "whatdya'mean" face and Charles launched into an explanation. "You have to see and hear like the narrator in a Great Russian novel."

A shiver of recognition moved up Fong's spine. He knew these words.

"Only when you're present – when you really see everything that's in front of you – when you hear not only the words your acting partner speaks but also the implication of the words and then the implication of the implication and allow all that data in your eyes and ears and pull it down with your breath to your heart, unencumbered with politics – unfiltered – unfettered with connotation – only then are you present – are you ready to act."

These words were slightly different but the "implication" of Charles's words were terribly familiar to Fong. He shifted in his seat to get a better look at the lie detector.

Dark, not squat but not long either, but alive in his centre – molten – and quick, very, very quick. Beautiful hands. And those old, old eyes.

When the class ended, an older black actor and a young Italian set to dismantling the camera equipment as Charles talked with three actors in a corner.

Fong stood and stretched. The class had started promptly at 6:00 and it was almost 11:00. Charles had taken a two-minute "half-time" break but was clearly present himself for the entirety of the five-hour class.

The confab in the corner broke up. An older actor with bushy eyebrows smiled and promised to bring coffee to the next class. The young actress turned away from Charles and headed towards the door, clearly hiding tears. A slender woman who parted her straight hair in the middle, evidently made some crack about the crying girl and Charles rolled his eyes. The slender woman rested her fingertips on Charles's forearm for just a moment too long.

Then Charles spun around and faced Fong. His eyes were suddenly bright, vibrant, as if he'd just run a race. "*Ni hao,*" he chirped.

Fong smiled and replied in Mandarin – if you speak the Common Tongue then I'm a chili pepper in a whore's armpit.

Charles smiled. Fong found himself liking the smile. "You got me. All the Mandarin I know is how to say hello." He then repeated, "*Ni hao.*"

Fong resisted correcting Charles's use of tones in the word. His childish approach to the word reminded Fong of student actors on the Shanghai theatre academy campus who loved to approach Westerners with loud salutations of the only English phrase they knew: "*Well, Come too Chey Na!*"

"Your class was very interesting," Fong said. "You are

very skilled. My name is Zhong Fong," Fong said in his textbook-perfect English.

Charles turned to the students who were still dismantling the video equipment, "That's enough, thanks. I'll do the rest."

"You going to join us for a drink?" asked the older black actor.

"Do I ever join you for a drink?" Charles asked.

"No, you don't."

"Right. But thanks for asking. One of these days I'll surprise you all and show up."

"We'll try to hide our astonishment."

"Just find the truth, breathe in the truth and say the stupid words."

"Good-night" and "Great class!" were offered by the actors and gratefully accepted by Charles. And then the actors were gone. Charles closed the main door behind them and opened the blinds on the south side of the studio. A full moon sat low in the night sky. Charles stared at it, doing what Fong's actress wife, Fu Tsong, used to call "breathing it in."

Fong allowed himself to breathe in Charles watching the low-slung moon. He sensed something almost ancient in this young man. Finally he asked, "Is there not madness in watching the moon?"

"No, there's no madness there, Mr. Zhong," Charles said without turning back to face Fong. "There is truth in the moon's movement."

"Truth in the moon? How can that be when the moon constantly changes?"

"The moon changes because it is about time – no, it is time itself. Trying to find truth between human beings without understanding time is folly."

"Is it truth between human beings that I saw you teach this evening?"

"No art is about the clever rearranging of the truth. It is by its nature a kid of deception."

"Then teaching acting is teaching lying."

"No. I never said that, although there are far too many liars who claim to be acting teachers."

"I'd like to talk to you about truth."

Charles finally turned to face Fong. The moon hung between the two. "I assumed we'd meet again. Once is a chance meeting. Twice is an odd coincidence that assumes the arrival of the third meeting."

"But this is only our second meeting," Fong said.

"Wrong. Third." Before Fong could respond Charles added, "Be that as it may, *ni hao*."

This time Fong corrected Charles's inflection. Charles accepted the correction and, much to Fong's surprise, repeated the complicated up and down tonal pattern – so foreign to English speakers – perfectly. Then he surprised Fong again. "You sit behind your eyes, Mr. Zhong."

Fong remembered conversations with his actress wife about the positions that actors "wear their eyes" – and how to change the position. He parted his lips and touched the tip of his left index finger to the end of his tongue. He tasted the bacterial mix on his skin. It moved him forward from behind his eyes. Then, as his eyes softened, he dropped down to his mouth.

Charles noted the movement of Fong's self from behind his eyes eventually into his mouth and nodded. "Who taught you that trick?"

"My wife."

"She's an actress."

"Was an actress," Fong said.

Charles got it. Implication and all. Fong's wife had been an actress. Fong's wife had died. Fong adored his deceased wife. Those facts were obvious to Charles.

What wasn't clear was, "Who taught her?"

Fong hesitated.

Then Charles smiled, "Poor Geoff." It was a statement of fact not a question.

Fong nodded. Then he surprised Charles, "And you taught Geoff, didn't you?" Again it was a statement not a question.

It was Charles's turn to nod. "He was older than me by almost fifteen years but he wanted to learn what I had to teach." He sighed deeply. "It's rare that an older man is willing to learn from a younger one. Geoff was a rare talent and in his own way modest."

Fong didn't know what to say to that.

Momentarily time stretched between the two men as the full moon outside the window perfectly framed the two and held the moment in time's viscous suspension – neither man took a breath – then the moment passed – breath and time resumed – the moon no longer centred the two men.

"Three meetings?" Fong prompted.

"Third meeting now. Second meeting in my rehearsal room at the Vancouver Theatre Centre watching twelve angry egotists. First meeting at the skateboard park."

"You were there?" Fong said cautiously.

"I go to watch and I saw you see."

"See what?"

"Don't lie. I'm quite good at knowing when someone is lying." Fong didn't respond. "When Stanislavski, the great Russian acting teacher, lost his faith in what he was doing – which, being a Russian, happened to him a lot – he would always go to the beaches of the Black Sea and watch children play. Watch them put their heads up into the pure river of a child's truth." Charles kicked the hardwood floor with a dirty shoe. "The Black Sea is pretty far from here, Mr.

Zhong – skateboard parks have a tendency to be closer. There's a kind of truth there. I make my living by perceiving truth. By sticking my head up into the pure flow of the jet stream and hoping it doesn't drag me back too far in time."

"Excuse me?"

"That's not important, Mr. Zhong. What is important is that just like me, you saw the truth in what those kids were doing – and, Mr. Zhong, I saw you see it. The powerful believe that they understand the truth and that everyone beneath them is influenced by the gyrations, fluctuations and even subtle movements of their truth. But they are wrong. Completely wrong. There are other pure rivers of truth. One of them was being played out before your eyes in the skateboard park.

"Remember the girl skateboarder? She brought something different by accessing the only commonly known pure stream: sex. It's the one that pornographers have been building ladders to, then elevators and finally high-speed modems. I don't care about the morality of what they do, only that they debase something that can be pure. They make it common, banal. The greatest threat the West poses to the rest of the world is its relentless pursuit of ways to bottle that 'jet stream' and sell it."

"But no one can commodify the ethereal," Fong said.

"Perhaps, but the effort to do so is the greatest sin of the West."

"And does the East have a greatest sin?"

"For sure."

"And that sin is?"

"The East demands obedience to gain freedom. They refuse to see that talent is needed to make the leap to the truth. And there is no talent without freedom."

"That's a touch elitist, don't you think?" Fong countered.

"Perhaps, Inspector Zhong, but there are real obligations imposed on people of talent – you know that yourself."

"I don't follow."

"Sure you do. Don't lie, Inspector Zhong."

Fong ignored the comment. "What kind of obligation does talent demand?"

"To share. Talents are to be shared. Ever hear of the parable of the talents?"

"Is that a TV game show?"

Charles laughed. Fong found the sound pleasant if disturbingly older than the sound ought to be. "If it's possible to be the opposite of a TV game show, the parable of the talents is. The parable tells us not to hide talents, in the case of the parable, beneath a bushel – because talents are to be shared."

"Do you share your talent, Mr. Roeg?"

"I teach, Inspector Zhong. It wasn't what I intended to do but it was where some of my talents led me."

Fong nodded.

"And you share your talents, too, Inspector Zhong."

Fong thought of Captain Chen and Lily and the dozens of young officers that he'd taken under his wing – but he said nothing, although he did smile.

And Charles Roeg smiled back. "No doubt merchants are already hard at work trying to bottle what the skateboarders have – but it's hard – skateboarding requires the one thing the West is not good at – dedication. But only with dedication can you reach up into the jet stream and fly with God." Charles took a breath and then began to coil camera wire. "Let's leave it at that."

Fong looked at Charles in amazement. As if the younger man had read his mind.

"You are a dangerous man, Mr. Roeg."

"No more so than you, Mr. Zhong."

Fong turned to the window and looked at the moon. "Can you really tell when a person lies, Mr. Roeg?"

"Charles – you can call me Charles."

"Thank you, Charles." Fong struggled to get the "rl" sound in Charles to work for him and was only partially successful. "Can you tell when a person is lying?"

After a beat, Charles said, "Yes, but when I agree to do so, I get paid handsomely. But I'm careful when I use that talent. Besides it's not why I'm out here in Vancouver."

"You are here to direct that silly play with the lawyers?"

"That's a favour I do. Something I return to the community that has been very good to me. I'm actually out here because I have a new girlfriend – she's a features writer for the *Vancouver Sun* – the West's national newspaper."

"I see," said Fong. "So have I been lying, Mr. Roeg?"

"You are inclined to lie, Mr. Zhong. Sins of omission are not strictly speaking lies. But you have committed many sins of omission. Who sent you to me? Don't lie . . . I'll know if you do, and if you do, I won't play my magic trick for you."

"Robert Cowens."

"The Toronto lawyer? How's his health?" Fong shrugged. "Sorry to hear that."

Fong nodded. "Mr. Cowens says you have reviewed final interviews with executives for high positions and offered your opinion as to whether they are truthfully answering the questions they are asked."

Fong watched the younger man get defensive, "Yeah, I've done that before."

"So there is a person who . . ."

". . . who you need me to tell you if he is a liar or not. Right?"

Fong felt ridiculous but that was exactly what he wanted – and after a bit of hemming and hawing said as much.

The restaurant that Robert Cowens sat in was terribly expensive and Allen Barton, of Henderson, Millet, Cavender and Barton, Attorneys at Law, was late. He arrived and ordered a single malt scotch before he even sat. Quickly he launched into the details of business dealings with the Chiang family who controlled the blood trade out of China.

Robert expertly guided the conversation to the silent partner.

Fong and Charles sat listening to the conversation from a small speaker in the back of Charles's girlfriend's beat-up Corolla. Fong was about to speak but Charles held up a hand. The conversation between the two lawyers continued for another ten minutes, then Charles reached over and turned off the speaker. "I've heard enough."

"So?"

"You want my opinion as to whether Mr. Barton was lying, is that right?"

"Yes, if you would."

Charles laughed, "I don't do this for just anyone."

"Poor people in Anhui Province are dying from AIDS brought about by the money that a silent partner supplies. These are desperately poor people who cannot protect themselves. You are not doing this for me. You are doing this for them." Fong took a moment to compose himself. "So is this lawyer lying?"

"About not knowing who the silent partner is?"

"Yes, about that!"

"No, Inspector Zhong, he's telling the truth about that. About other things he's lying: his belief that Robert is representing a syndicate of money from the East, his pleasure in seeing Robert again, his upcoming meeting – fuck, even his love of single malt scotch is a lie. But not knowing the silent partner – that's the truth." He looked at Fong's face. "Sorry. I assume it's not what you wanted to hear?"

But Fong wasn't listening. He was running towards the restaurant.

Fong charged into the restaurant the moment the lawyer left. Robert was momentarily stunned at his arrival. "Do you believe him?" Fong shouted.

"Sit down, Fong. This is what is known in this part of the world as a fancy restaurant and they don't think kindly of either shouting or standing."

Fong grabbed a chair, pulled it out and sat. "I'm sitting."

"Good." Robert pushed his plate away. "What did Charles say?"

"Never mind about that. I want to know what you think. You were sitting across from him, so was this man telling you the truth or not?"

"I think he was."

"Telling the truth?"

"You know that's what I meant. Yes, Fong, I think Mr. Allen Barton was telling me the truth when he claimed that he didn't know who the silent partner was."

"So he doesn't know who the money is behind the Chiang operation in Anhui Province?"

"Are you asking me or just pissed off that we did all this work for nothing?"

"Asking you."

"So, yes, that's what I believe. That Barton doesn't know who supplies the money for the blood-trading operation." Robert shook his head. "What did Charles say?"

"He agrees with you that this lawyer wasn't lying."

"Now what?" asked Robert.

Fong stood and looked at the table. Two untouched pastries sat on a plate. Pointing to them he asked, "You don't like sweets, Robert?"

"No. They upset my stomach." He reached in his pocket and then swallowed two pills each about the size of a pencil stub.

Fong looked at Robert, awaiting an explanation for the pills. When it became clear that Robert wasn't going to supply one, Fong turned to go. Over his shoulder he heard Robert say, "Where to now?"

Fong turned, about to say something about speaking loudly in fancy restaurants when he saw Robert smiling broadly. As he approached Fong, he said – loudly – "I always hated pretentious places like this. Why do lawyers always want to take meetings in these beer joints?" Fong smiled. Robert turned to a matronly woman with a shocked look on her face and the tiniest dab of horseradish mixed with roast beef juice on her pointy chin and said, "Enjoy your dinner, Agatha."

As Robert and Fong drew every eye in the restaurant, an elderly Chinese man dabbed his lips with a linen napkin and rose from his seat. Passing Robert's table, he nimbly slipped one of the sweet pastries into his coat pocket then continued out of the restaurant, careful to keep his distance, but also careful not to lose sight of Robert Cowens and Zhong Fong.

Fong hailed a cab and shoved Robert into the back seat. "Go to your hotel. Rest. I'll call you." Robert resisted, but only for a moment. Then he sat back and closed his eyes.

Alone on the dark streets again, Fong re-envisioned the columns on the desktop back in his Shanghai office and mentally swept the column headed by LAWYER into the garbage can. He had actually thought it was their best chance. But now that it was gone he turned his attention to the second column, the one headed with the family name, CHIANG.

Gelati-eating couples passed by him as he leaned against a building, pulled out his cell phone and pressed #9 on his speed dialer. Once again the eighteen numbers were dialed and the young Shanghanese cop with Special Investigations answered.

"*Wei.*"

"Is everything ready?" Fong asked.

"Yes, sir." The young cop's voice had a waver in it. Fong thought about that, considered cancelling his plans, then thought of AIDS in Anhui and said aloud, "Fuck it."

"Sir?"

"Start the plan we discussed. Now. This very moment."

Fong hung up.

Within twenty minutes of Fong's call the wheels of his plan were set spinning. By the end of the day the streets of Shanghai literally ran with blood and blood products that had been ransacked from warehouses by incensed Chinese mobs shouting, "Chinese blood for the Chinese people." At the same time a massive sweep of blood heads began in Anhui Province. Hundreds were arrested, dozens of officials publicly shamed – many were badly beaten. Within twenty-four hours China was alive with protest and the blood business was in a shambles.

Fong knew this would not last long but he hoped it would be enough to force the Chiangs' hand.

Fong was alone on the streets of Vancouver and the night was deepening – and, although he couldn't see anyone else, he knew he was not alone. He turned – and began to run.

Back in Shanghai, the four Anhui peasants were flushed

with excitement. "The Middle Kingdom is rising – rising to revenge our shame!"

CHAPTER TWELVE

MEETINGS AND PURITY

"Sit down, Suzanne." Old Chiang's voice was hoarse. He tightened the plastic oxygen mask on his face and breathed deeply. The Chiang sons stood to one side as Suzanne sat down at the fifties-style Formica-topped kitchen table across from their father, her grandfather.

"I read the articles too, Grandfather. But will the Beijing government really pass laws against the blood trade? Many peasants make their living by giving blood. To say nothing of all the government officials who have bought new Lexuses with their share of our business."

Old Chiang thought about trading Chinese blood for Japanese cars. "Suzanne, you must remember that we are now talking about taking blood from our people and bringing it to the Golden Mountain." His voice sounded thin through the plastic. "This is about blood. It is about the black-haired people." He took a deep breath then took off the mask and inserted the plastic clip into his nose. "There are already mobs on the streets of Chengdu and Nanjing and Shanghai. Two of our warehouses have been destroyed and some nuts are running around jabbing stupid Round Eyes with needles."

"It won't last."

"Don't be too sure." The Chiang patriarch was referring not only to the mobs but also to the ominous articles in opposition to the blood trade that had begun to appear in Chinese newspapers. He had no way of knowing that Fong had planted the newspaper articles before he left Shanghai.

Fong's timing this time had been impeccable. The first newspaper articles had come out just before the ship arrived and then at least one had been in the paper every day since.

"What do we do, Grandfather?"

Old Chiang allowed the sounds in the room to come into his consciousness. He knew he was at a crossroads. He looked at his beautiful granddaughter and knew that the path he took would determine her future as well as his. He turned to his sons, "Leave us."

Slowly, with open malice, the boys left their father.

"Was that wise, Grandfather?"

He spoke slowly, "Family and business do not always mix well. Remember that." He winced and readjusted his breathing tube. "Now, we have lost some money."

"Yes."

"But our partners lost significantly more than we did."

She nodded. She always knew that there were silent partners but she never knew who exactly they were. Was he going to tell her now?

"And who would these new Chinese laws against the blood trade hurt most?"

"Depends how much of our business is our money and how much belongs to the silent partner or partners."

"Partner, Suzanne – partner."

That surprised her.

"Ninety/ten split," he said flatly.

She held her breath. Ninety percent from us or ninety percent from them?

"You must learn not to wear your questions on your forehead, Suzanne. You have known me a long time. Would I really put up ninety percent of any investment in the Middle Kingdom?"

Slowly she shook her head, "Of course not."

"Suzanne, we are Chiangs. We supply infrastructure and expertise. Skills, connections and our family's history. We are middlemen. We get paid both coming and going. Only fools put forward their money to make money. Fools and harlots. Your brain and your abilities and the family's historic contacts allow you to make money – not investment capital." The last words were spat out like a curse.

She paused for a moment then asked, "So how much did we lose in this shipment, Grandfather?"

He smiled. For the barest moment, the handsome young man he had been returned to his face. "Nothing. I sold our percentage long ago to a broker."

"Then we have no problem since we lost nothing," she said.

"Not true, Suzanne. We lost nothing but our partner lost much."

"But surely that's their concern."

"They are our partners and have been for generations. We can work here because of them and they can work in the Middle Kingdom because of us. If they are hurt, we are hurt."

"I see."

He didn't look at her. Was it possible that whoever was behind all this was trying to hurt his silent partner? He didn't know. But he knew he still needed the family's historic Long Nose partner. Then he took his first step down the new path by saying, "I think it's time you met our partner in this business." After a moment of silence he asked her, as if it were the natural next question, "Do you ever read the *Vancouver Sun*?"

"No, Grandfather."

"Well I do. Every day. The personal ads are most interesting."

For a moment she didn't follow him, then she smiled, "Is that how you contact our silent partner?"

"It is. If I want a meeting I place an ad with the words 'Gold, Desire and Mountain.' If our partner wants a meeting the ad always includes the words 'Gold, Purity and Illness.' The meeting always takes place at noon on the following day. I grant it is clumsy but it is also secure. Everything that promotes speed permits unwanted intervention. It is a trade-off."

"You have already placed the ad, haven't you, Grandfather?

"Naturally, one must consider the feelings of one's silent partner."

"He did what?" Fong demanded so loudly that the warehouse echoed momentarily then returned to its dirty silence. All eyes turned to him.

The Tong guy stiffened at the rebuke. Not for the first time, Fong questioned the wisdom of using these thugs. But what choice did he have?

"Like I said, the old guy placed a personal ad in the *Vancouver Sun*."

"That's all he did?"

"You heard me. He placed a personal ad. Then his granddaughter, the icicle princess, came to his place in the British Properties."

"And there's been no more phone activity since then?"

"None."

Fong thought about that. Personal ads to communicate? Finally he said, "Is it still the Cold War here?"

"Chiang's been around a long time."

That was true. Fong also knew that personal ads although slow were usually a secure way of communicating. "You don't have anyone on the newspaper . . ." He didn't bother completing the question.

"So what do we do?" Matthew asked.

"We wait," Fong said, "and increase our surveillance. Their mutual business interests are going up in flames. They'll have to meet and we have to follow them. It may be our last chance of getting to the silent partner."

The Dalong Fada men looked at each other, then sat. Matthew and his men did the same. The Tong guys ordered food and drink. Then they all waited.

The guild assassin watched the shadows moving in the warehouse windows, then pried open a rusted door hinge and slipped in. Soundlessly, he climbed a metal ladder into the overhead I-beam superstructure. He checked to make sure his cell-phone ringer was off then he curled up on a large cross-span and watched the men below him – like a snake in a tree eyeing its prey.

The air in the warehouse was stale and stunk of unwashed men and cigarette smoke – and more of that damnable General Tso and his stupid chicken. After more than thirty hours in the room, the phone finally rang. The Tong leader grabbed it, listened for a moment, then put his hands over the mouth piece, "They're moving."

Midday traffic in Vancouver is not as bad as in Shanghai, but it was challenging to get from the warehouse upriver near Deep Cove to the Gastown area of Vancouver with any speed at that hour. But they barged and honked and shouted their way there.

Outside the forty-storey building they were met with another surprise.

Police officers everywhere.

The building was cordoned off. The head of the Tong surveillance team raced over to his boss, "The cops arrived moments before Chiang and his folks entered the building."

The Tong leader swore. "Did you at least see where Chiang was going?"

"We tried, but the cops kept us outside and they kicked out our guys who were already positioned when they cleared the lobby. One of them did manage to see Chiang and his people get on an elevator. That's all he saw before he was thrown out. The cops claim there's a sequence from *Star Gate* being shot in the lobby."

Fong sneaked a peek. There were cameras set up in the lobby and officious-looking technicians making as if they were important walking around. Fong approached Matthew. "Would there be hair and makeup people there?"

Matthew nodded.

Fong raised his shoulders and said, "So what are you waiting for?"

"Not all hair and makeup people are gay!"

"Oh, please, this is hardly the time for correct politicalness or whatever you people call that! Is there anyone in there that could help us?" Fong shouted.

The silent partner was thinking about purity. The silent partner often thought about purity – actually, about the price of purity – whenever they had to meet face to slant-eyed face with the family's traditional Asian business partners. At least fewer of them smoked now – but it still remained a room of rotted teeth, rice-paper dry hands, toad-belly skin and . . . them. True, the old man brought along the granddaughter this time. Pretty thing. A no-doubt frigid MBA from somewhere expensive. But it made no difference. You always felt as if you had to swallow a large soapy facecloth inch by sodden slimy inch when dealing with them – while protecting the purity of this ungrateful land.

The silent partner thought about ingratitude of Canadians, then about disease and sickness, and then looked at the "partners" – the family's historical partners – the bringers of contagion whose coils were wrapping tighter and tighter, bringing the British Columbian deeper and deeper into the silence.

The silent partner glanced out the window towards the mountains – the purity. Between where they stood now in this tastefully furnished flat and the mountains was clear evidence of the ingratitude of this land's newcomers. The detritus of those who came to Canada for only one reason: to take her money, then return "home" with their booty. The silent partner was always furious upon returning from speaking in San Francisco or New Orleans or Chicago. The magnificence of the architecture of those cities was the direct result of the beneficence of those who left buildings behind in gratitude to a land that had given them refuge, honoured them and made them wealthy. But not here. True, Vancouver was not as atrocious as Toronto – the physically ugliest big city in the entire Western World as far as the British Columbian was concerned. None of the whores there – the wops, the Caribbean Negroes and the kikes – left any sign of their gratitude to the place that had allowed them in and made them welcome . . . and made them rich.

Things really began to go to hell in this country in the late 1960s with the advent of multiculturalism.

Multiculturalism, hell! Non-gratitudism, non-nationhood-ism would be more accurate terms. Come on in, we'll hold the country still, spread her legs, while you assault her! Nah, pay no attention to the people who made this country from the heathen rock, ignore their values, blaspheme their churches, degrade their language – mock their ways – and we are to roll over and agree? We never did in the past, we do not now.

Let them freeze in the dark!

Oh for the days when you wanted to buy something you got your fat little fanny down to Eatons or Woodwards. Our stores, not theirs. Then in the early 1970s discount stores from the East tried to what they called "open up" Vancouver – to upset our world. Funny how their trucks kept slipping off the roads in the mountain passes. Funny about that. One's an accident, two's suspicious . . . nine and they got the message – NOT WANTED OUT HERE IN GOD'S COUNTRY!

Going back a little further in the family history, there was the ill-fated raid on Japtown that ended with six white men hanged from the lampposts in that ill-begotten part of Vancouver. Then when the Supreme Court of the land couldn't figure out who to punish – so they punished no one – our anger went into dormancy. But it did not die. Our anger never dies. Eventually the war came and our revenge fell upon them. Not a stick of furniture, a garden, a home or a farm was left in the hands of the Asians. We shipped their sorry asses to southern Alberta to live out the war in the harshest climate in the country – without so much as a twig of firewood to heat their badly built sheds. Welcome to Canada, fellas!

Purity has a price and part of that price was sitting in the room with these slant-eyed monkeys. They were talking again – they were always talking. True, they were better dressed now but they were still monkeys freshly down from the rutting trees. The Chinese men spoke quickly to each other in Mandarin. The silent partner wanted to smile but didn't – all these years and they still didn't get it that the British Columbian spoke their doggerel tongues. All of them – Mandarin, Cantonese, Hakka – even the highly idiomatic Shanghanese. The silent partner listened a little further. So they wondered aloud if the complexity of the situation was understood by the stupid Round Eye – if their Long Nose partner had gone senile since their last meeting. The British Columbian allowed their Mandarin slanders for a few more highly insulting moments then said, "So the shipment is totally spoiled?"

That swung Chiang's head, breathing tube and all, in the silent partner's direction, "Totally spoiled."

"That was two months' collection?" the silent partner asked, knowing full well it was a lot closer to four months of collection.

"Actually three months," Old Chiang replied, knowing as well that they were talking about four months of work down the proverbial drain.

"Do we have a figure?" the British Columbian asked.

The granddaughter handed over a spreadsheet. The British Columbian touched her pretty hand. Very nice. Then he handed it to the handsome young cop whose unbelievably light blue eyes turned dark with anger. The British Columbian said, "Easy, Son. Are you still tracking the car?"

"The bug works just fine," Blue Eyes answered.

The British Columbian took the spreadsheet and handed it back to the head of the Chiang family. "The loss is yours. Your error – your responsibility. I'll expect prompt reimbursement of my investment. Surely you insured the shipment?"

The youngest Chiang spat on the floor – old habits die hard. "No insurer would touch this shipment," he barked.

The British Columbian thought about that. There was technically nothing illegal about their business dealings. However the deal, like so many before it with the Chiangs, was unsavoury. Thus, insurance companies, ever wary of their public image, wouldn't consider being caught making money off the transfer of blood from Asia to North America.

The railway business was not so different from the blood business. Totally legal – significantly unsavoury. The country is desperate for blood products but doesn't want to know where or how the blood is attained. Just as long as the blood is safe – who cares how it gets into our hospitals. It was the same in great-grandfather's time with the railways. The country wanted a transcontinental railway built within a specific period of time for a specific amount of money. So what if the Chinese labourers were lied to when they agreed to come to the Golden Mountain. So what if every dangerous job was given to the Chinese. So what if Chinese men made less than twenty percent of the wage that white men doing the same or less arduous jobs made. So what if thousands of Chinese men lost their lives building the railway. So what if once the railway was completed (the greatest act of industrial conspiracy in Canadian history that guaranteed a fine income for the families behind all this) we kicked the Chinese out on their skinny asses, then charged them a fortune in head tax to get back into the country they helped build. And even then we did everything we could to keep their women out. No Chinese breeding here! So what!

The British Columbian thought about the connection between blood and purity – the longevity of that connective – the essential nature of it. The Nazis went too far, but the whole world knew what was happening over there and no one raised a finger until the Germans threatened the real power structures of the West, England and the United States of America. Until then the world was content to allow the prerogatives of purity to play themselves out. Even after the war ended, when Canadians were asked which nationalities they didn't want in their country, the order of the unwanted was Japanese, Jews, then Germans (Chinese were already blocked entry by the *Exclusion Act*). The nation had just fought a war against the Germans but preferred them to Jews. The prerogatives of purity were still in play. It always made the British Columbian laugh when hearing Ontario liberals twist themselves into logic pretzels in their effort to support the purlaine racist policies of Quebec – asymmetric federalism, my fanny!

They were talking again. More Mandarin mumble-mouth. Finally, the silent partner painfully rose. The gabble stopped. "The guild assassin is in place."

The eldest Chiang's mouth flopped open. The grand-daughter's shock was deeply gratifying.

"My family has dealt with problems in China for many generations. We have many sources of power there. Now, there are two things that need doing post-haste. One, you need to reimburse me for my losses due to your negligence and two, it is time to put an end to this Shanghai investigator's investigation. We could sic the Vancouver police on him," the silent partner pointed towards son Doug, "but that could get unnecessarily complicated. The guild assassin is in place – I'll activate him." The British Columbian turned towards the mountains, "After all, what's one more dead Chinaman to the city of Vancouver?"

The British Columbian smiled then added, "It's time for you people to go."

As they left, the silent partner thought about Shakespeare and Dryden and Pope and Longfellow – and the beauty of an Anglican boys' choir. They were the beauty of this life. They were us. Not them. Ours. Not theirs. Unique, special, unmatched in any other culture, unparalleled – a sacred trust to be protected at all cost.

It took Matthew very little time on his cell phone to determine that the third assistant director on the shoot was a member of the community, and very little time after that to get someone he knew who knew the man and contact him.

Shortly, a chubby man came out the front door with a clipboard in his hand, an earpiece plugged into his left ear and a quizzical look on his face. "Are you Matthew?"

"Was your shoot always planned for this location?" Fong demanded.

"Yeah."

Fong believed in coincidence, but not like this.

Then the man added, "It was always planned for here but next week, Thursday night. Suddenly out of nowhere we get a call to haul ass over here. It's crazy, but this is a crazy business."

"Better," Fong said. "They're scurrying to cover their tracks."

"Better than what?" Matthew asked.

"Nothing," he said, then turned to the third AD. "Can you get me into the building with you?"

Matthew whispered something into the third AD's ear and the man said, "Yeah, but just for a peek okay. The male stars are really touchy on this show. They've begun to think they really are superheroes or something. They hate looki-loos."

Across the street, the guild assassin watched Fong talk to

the plump man then go into the building. He sat back and opened his second Nanaimo bar of the day. The chocolate-covered chocolate squares were as close to perfect as the old assassin had ever experienced. Sugar's version of nirvana. He thought about buying a third bar then decided he would wait until it got dark to treat himself again. He checked his cell phone. Still no call. But it had to be soon.

His revenge could not wait forever.

Fong entered the lobby of the building behind the third AD and then slid to one side beside a "WATCHDOG PROTECTS THIS BUILDING" sign. He wanted to see the elevator banks. To see the numbers as they descended. All four elevators were at lobby level. He noted that there were over forty floors and from the size of the lobby probably many offices on each floor – way too many possibilities.

A striking blonde woman, dressed in an army fatigue costume, passed by him. She carried a small baby and cooed, "Olivia," to her. She noticed him and smiled. He smiled back. An actress, he thought.

There were a series of commands shouted from various assistant directors, and many walkie talkies responded. Lights were thrown on the walls and massive black draperies were dropped over the windows. Naturally Fong thought, they were supposed to shoot next week, at night, now they have to shoot in the daytime so they have to modify the light. Fu Tsong's phrase "day for night" came to him.

He looked back at the elevator banks. The far one was rising from the ground floor. The others were all still. A camera crane moved between him and the bank of elevators. He took a step forward to see past the crane and a hand landed on his shoulder.

Fong spun and couldn't believe his eyes. "So there you are, Zhong Fong," said his young well-dressed Beijing minder whom he thought he had lost in Calgary. "I didn't know you were a fan of this show."

"What show?" Fong said.

"*Star Gate*. Very big hit at home, Zhong Fong. Very big. I couldn't miss the opportunity of getting to watch them film an episode. Very exciting."

Fong tried to step past the man but the Beijing man stood in his way. "You're not going to disappear again are you, Inspector Zhong?"

Fong couldn't see the bank of elevators because of the crane. Finally he said, "I hope you enjoy yourself," and shoved his way clear of the man. He stepped past two technicians and turned quickly to see the elevators. The elevator was already descending past the twenty-seventh floor.

"Damn!" he said aloud.

"Quiet," three people yelled at him.

Then the elevator opened and he had his first look at an ancient evil and the beautiful young dowager. The Chiangs stood for a moment in the light of the opened elevator as if they were the stars of the event – which as far as Fong was concerned, they were.

Later that night Fong faced a serious truth. He had no way of knowing which of the floors above the twenty-seventh floor, let alone which of the offices on those floors, the Chiangs had gone to. Despite that, he jotted down a note to get an exact list of the occupants of all the offices above the twenty-seventh floor of the building. He remembered the three columns of cards on his desktop back in Shanghai. The first column led from the lawyer to THE MONEY. That had failed. And now his second column through the Chiangs to THE MONEY had also failed. He had no more tools to force the Chiangs to contact the silent partner again.

He mentally moved to the third column of cards he'd left on his desk back in his office on the Bund – the column headed by the card with the large question mark.

CHAPTER THIRTEEN

A GUILD ASSASSIN

The guild assassin watched the shadows move in the dirty windows of the warehouse. He was about to re-enter and resume his watch from above when an elderly stooped Chinese man walked past him and instinctively averted his eyes.

The assassin stopped and rage filled him. He hadn't even noticed the man's approach. He felt the surge of his blood as it circled the eye marks on the hood of the cobra on his back. A mistake! He had to be careful. There should have been no way that an old man could have gotten that close to him. Then his cell phone purred in his pocket and he felt the hood flare – open – ready.

The fading light slitted through the filthy windows of the deserted warehouse. Fong wondered, not for the first time, why Tong guys liked meeting in storage rooms like this. In Shanghai this place would have been across the Su Zu Creek north of the city, the reek from the creek's junks pungent in the air. Here in Vancouver they were in a dock area far up the estuary past Deep Cove. The Tong guards were not obvious, but Fong knew they would not be far away.

Fong stood beside Robert. Matthew and the head

waiter of the restaurant stood to one side. The Dalong Fada guys stood near a pyramid of rusting barrels in a corner. The Tong leader, followed by six of his men in a tight phalanx, entered the room as if he were entering the Forbidden City at the head of a conquering army.

"We called in a lot of favours, Inspector Zhong, to get you this far." The Tong leader's voice was tinged with warning, like a poufy white dog giving notice that he'd had enough of whatever it was he didn't want repeated. "You owe us an explanation, Inspector Zhong – so explain."

Fong was careful to hide his distaste for the man. "Okay," Fong said. "I set events in motion in China, then followed the Chiangs' reaction, hoping they'd lead us to their silent partner. All we learned was that they met with someone in the EA Building in an office above the twenty-seventh floor."

"Not terribly useful information, Inspector," the Tong Leader said.

"I agree. As well, I tracked down the lawyer who handled the Shanghai blood company's business in Vancouver, but that proved to be a dead end too. The lawyer has been working in a legally structured blind where he never meets or even knows the name of the silent partner. He has no record of the silent partner's name. All contacts are made through Internet sites. All payments are made through account transfers in offshore bank accounts."

"So you have no idea whose money is behind all this. You have found nothing!"

Fong again reminded himself that although he really didn't care for the man's approach he could not afford to lose the Tong leader as an ally if he was going to get anywhere with this. "I'm sure that the lawyer is not the man, nor is anyone else in his firm, nor does he know who the money is behind the Chiang's blood-collecting operations in Anhui Province."

"The Chiangs have enough money to fund such an operation themselves," the Dalong Fada guy suggested.

"No doubt, but the Chiangs' history suggests that they never spend their own money on anything. They provide muscle, contacts and expertise – but not money."

The Tong leader looked to the smallish bespectacled man in his entourage. The man nodded his head. "And you think this lawyer is telling the truth?"

"I know that he doesn't know who the silent partner is."

"And you know this exactly how?" the Tong leader demanded.

Robert coughed. Fong thought Robert was warning him not to reveal Charles Roeg; then the man's cough increased, sending wracking spasms through his body. Robert threw his hands over his mouth.

Flecks of blood seeped through his fingers.

"Are you all right?" Fong whispered.

Robert nodded but kept his hands tight to his lips.

Matthew turned away, stared out a window and thought of his grandfather. Finally he said, "So what do we do next?"

"Perhaps we walk away from this," said the Dalong Fada guy. "There are other battles to fight." He slid off the barrel and straightened his sweater.

"Where's the rag man?" Fong asked.

"Who?"

"The rag man. The guy who warned me on Pender Street. He's one of yours, isn't he?"

"Yes," said Matthew.

"So where is he?" Fong demanded.

"Why?"

"Where is he?" Then Fong surprised them all. He raised his voice and ordered, "Find him! Now!"

* * *

Robert was curled in a corner of the warehouse trying to sleep through the waves of pain when the waiter from the insulting restaurant ran into the warehouse. "He's dead."

"How do you know that?" demanded the Tong leader.

"Gay men are nurses throughout Vancouver – in the morgues too. I sent out the word and back it came. The 'rag man' was named Larry Allen. He was a lecturer at Langara College."

"I need to see the autopsy report," said Fong. No one moved. Fong turned to the Tong leader. "That shouldn't be so hard for a connected guy like you?"

"Forensic labs are run by Japanese, not Hakka Chinese. You may recall our history, Inspector – there is no love lost between our two nations."

Fong threw up his hands.

"Would the autopsy report go into a database?" the Tong leader asked.

"I would assume as much."

The Tong leader looked to the young glasses-wearing member of his "boys."

"So?"

"Shouldn't be a problem."

"How long?"

"Ten minutes, twenty, tops." The voice was confident but extremely high. Like that of a teenage girl's.

The Tong leader read the data from the computer screen over his IT guy's shoulder. "They found the rag man's body in an alley behind Pender Street." That stilled the movement in the room. Then he added, "He was cut into pieces. Severed cleanly at the joints. The coroner makes a notation that the work was done with 'tremendous haste but great accuracy.'" He lit a British cigarette that had a gold-coloured filter then added, "You'll love this. The heart was cut out of the guy's chest then slit in half. They only found one of the halves at the crime site."

"What!" The single word leapt out of Fong's mouth with such force that every eye turned to him. "Say that again!" he ordered.

The man repeated the details of the severed heart. Fong couldn't believe his ears. "I want that confirmed." He turned to the Tong leader and said again, "Can you get confirmation of that?"

"Why?"

"Because if it's true then none of us in this room, yourself included, smart guy, are safe. Is that a good enough reason?"

"Why would that . . ."

"Because that's the signature of a guild assassin."

"Oh come on that's nothing more than . . ."

"Myth? Fairy tale? Listen to me! Nine years ago I killed a guild assassin. He butchered two men on the streets of Shanghai in broad daylight. In each case the bodies were left like human jigsaw puzzles and the hearts had been pulled from the victim's chest, then cut in half. The half that was found, in both cases, had a piece bitten out of it."

"But did this one," asked the Dalong Fada leader, "have a piece bitten out of it?"

"Scroll," the Tong Leader ordered. "There." A strange smile came over the Tong leader's face. "No. But there were markings on the cut side of the heart that the coroner couldn't identify."

"What kind of markings?" asked Fong.

"The coroner called them soft impressions."

Fong tried to put that together but couldn't.

"What does all that matter? Nine years ago you killed a guild assassin – you got him. So he was just . . ."

"It wasn't my skill that allowed me to kill him. It was him," Fong paused unwilling to put on the table his surmise that Loa Wei Fen had in fact committed suicide. Fong knew he had to offer up some sort of explanation for the young guild assassin's death. All he could think of saying was, "Something was wrong with him."

There was a lengthy pause in the room. No one knew what to say next. Finally the Tong leader said, "So this assassin is here, in Vancouver now?"

"I sensed that I'd been tracked for some time." He didn't bother mentioning the feeling of someone tracing the outline of his heart as he slept on Jericho Beach or the image he'd seen in the running-shoe-store's plate-glass window. "He's here. A guild assassin in your city."

Fong looked at the men in the room. The heads slowly nodded as the idea of a guild assassin in their midst solidified in their minds.

"But he may also be our last point of access," Fong said.

"To what?"

"To whom," Fong corrected.

"So to whom?" demanded the Tong leader.

Fong ignored the question. "The guild does not kill at random. They are sanctioned by the state. They are a last resort. I can only assume that the reason he hasn't attacked yet is that he hasn't been given the order to kill."

"He killed the rag man."

"Mr. Allen must have been unfortunate enough to have seen him up close."

"But who would give the order?" Robert asked in a hoarse, weak voice.

"The money behind all this. The silent partner."

"But who would be his target?" asked Matthew.

As all eyes turned to Fong, Fong's mind was far away. Of course he would be the target. But the problem was that even if he could stop the assassin, how could he get the man to tell them who gave him the order to kill – in other words, who the silent partner was.

Dirty sunlight splashed across his face. He looked out the filthy window. It was another day.

As the assassin tracked Fong from the warehouse he felt the snake skin handle of the swalto blade turn towards his hand. "Soon," he cooed softly. "Very soon." He felt the weight of the ancient snake on his back. He felt purpose. He felt strength. He felt the presence of Loa Wei Fen at his side, begging him to revenge his death.

"I need it and I need it fast, Lily." Fong was speaking too loudly into his cell phone and he knew it but he couldn't stop himself. He was walking east on West Georgia trying to stay in the midst of as many people as possible. He knew it was no real defence, but it was all he could think of doing.

Lily hesitated but finally responded, "It was a long time ago Fong. Another world."

"But the old coroner kept great records. Lily, I know this is hard. I know you cared about him. But he's been dead a long time and he was the best coroner Shanghai ever had – and he was a meticulous record keeper. Lily, please. Get me those records."

Again Lily hesitated. Fong heard her take a deep breath and then let it out slowly. When she spoke her voice was more centred – in fact, it was determined. "Will it help catch the people who are making this happen in Anhui Province?"

"Yes, Lily, I hope it will."

"Not enough good, Short Stuff," she said switching to her version of English. Then in her elegant Shanghanese she finished with, "Promise me. Promise me for our daughter, for Xiao Ming, that you will get these bastards."

"I promise," he replied in English, although he had no idea if he could fulfill his promise.

Lily held her breath and entered the old coroner's office. As a young forensic specialist she had spent many hours in the old coroner's domain. Never having known her own father, Lily often thought of the old man as her– well, as her father. When she turned on the light in the old autopsy room in the basement of the Hua Shan Hospital she was immediately flooded with memories. She felt that at any moment he would appear at her side hacking his guts out which was his normal "good morning, how're ya" greeting – a lit cigarette on a constant dangle from the corner of his slightly downturned – or was it just his basic snarly – mouth. He never acknowledged it but he loved to teach and Lily was an avid learner. Over his shoulder she watched his remarkably delicate hands take apart the smallest sections of human tissue and pronounce upon the trauma evidenced there.

The old autopsy room had been converted into a storeroom when the Hua Shan Hospital finally completed its expansion. They hadn't bothered to remove the slanted metal table and now it, as well as most of the available floor space, was piled high with the old coroner's file cases.

Lily shook off the sentimental world of memory and forced herself to concentrate on why she was in the midst of this room stacked high with mouldy paper. Anhui –

AIDS – a peasant man now walking some 1,000 kilometres to an empty home.

A rat skittered across the floor and disappeared behind one of the boxes. She walked calmly over to the box and shoved it hard against the wall. A momentary high-pitched squeal pierced the quiet of the room – then was no more. Lily didn't wince. Killing rats was important for the health of the hospital and its patients. Finding rats was important for the health of defenceless peasants in Anhui Province who were dying in the thousands.

She grabbed the first file and scanned for dates.

It had been a while since the old assassin had seen his own blood.

He held up his hand and turned it in the morning sun. The blood that came from the back of his hand and circled its way down his inner arm didn't bother him although he was taken aback that so much blood had been caused by such a little knick. He was however stunned that he had accidentally hit his hand. Control of both body and emotion had been central to his talent for so many years that he took it for granted. Then this.

He kicked at the sand, sending a spray of pebbles far out into the water. In the inlet a small boat ferried people to Granville Island and its overpriced tourist shops. The boat looked like a bathtub with a motor.

He turned back to the rock structure that he'd inadvertently smacked his hand against. It was a series of granite rocks that were balanced one upon the next, forming a rough image of a human. From the literature he'd read he knew that these were the works of aboriginals. He stepped back and examined the rocks. His blood stood out starkly against the colour of the stone in approximately the position of the sculpture's nose – if it had a nose.

The sun glistened off the blood smear and he stepped away from it. Again, more inadvertent than intended. He shallowed his breathing and reminded himself of the need for patience. But his patience was running short. Loa Wei Fen's ghost was screaming in his ear for revenge and Zhong Fong was there on the beach waiting for something.

"I found it." Lily's voice was tight, tense.

"Are you all right, Lily?" Fong asked.

"I've been better."

"I'm sorry I had to ask you . . ."

She didn't want to hear an apology. She wanted to hear that he was going to be all right. That the father of her daughter was going to return home safely. "Shut up, Fong and listen. I found the file on Loa Wei Fen's death. And there's something in it that might help us."

"What?"

"The coroner completed the autopsy on the body then it was shipped back to Taiwan. There's a notation in the file that the body was picked up from the airport over there by a group of people."

"Who were they?"

"There's no mention in the file, Fong. But Taiwan is paranoid when it comes to security so I'm sure there are video surveillance images available." She paused, then added, "In Taiwan, which is not exactly our best friend these days, Fong."

"Joan could help." There was a very long pause. "You still there, Lily?"

After another very long pause Lily answered in her own hybrid version of English, "Now my ex me wants to talk to his new non-ex, neh?"

"Call her, Lily, she might know a way to get hold of the surveillance tape."

Lily thought about that for a moment. Then she remembered the deep sadness in the peasant's eyes when she told him that his wife had died and said, "Same number, Short Stuff?"

"Yes, Lily, it's the same number."

"Fong?"

"Yes?"

"It's raining here."

Although it was brilliant sunshine in Vancouver, Fong replied, "Here too."

Joan had to ask a second time, "Who is this?"

"Fong's Lily wife."

Joan took a deep breath and tried to steady herself. "Is Fong hurt?"

"Not yet."

"What does that mean?"

Lily was tempted to say, "Don't talk like that, young lady" but knew it made her sound old. She switched to Shanghanese, "Fong needs information from the Taiwan security police."

"Special Investigations has . . ."

". . . a liaison officer, I know. But Fong needs this information now, not after days of negotiation."

"So what can I do?"

"You're from Hong Kong, dammit. It's almost the same as Taiwan. Pick up the phone and call someone – now!"

Joan had to call four different sources, each of whom called two others. Then she waited. The ding from her computer momentarily set her heart fluttering. Then up scrolled a high angle shot, evidently from the open cargo bay of an airplane. The coffin with Loa Wei Fen's remains was on a dolly of some sort. A very young woman and three clearly athletic men had their hands on the coffin. There was a fifth figure. An old serving man who pushed the dolly.

She waited for further images. None came. At midnight Shanghai time she emailed the image to Fong's BlackBerry.

Fong sat with his back against the railing of the small ship that had attempted a northwest passage. He'd spent much of the day on the dry-docked vessel. It struck Fong as terribly ironic that the Golden Mountain only existed because Europeans were so anxious to find China and they had used boats like this to find the way. The cramped quarters of the boat didn't bother Fong and he found the narrow access to the boat a kind of safety. From his position on the railing he could watch everyone who bought a ticket and came on board – and there were a limited number of tickets sold at one time which also helped him.

His BlackBerry sounded. He punched the Receive button, and up came the pixelated photo from the Taiwan airport.

Lily's comment, "Only picture we have," appeared then disappeared.

Fong scanned the picture carefully: a simple pine-box coffin on a hand trolley wheeled by an old serving man towards three fit young men and a young girl who waited by a black hearse.

Fong manipulated the scan so that each face filled the entire screen. He ignored the girl who seemed only eight or nine years old and examined the three men's faces closely. But nothing jogged a memory. No face, even taking into consideration changes that could have taken place over nine years, matched the rogues' gallery in his head.

He saved the image in a JPEG format then turned off the machine. The image dissolved irregularly with parts from one section disappearing to wherever it is that pixels disappear to before parts of other sections.

He put in a call to Matthew and within an hour was standing in the deserted warehouse with his "troops."

Matthew had made copies of the BlackBerry image and gave them out.

"Oh, hey, the girl looks tough," the Tong leader snarked.

Fong thought, this image is nine years old. She could be quite tough now. "Do we have any way of identifying the three men?"

The glasses-wearing Tong youth shook his head. "I could put the three images through time-lapse. Nine years isn't all that much but the changes could be interesting. As well, I'll do images with facial hair and glasses."

"How long?"

"Seconds." The dweeb plunked and scrolled and punched his computer, and out tumbled three images of each of the suspects. Everyone grabbed copies and stared at the faces.

"Now what?" asked Matthew.

"Robert gets his car."

Fong helped Robert to his feet. The man was exhausted and clearly in pain.

"I thought it was bugged," Robert said.

"It not only was, but it is bugged," Fong said. "Now we lead them."

"Into a trap?" asked the Tong leader.

"The art of war is very clear on how to do this."

"I know. Just tell me where?"

Fong thought for a moment. He wanted as few Asians around as possible so that the guild assassin would stand out. "Up towards the Capilano swinging bridge. Have your people set up a roadblock on the way. The road is steep and only two lanes. There are parking lots along the side. Robert and I will lead them up; you cut them off."

The Tong leader smiled.

Robert coughed blood onto the steering wheel. "We should take you to the hospital."

"Timing's not so good for that, Fong," Robert said as he swung the rental car out into traffic. "Besides, if I check in I'll never check out." Fong was about to respond when Robert added, "Like a roach motel."

"A what?"

"Never mind. So should I drive slowly or something?"

"No. The opposite. Drive aggressively. It will imply that we're running."

The yellow luminescence on the cell-phone screen began to move. And so did the guild assassin. And others.

Traffic jammed the way across the Second Narrows Bridge, but Robert kept his foot on the accelerator any time he could. His stomach felt like it was dropping through his body, through a pool of warm cancer-soaked crap. He put a hand on his belly and pushed. The pain almost made him cry out.

Fong was watching the traffic that finally thinned as they left the bridge. Fong had given the Tong members lots of time to set up their fake roadblock and insisted that they set up a second.

Robert took the hard right-hand turn and headed up the mountain gorge. He was having trouble steering. His mind drifted. Fong seemed far away. The trees seemed beautiful.

It was the pale blue eyes that got the Tong leader. The itch he sensed behind them. The violent purity of the racial hatred. "You boys always dress like cops or is it Chinese Halloween already."

The Tong leader went for his cell phone only to find the pale blue-eyed cop's gun pressed hard against his right eye. "You can make a call at the station, if you're real nice."

The large force of cops behind the blue-eyed cop quickly disarmed and "uncellphoned" the Tong members.

"I should have gotten a call telling me that they're set up," said Fong.

"They called that they were already there."

"Yeah but I asked them to confirm that both road-blocks were fully functioning."

"And?"

"And I haven't heard dick and I can't get through to them." A shiver of fear snaked down Fong's spine as they swung around a huge bend in the road and headed farther up the gorge.

The assassin loped along with a simple elegant stride. His teeth were bad but his body was well toned. A ten-kilome-tre run was a nice way to prepare oneself. As he ran he sensed that he was not alone. He didn't look but he was sure that Loa Wei Fen was running, step for step, beside him. Their every footfall in perfect synchronization. Two as one. He headed deeper into the forest and turned straight up the gorge. He checked his cell-phone's screen – the yel-low luminescence was indeed heading towards the Capilano swinging bridge. A fine place for a killing.

He returned the cell-phone, whose one and only call had released him from his waiting and set him on the kill, to an inner pocket.

"There was supposed to be a roadblock there," Fong said as he turned and craned his head to see.

"What do we do, Fong?"

Fong looked out either side of the car. Traffic was thin but there was no way to turn around on the steep mountain road with the fall off several thousand feet on each side.

"Drive."

Two more kilometres up the road and Fong knew that they were on their own. The second roadblock wasn't in place either. Fong pointed to a scenic-view spot on the opposite side of the highway. "Turn around. Let's head back."

The moment Robert pulled into the lay by, two cop cars screeched to a halt, preventing him from turning around. Robert got out of the car only to find himself pushed back into the driver's seat. "Nice to see you again, Mr. Cowens," said Doug, tilting up his mirror sunglasses to reveal those pale blue eyes. "Sorry for the inconvenience, fellas, but there is construction on the road, as you may have noticed if you weren't too busy and we're insisting that people go to the head of the road before they turn and come back. Okay?"

Robert slowly turned the car and waited to find an opportunity to, once more, head up the gorge. Suddenly a hand smacked hard against his window. Robert turned. Doug's face almost filled the entire windowpane and his lips were not hard to read, "Your taillight still needs fixing!"

* * *

As the car climbed it began to rain. Robert coughed and the blood from his mouth splayed on the windshield. "Fong . . ."

"Pull over, Robert."

Robert pulled the car as far off the road as he dared

then set the emergency brake. Fong hopped out of the car and came around to the driver's side. "Does the seat recline?"

Robert pointed at a slider on the side of the seat. Fong tilted it backwards and Robert's seat slowly reclined to an almost flat position. "Listen, Robert, are you listening?"

Robert nodded slowly.

"They want me not you. I was going to leave you at the reception centre. There's no reason for you to be in danger."

"Fong . . ."

Fong covered Robert with a blanket from the trunk then took out his cell phone. "Is there an emergency number here?"

"911."

Fong turned towards the highway, wiped the raindrops off the cell phone and dialed. "There is an extremely sick man in a car on the side of Capilano Road not far from the reception centre." He listened and said, "How long . . . fine. His name is Robert Cowens."

When Fong looked back, he was surprised to see Robert's head shaking from side to side. "What?"

"If they take me to a hospital I'll never leave." Then he said something peculiar. "If I die there I will never fly, Fong." He breathed heavily, pain clearly etching its lines on his face. "Do you remember the kid in that song?"

"What song, Robert?"

"That Tom Waits song you hated. The one about the kid in the hospital and his friend sending him 'down the rain pipe to New Orleans in the fall.'"

Fong remembered – he also remembered the image of the man jumping from the World Trade Center – and flying to his end.

"I need a friend, Fong."

"I'm your friend, Robert."

Robert closed his eyes. Fong thought about friendship for a moment. Then he thought about the peasant from Anhui and he reached over and pried off the bug – and shoved it in his pocket. As he did, he muttered, "Come and get me."

Fong was running. Just as he had run nine years ago in the Pudong. He crashed through the brambles and tight vines at the side of the road and plunged into the dense underbrush beneath the cathedral tall Douglas Firs.

He ran and ran – ran for his life. If he could make it to the bridge the assassin's advantage would be limited by the width and swing of the treacherous thing. He wasn't thinking, at that moment, about getting the assassin to tell him who was the money behind all this. Now all he wanted was to live another day.

The assassin approached the parked car at the side of the road and looked into the eyes of the dying man in the driver's seat. "Wrong one," he thought as he circled the car for signs of Fong. He noted that the bug was gone from the side-view mirror. He pulled out his cell phone. The luminescent dot was in motion. "You want me – you got me," he mumbled. Then he heard the wail of an ambulance siren coming up the mountain road and he stepped back into the brush – and returned to the chase with a seemingly effortless loping stride.

Fong was hearing things and he knew it. But he was hearing things! He dashed across the parking lot of the reception area and past the restaurant, then climbed a small hill and looked back. The drizzle had increased to a full-fledged rain. People were emerging from their cars with either umbrellas or their hoods pulled up on their anoraks.

Both made it hard for Fong to see their faces – to compare them against the images in his head of the three guild assassins meeting Loa Wei Fen's coffin. Then a sleek Mercedes pulled into the lot and out hopped three Chinese men in their early thirties. The rain didn't seem to bother them.

Fong turned and raced into the dense woods.

The assassin stood by the back entrance to the reception centre restaurant and surveyed the landscape on the park map in his hand. He placed the luminescent yellow dot into the geography of this place. Then he smiled. "Very good, Zhong Fong," he said aloud. If I were being chased, that's the kind of place I would seek out too. His body ached to run after Fong but the voice of his teacher came to him again, "*Choose the place carefully. Never fight on the target's ground. Strike from either above or below, never on the plane your opponent expects. Patience is the only knowledge available to all.*"

Then an elderly Chinese waiter stepped out and lit up a cigarette. The elderly man smiled at the assassin, "Wanna smoke?" he said holding the pack out.

"Wanna smoke" were the man's last words.

Fong waited in the centre of the swaying bridge. He tried desperately to contact any of his "troops" on his cell phone but the gorge evidently created problems. Over and over again he got the message: "This call cannot be completed. The customer you are calling is out of your calling area or has his phone turned off."

The rain had slowed a bit, but the boards of the swinging bridge were slick underfoot. Fong watched every person who ventured onto the bridge, waiting for the three assassins from the BlackBerry image.

Finally they arrived. Without umbrellas. Without hoods. They allowed the water to drip down their faces and headed directly toward Fong . . . and then past him.

Fong couldn't believe it.

Half an hour later Fong finally was able to get through to Matthew, "I'm in the restaurant at the reception centre at Capilano Park."

"Are you all right?"

"Fucked up but all right." He had the BlackBerry on the table with the image of the three men with their hands on Loa Wei Fen's coffin. A Chinese waiter approached his table, "More tea?"

Fong nodded.

The waiter poured the tea; a little splashed over the side onto Fong's lap. "I'm so sorry, sir. I'll get a cloth," the waiter said, as he walked back to the kitchen.

Fong smelled chocolate. Chocolate?

He stood and looked around. In the reflection of the big mirror on the west wall of the restaurant he noticed his waiter clearing a table. Fong was about to sit when he saw the man deftly scrape a finger along the top of a piece of half-eaten chocolate cake then quickly suck the icing off his finger.

Chocolate.

The squiggle taken off the top of the Hostess Cup Cake in the refrigerator of Kenneth Lo's apartment.

"Sweets are only of interest to the young and the very old," the Yale nurse had said to him.

Fong's heart felt like it had stopped in his chest.

Two coal-black eyes reflected in the shoe-store window. An old man standing on one leg on Jericho Beach. An old man on the airplane. An old man standing on a bench on the raised promenade on the Bund looking at him. No. Looking through him.

A heart cut in half with soft impressions, soft impressions because the aged assassin's mouth had so few teeth left!

Fong sat and looked at the BlackBerry image again. This time not at the three men by the coffin but at the one older man – the servant – who was pushing the cart.

"So sorry, sir." The man's voice was terribly loud. He reached towards Fong with the towel.

"Not a problem," Fong said through the fog of his fear. Then he looked the old assassin in the eyes. "You like sweets."

"Sir?"

"You explode bombs in apartments of innocents, including a baby, a sleeping baby."

"Really . . ."

"You work for rich white men against the interests of our people. Who employed you?" This last was said so loudly that the entire restaurant turned towards them. "Why not kill me here, in front of all these nice white people?" Fong screamed. "You take their money, you do their dirty work, so go ahead and kill me here. Who gives a fuck about peasants dying in Anhui Province! You don't give a fuck about anything . . ."

Not true, the assassin thought, I cared about Loa Wei Fen. The swalto blade pierced Fong's shoulder and sent him spiralling to the ground. Instantly the assassin was on the table – from above – and launched himself at Fong.

Light flickered off the blade and Fong rolled. Rolled beneath the next table. Patrons scattered everywhere and Fong scrambled to his feet and threw himself out the open window to the wraparound porch. He landed on his side and the pain roared down his arm.

He heard screaming from within, then he was running.

Running through the fishery ponds and back towards the swinging bridge.

The assassin's heart was beating heavy in his chest. He had never felt that before. He disentangled himself from the terrified restaurant patrons and dashed out the door. Fog had replaced the rain. "Good," he thought. "This night you return to the fog, Zhong Fong."

On the bridge Fong made his way carefully to the very centre and yanked out his cell phone. No connections. Then he remembered his BlackBerry. Captain Chen had said something about a different network system for it. Something about it being powerful. Something about how the fuck to use the thing as a phone.

The assassin approached the swinging bridge from beneath. He'd spotted Fong's position from across the way. No need to walk right up to him when you can approach from beneath. He put the swalto in his mouth. The snake-skin handle tasted sour; the cobra on his back flared. Then he reached up and wrapped a strong hand around the metal cable that ran beneath the bridge.

Menu. It's in menu. Fuck, everything in electronics is in menu. But where in menu?

The river sang to the assassin as it thundered beneath him. He looked down. There in the shallows of the river was a native stone statue of a man. Six beautifully balanced stones – too much like the one upon which he had bled only yesterday, he thought. Then he nodded. If it is so, it is so. He hung there by one hand as he undid the buttons to his shirt and then allowed it to slip off his back and into the river. He turned and grabbed on with the other hand – the cobra now fully alive on his back.

The BlackBerry yakked. He turned up the volume. "Where the fuck are you, Fong?" screamed Matthew Mark out of the thing.

"In the centre of the Capilano . . ."

He said no more. Pain roared through his foot. He looked down and the point of the swalto blade peaked out from the top of his left shoe. Blood added to the slickness and he staggered. But despite the fact that the swalto had split the board cleanly in two, the knife held him fast to the broken board of the bridge.

Then the cobra came over the side and perched on the railing of the swinging bridge, its hood filled with blood, its eyes black with hatred. And it spoke, in an old man's voice. "You killed the boy I loved. I loved." The cobra seemed to sway on the railing. "I have seen so many things – the end of the Manchus, the rape of Nanking, the liberation of our country, the rise of our power. But things of beauty I have seen very few. But he was beautiful. Beautiful. And you took him from me."

The cobra leapt off the rail and landed with a surprising thud on the decking of the bridge.

Fong forced himself to stop shaking and slowly inched his foot up off the swalto blade.

Then the cobra hit Fong across the face so hard that his head smacked into the planking with a sickening thud. Before the pain set in Fong had a flash of thought, Not my teeth again. Please not my teeth.

The next blow broke two ribs on his left side.

Fong rolled over to protect his ribs and waited for the next blow.

And waited.

Then he heard the assassin whisper in a hoarse voice, "Why do they call this place the Golden Mountain? This is not our Golden Mountain. It is our doom."

Fong reached for the swalto and yanked it free of the split board. The thing flew from his hand – a foreign object – careened off the railing and pierced the old assassin beneath the right armpit.

The man turned to Fong, a strange look on his face. He made one attempt to take the swalto from his body then turned – and the cobra fell forward, over the railing – towards the rock statue of a man that stood on the river's bank.

As the old assassin crashed to the ground, the tip of his nose caught the edge of the jagged stone and he heard, deep in his mind, the snap of bone and, as his hands flailed for but failed to find purchase, the grinding of cartilage and snap of ligaments as the bone shard slid between his eyes and pierced his thinking self.

A moment of blossoming pain – then light.

He was young again and in the centre of the Guild Academy's contest ring. His left arm was raised and blood coursed down it as he sunk his strong teeth into the half of a heart he held aloft in his right hand.

Then he bit down hard and tasted his opponent's essence – then he spat it hard into the dust as the cheers of his teachers and fellow students filled his soul.

His first victory. His first kill. His life journey just beginning.

The carved cobra on his back leapt to life as he took his swalto blade and threw it with all his might straight up in the air.

The Tibetan knife flew perfectly straight then, as if on

some godly command, turned, flattened out and seemed to embrace its return to the earth.

But just millimetres from the ground an elegant boy's hand grasped the handle of the swalto and with a wild cry threw it high in the air a second time. Then the hand moved to a mouth – Loa Wei Fen's mouth.

So beautiful.

"Forgive me, Loa Wei Fen, I have failed you."

"You stink of wet paper, old man!"

The swalto seemed to give off a high-pitched, woman's scream as it came back to earth, slicing through Loa Wei Fen's shoulder and splitting open the boy's torso to the waist.

The snakeskin handle of the knife slowly turned crimson and everything changes.

A hand, a female hand, reaches in and wraps its fingers around the snakeskin handle of the swalto blade – and in a single move cuts open the chest cavity and frees the heart of its ligament moorings. Then, holding it aloft, slices it in half and bites down hard.

Blood sluicing down her chin and neck, crimson outlining her young breasts beneath the cotton shirt, she turns and bows to the old assassin.

Yes, now he remembers, it had been a young woman who had surprisingly won the Guild tournament to honour the death of Loa Wei Fen.

He smiles.

She smiles back at him. She opens her mouth – her teeth are etched in blood.

He senses the cobra on his back turning.

"Sleep now, Grandfather. Sleep. You have earned your rest."

"But I failed." His voice sounds like sand scraping against stone.

"Allow your cobra to sleep. It is now my job to avenge Loa Wei Fen's life." He feels the snake on his back free itself from his skin and crawl down his leg. He wants to cry out for it to stay. But the great beast is already moving down his calf, then slithering off his left foot – then is gone. He feels himself stumble and her strong arms catch him and hold him tight. "Zhong Fong will pay with his life for your life. I swear it by the cobra on my back, Grandfather. Now sleep and dream the dream of dreaming."

"A girl is a good disguise for an assassin – a very good disguise," he thought. Then he wondered if she had a candy, something sweet for him.

Even as he thinks this he knows it is his last thought on this earth.

A blood vessel tears open behind his eyes and his last vision of this world comes from behind a crimson curtain of his ancient blood. And there he is, Zhong Fong, as he must have been nine years ago in that construction pit in the Pudong – a killer of assassins, a tamer of cobras – a man destined to die at the hands of a girl.

He wanted to bow to Zhong Fong, to acknowledge his talent, but he was already on the ground, his face pressed hard into the moist earth of the Golden Mountain. And he knew that he would shortly return to the earth from which he had come.

Fong watched as he had watched the death of Loa Wei Fen, breath rasping in his chest, head alive with terror, nightmares accumulating, ghosts enwrapping him. Then he reached down and grabbed the old assassin by his shirt and slammed him hard against the stones of the ancient statue. Then again. Then again until his hands were red with blood and rage.

Then he looked at the night mountains and took a full

lungful of the clean air of the Golden Mountain and flung the old assassin aside.

The man landed like a pile of rags – a pile of rags with a clink.

Fong hobbled quickly over to the man. Ignoring the blood, he tore off the man's clothing.

In an inner pocket he found the man's cell phone.

Fong was screaming into his BlackBerry. Captain Chen on the other end in Shanghai was trying to get him to slow down.

"What is broken, sir? Exactly what on the assassin's phone is broken?"

"I don't know what you call it."

"The antenna, the body of the phone, the screen?"

"The screen. The screen is cracked, no, it's completely black."

"Is the power on, sir?"

"Yes, that light is on the side."

"Okay, sir, so the liquid display is broken. So you can't see anything like the number when you dial out."

"I don't care about that. I want to see the last number that called him." There was a long pause. "Chen, are you still there?"

"Yes, sir. I'm still here. The last call would have come from whoever activated the assassin, is that right?"

"That's my hope."

"Okay, sir. Take off the case, carefully. There are serial numbers. Find them and tell them to me."

It took Fong a while but he finally found them and recited them slowly to Captain Chen. "Okay, sir. Don't touch the assassin's phone anymore. Call me back in ten minutes on your phone."

"So?"

"The assassin's phone was manufactured in China, sir, under a special government contract. It's a single-use phone. It can receive one call and respond only to that call. Do you understand, sir?"

"No."

"The phone was set up to receive only one call and by pushing any of the number keys the phone will dial back that number."

"So we can get the number off the phone and trace it."

"Not if the liquid display is cracked. The memory chip is set up to refuse tampering. If you open the chip, it disintegrates."

Fong paused. He looked across the water then he spoke very carefully. "But if I press any one of the keys of the phone it will call the phone that called it. Right?"

"Yes, sir."

"And I can only do it once?"

"Just once, sir."

Fong thought of offices above the twenty-seventh floor of a building and what could get all the occupants of all those offices to gather in one place.

One place where he could place a phone call by pressing any key of the old assassin's phone.

And the words WATCHDOG came to him from faraway.

The Tong boys and their computer whiz kid found little resistance when they took over the WATCHDOG command centre at the EA building. Once they were ready, they called Fong's cell, "You ready, Inspector?"

Fong looked at the large empty room with its reinforced walls and ceiling – the safe room. Personally Fong doubted there was such a thing as a safe room. He put his cell phone to his lips and said, "Do it." The Tong leader threw the WATCHDOG emergency switch – and every computer in the EA building blinked out. Then all hell broke loose.

An hour and twenty minutes later every tenant of the EA building, except six who had booked off sick, were checked off as present in the safe room. Fong took out the guild assassin's damaged cell phone, hoped to hell that Captain Chen was right and pressed "Return Call."

When his cell phone rang, Evan felt mildly embarrassed – as if he'd farted in church. But then he looked around and saw that dozens of other people in the room were on their cell phones. So he flipped his open to take the call.

Across the room on a small raised dais, Fong saw Evan Balderson answer his phone and when Fong snapped his phone shut, Evan reacted, as he should, like someone had just unceremoniously hung up on him.

Fong made sure he had Evan in his line of sight, then put away the guild assassin's cell phone and pulled out his own. He called the Tong leader in the WATCHDOG command centre. "Sound the all clear."

Ten minutes later Evan was outside his office punching in the door code. When the door opened, he found himself thrown head first into his office.

Fong shut the door behind him and bolted it shut.

Evan staggered to his feet, "Who are you?"

"I'm the one who called your cell phone just now."

"So?"

"I called. You answered."

"Yeah, I answered my wife's cell phone. So what? She asked me to get it fixed and . . ."

"Your wife's cell phone?"

"She's in the flat above my office, she's . . ."

Evan never got out the word "sick" before he found himself bound and gagged. Shortly Fong found Evan's key ring and shortly thereafter he stood in the beautifully furnished apartment of Mrs. Evan Balderson.

"Who are you?" she demanded as she used her two crutches to rise.

Fong's explanation was short and to the point, his proof that she was the silent partner and the guild assassin's employer, even briefer.

Then to Fong's surprise, she made her way laboriously to the bar and poured herself two fingers of fifty-year-old brandy, took a sip, then said, "So fucking what?"

CHAPTER FOURTEEN

THE SILENT PARTNER

"So what are you going to do, Mr. Zhong? You've found what you sought so diligently – well, I'm here in front of you – now what?" She walked, leaning heavily on a silver cane she had picked up by the bar. "This is Canada, our business is legal, it's even registered with what you would no doubt call the 'authorities.' Now, we may have been bending the laws of God – but then again you don't believe in God and hence he could not have laws that I or my company could possibly break. So where does that leave us, Mr. Zhong? Actually, let's start with you – where does it leave you?"

Fong paused – the woman's words just flowed out of her like water from beneath the ground. "So this was just about money?" Fong finally managed to say.

That seemed to momentarily stop her. Then she found his voice, "Only those without money would use the phrase 'just about money.'" She took a step towards Fong and raised her silver cane. "You have no jurisdiction here. No right to judge. This is the Golden Mountain and you are nothing but a foreigner here. A monkey fresh down from the trees." She turned her back to Fong. "See the beauty out there? The mountains. Our mountains! Not yours, ours!

Pure. Not half-monkey, half-coolie like you."

Fong couldn't move, couldn't shut out the woman's words. Suddenly he felt himself falling. Somehow or other this crippled woman had pushed him over the lip of a well, backwards, on a starless night.

He plummeted down the well, past the deaths in his life – Fu Tsong, the men he'd seen executed, the man he'd shared the cell with west of the Wall, the assassin Loa Wei Fen – and finally his own father who had disappeared into the night to fight for the liberation of China when Fong was four, never to return, never to lean over Fong and tell him bedtime stories or explain the moves in the Peking Opera, never to touch him with his soft hands, never to point his moral compass – "So, here you are, Fong." His father's voice was still light, his breath tinged with tobacco. "So, you are here, Fong," he repeated.

"But you're not– here, that is," Fong replied.

"As you wish," his father said and retreated back into the recess in the well in which he stood like a statue in a church niche.

"Come back, Father."

Fong's father re-emerged from the recess and shrugged his shoulders.

"Was it worth dying for China?" Fong asked.

His father bowed his head as if in thought, then said, "I'm not sure – how could I know what I missed – what life I would have enjoyed – if . . ."

"How did you die, Father?"

"With suddenness – and blunt force – at the hands of a man who fought to make money to feed his family."

"Was there pain?"

"Yes, and loneliness – and this place." He indicated the well shaft with an outstretched hand. Fong noted the long tapered fingers and the delicate skin. He looked at his own hands – they were identical. "You look old, Fong."

"I feel old, Father. I'm over twice as old as you were when . . ."

"I died – yes, you are. But it is not age that makes you old, Fong, it is the sadness you carry. Have you found no love in your life, Fong?"

"I have. I have been very blessed with love, Father. More blessed than I deserve."

His father smiled. His teeth were bad. "I'm glad to hear it – I was never so blessed."

Fong wanted to ask about his mother, whether his father had loved his mother, but didn't know how to even phrase the words.

"If you have found love, Fong, why are you here and why so bent beneath your burden?"

"I don't know the way, Father. I don't know anymore how to determine right from wrong – moral from obscene . . ."

". . . sacred from profane?" Fong's father asked.

"I don't believe there is a difference between sacred and profane."

"Of course you do, Fong, or you wouldn't be here. How can you possibly justify talking to your dead father if you don't believe in the sacred?"

Fong thought about that, then he heard his father laugh – a tumbling sound that fell upon itself then rose only to fall upon itself over and over again – like a crease in the water on the downstream side of a large rock in a raging river. And Fong fell into the very centre of the crease – the laughter all around him. Then he was laughing – laughing and running back to the present.

"What's so funny, Mr. Zhong?" Meredith Balderson asked.

"You. You that you think you are above time – beyond

the pull of the earth – outside of the rest of us. Your wealth may not be based on our poverty – but our poverty supports your wealth – taints it – disgusts it – like a spider in the bottom of your flute of champagne."

"That's almost Shakespearean of you."

"From *A Winter's Tale*, isn't it?"

"You are full of surprises, Mr. Zhong."

Fong didn't answer but an idea blossomed in his consciousness like a seed in the early spring rain. Full of surprises, he thought, like a human lie detector with a girlfriend who writes for a local paper – that kind of surprise.

Fong began to nod his head up and down and the laughter roared out of him – because he had finally figured out how to think from the end of the puzzle – how to put the three towers one upon the other upon the other – to bring Mrs. Evan Balderson's world crashing down.

CHAPTER FIFTEEN

AFTER THE FALL

Matthew Mark handed the *Vancouver Sun* delivery guy ten bucks as he snapped the wire on the stack of next-day's papers. It was two o'clock in the morning and the city was quiet.

And there it was on the front cover – entitled "Anhui Story."

Fong sat in the back of the cab and nodded. His wounds ached beneath their bandages but they could have been much worse.

"You should be happy, Inspector. I think we won."

Fong didn't know about winning. As long as there were extremely poor people they were vulnerable to the likes of the Baldersons. There would always be those whose only asset was their blood. He sighed and forced himself to smile.

Matthew beeped the cab's horn gaily then said, "Where to, sir?"

The hospital room blinked in the darkness, its machinery little more than red lights in the gloom. On the gurney bed Robert turned his head and the two large morphine drips swayed on their stands. Fong closed the door quietly and sat by the bed. Fong read the fear in Robert's eyes. For the first time in his life Fong wished that he was religious. Maybe then he would have words to offer, comfort to give.

Instead he told Robert of their success. He spread out the Vancouver paper on the sheets of Robert's hospital bed. But Robert didn't look.

"Are you my friend, Fong?" The voice was little more than a soft whisper. Then Robert shifted in the bed and dark crevices of pain erupted on his face. "Are you?"

Fong nodded slowly.

"Then take me from here. I don't want to die here."

Slowly Fong said, "Slide down the drain all the way to New Orleans in the fall?"

"All the way to New Orleans in the fall," Robert replied.

It wasn't hard, with Matthew's connections in the hospital, to get Robert out of the building. It was harder to get the big man into the cab. And hardest to get him across the meadows then down the steep path to Wreck Beach.

And there Fong sat with him as the night got colder until slowly the dawn came.

"I'm ready," Robert said, holding out the bottle of pills that his doctor had given him all those months ago in a fancy Annex office in downtown Toronto. "Feed me them, until they're all gone."

And Fong did.

And Robert – as his doctor had told him he would – flew.

And by the time the first bathers arrived and removed their clothes, Robert Cowens was no more.

When Fong hobbled out to the road he was surprised to see two men in dark suits approach him. "Hold it right there,

Inspector Zhong." A black Passat pulled up behind a Subaru Outback and two more dark-suited men got out. The nearest man took a wallet from his pocket and flicked it open.

Fong read the CSIS ID card closely. "Am I under arrest?"

One of the men frisked him quickly and efficiently. Fong looked at the Passat and the Subaru. "I've seen those cars. You and two other cars tailed me the first day I was in Vancouver."

"Yep, and we have every move since . . ."

"Then why didn't you step in. Why didn't you interfere . . ."

"Why should we? You did so well. We had a problem. Chinese blood products coming into the country. It's legal, but it's immoral and everyone knows that – but it's legal. Then we have you. You're moral but illegal. We let you do the work that we're not allowed to do – and you did it very well, Inspector Zhong. My congratulations."

Pointing back towards the beach, "Are you going to arrest me for . . ."

"For Mr. Cowen's death? No."

"Just another moral dilemma that I'm the solution for?"

"If you want to think of it that way – sure. But Inspector Zhong, now it's time for you to shut up and get into the Passat. We'll be escorting you to Vancouver International Airport. You're booked on the midnight flight over the pole to Shanghai."

"Could I ask one thing?"

The CSIS man nodded.

"Could I have a cigarette?"

The man lit Fong's cigarette and Fong inhaled deeply, an old smile returning to his face.

"Fine. Now get in the car, it's time for you to leave the Golden Mountain."

Fong was asleep before the plane left the runway.

He awoke with the dawn as the plane crested the Aleutian Islands – the stepping-stones to the Golden Mountain. He counted them as they disappeared beneath the belly of the plane. One after another until solid land – Asia – filled his window and the plane turned south.

He crossed to the other side of the half-empty plane and sat in a window seat and watched the sun rise – the dragon out of the east that brings a new day to the East.

For an instant the ghosts surrounded him – Kenneth, his wife, his daughter, his baby, Robert, the rag man and finally the old guild assassin whose toothless mouth sucked on a sugar cube.

Then he thought of Joan Shui, and the ghosts departed. She would be waking soon and starting her day. The very thought of that brought a smile to Fong's face. He rested his head and closed his eyes. The last thought in his mind before sleep took him again was, If there is a god, love is surely his gift.

Joan Shui twisted to one side to avoid the oncoming bicyclist carrying a small refrigerator on his handlebars. An eel seller yelled at the refrigerator man. The green-vegetable seller screamed at the eel seller to shut up. Then others hollered their complaints. The five-spice egg seller closed an ancient nostril with a filthy forefinger and blew hard. The extrusion missed her cooking pot by less than an inch. The maestro fixed one bicycle while he bartered with two men over the price of a bike chain. The sounds of cha-cha-cha came from Renmin Park as old folks learned how to Western-style ballroom dance, and the sounds and the smells and the sights of another Shanghai morning.

Joan took it in, breathed it in – and smiled.

The digital image of Fong getting onto the plane at the Vancouver International Airport pixelated on the computer screen. The young female guild assassin hit the print icon.

As she picked up Fong's image from the print tray, she felt the cobra on her back fill with blood – and her *chi* race through her body.

The peasant slipped off the back of the oxcart. "I will walk the rest of the way," he said. As he watched the cart disappear over the hill he thought of all the kilometres he had walked from Shanghai. He stepped off the road and found the old footpath.

He passed the place where he and his wife had made love the first time, then where his wife had found the valuable herbs, then he felt her – his body parting the air that her body had once parted. That they had parted together.

His feet felt heavy, his hands wet. He stopped and looked down at the rice paddies of his family farm, at the small plot that he had cleared for their house – and his hands flew up in the air like doves at the end of their tethers and his knees gave out and a howl came from him that filled the valleys all the way from the Green Mountains to the sea.

Xiao Ming awoke with a start. She pulled back the blind. Shanghai's summer sun lit her face from without but it was the joy from within that made her luminous as she shouted to the world, "Daddy's coming home today."